split ends

split ends

kristin billerbeck

Published by
THOMAS NELSON
Since 1798
www.thomasnelson.com

Published in Nashville, Tennessee, by Thomas Nelson, Inc.

Thomas Nelson, Inc. books may be purchased in bulk for educational, business, fund-raising, or sales promotional use. For information, please e-mail SpecialMarkets@ThomasNelson.com.

Library of Congress Cataloging-in-Publication Data

Billerbeck, Kristin.
  Split ends / Kristin Billerbeck.
    p. cm.
  ISBN-13: 978-1-59145-508-0 (pbk.)
  ISBN-10: 1-59145-508-1 (pbk.)

1. Hairdressing—Fiction. I. Title.
PS3602.I44S65 2007
813'.54—dc22

                                    2007005263

Printed in the United States of America
      07 08 RRD 6 5 4 3 2 1

Dedication

To Rich and Christina Girerd: I don't know how to explain friends like you. People who are there for others while facing terminal cancer together? I mean, what kind of people are those but incredibly-gifted-with-the-Spirit kind of people. I can say with the utmost certainty, there aren't enough people like either one of you.

Gosh, we have weathered single groups, weddings, and parenting together. My life is so much richer because of you both. Christina, thanks for the generous use of your husband when I needed a handyman or tech geek. Rich, thank you for all the organization and fun you brought into my family's life. You will be greatly missed.

There aren't many friends willing to risk bodily harm to say what needs to be said. You're both those kind of people, and may God bless you both for it. Rich, your legacy will remain.

Acknowledgments

Thank you to Leslie Peterson, who got more than she bargained for in editing this manuscript, and to Jeana Ledbetter, my agent (the only agent I know willing to dine with four children, who aren't hers, on a Disney high), who believed in me despite a few setbacks. I appreciate you both more than you can understand, more than I communicate.

To my writing groups, ChiLibris and American Christian Fiction Writers, thank you for being there when I need to vent, ask questions, and just have a little human contact.

And to Nancy Toback, who helped me find the voice of this book when it was lost in the wilderness that is my chaotic life. I love you, girl!

To the ladies of Andrew James Salon—Heather, Vanessa, Natasha, and Dana—who gave me the first good hair days of my life. Talent is worth paying for! The best thing I ever did for my wild Italian hair is research this book.

Lastly, thank you to Coffee Society in Cupertino and Red Rock in Mountain View, without which I very much doubt I would have been able to finish this manuscript.

Prologue

If I had known what success would cost me, I would have paid my fees for failure and called it a day. I thought my quest for financial solvency was a higher calling, a way to prove to my hometown that my mother and I had value and worth. In the end, I stand here with my feet in two separate worlds, belonging fully to neither.

There are two engagement rings before me on the expansive, stainless steel countertop. One is from Tiffany's, a classic platinum band and solitaire that I'm sure comes with all the proper GIA ratings. The other is from a mall jewelry store, miniscule and flawed, but sparkling with promise. This might give the impression that there's a choice to make, but there isn't. The sad truth is neither man would have made an offer of marriage had they known the truth.

Everyone wants to be Cary Grant.
Even I want to be Cary Grant.
~ Cary Grant

Μy entire life is strewn across the front yard, laid out for all to bear witness to my pathetic existence. I'm just glad I'm not dead yet. Can you imagine if this is what I had to show for my life?

Bottles of professional-grade shampoo: $3

"I'll give you six for it," Janey says.

Lee Jeans, size 4: $5

"Will you take ten?" Mrs. Rampas asks.

Now, I don't mean to be rude, but Mrs. Rampas hasn't seen the likes of a 4 in, oh, at least a quarter century.

"I'm having a garage sale!" I shout to my various neighbors. "Not passing the hat. You're supposed to be jigging me down in price."

"Darling." Eleanor Gentry, who is the epitome of what all good Christian women strive to be, strokes the back of my neck. "Darling, this town is so proud of you. We want to send you off in style. If we can help just a little, it makes us feel good."

"Don't rob us of the blessing," Mrs. Piper adds.

"If we were young again, we'd go with you in a flash," says Mrs. Rampas. "As it is, we're brittle and on too many medications to stray far now." They all cackle together. Truth be told, any one of them could probably run me into the ground on sheer strength.

"Hollywood!" Mrs. Piper crows. "Can you imagine the excitement?" She drapes a summer dress of mine over her elbow.

"You have to take a lot of pictures and stand on Clark Gable's star for me, will you, dear?"

"Absolutely. I'll make it my Sunday outing. I hope to get to every star you introduced me to all those Saturday mornings."

I look up and see my friend Ryan, large and gentle (think the Baby Huey of men), huddled in between another group of church deaconesses. "Excuse me, ladies."

When I walk up the cracked driveway, Ryan flinches, stuffing a paper bag behind his back.

"What do you think you're doing?"

"Nothing," he says with mock innocence.

"What's in your hands?"

"Nothing."

"Let me see them, then?"

A crackling of paper and then his palms appear. Ten- and twenty-dollar bills float down behind his feet.

"What the heck? Can you produce men in that bag?" Inspired, I launch into song: "It's raining men, hallelujah!"

Ryan bends over and pecks at the bills until they're all returned to the crunched paper bag. "We're just having a good sales day. You asked me to help."

"Ryan, the sum total of my life is worth about forty-five dollars. I saw at least that there, and it doesn't look like anything's gone. If you want to help me—"

"Furniture gets good prices at garage sales." A broad

smile covers his face. "I got twenty dollars for that computer desk alone."

"I didn't pay that much more for it five years ago." I look over at the desk, which is listing to one side, the keyboard drawer hanging miserably from underneath it. "If you sold it, why's it still here?" I challenge him.

"I offered to deliver it."

"To the dump, is that what you're saying?"

Ryan leans in close, pressing the paper bag full of cash into my stomach. He whispers into my ear (although all the townsfolk are watching us, so he might as well shout it), "Take it, Sarah Claire. Think of it as a dollar donation for every pin curl you ever blessed this town with. It's their way of giving you their blessing."

"Your wife's going to be doing all those pin curls, you know."

Ryan's fiancée and my best friend, Kate Halligan, is not here today. She's at the Hideaway Hair Salon, working double time so all the ladies will be freshly curled, permed, and frosted for the church potluck tomorrow. Although it seems as if many of them are here, the truth is when social security checks are doled out, Sable is on fire with action.

The salon is "base" in Sable, Wyoming. Home free. The only place I ever truly felt a part of something. For most people, I imagine that's home. But most people don't have to live with crazy rules and my mother. Even First Community Church, where many were warm to me, harbored the underlying current that I am my mother's daughter and the apple doesn't fall far from the tree. As the resident "bastard" in town, I didn't belong among God-fearing people, especially if they had dateable sons.

The church divided into camps, if you will. Those who fell into the "enemy" camp got their hair done elsewhere and left the Hideaway to me and those who offered the mothering and love I so craved. I imagine every church is that way to some extent. There are those who believe in blind truth (the law), those who believe in blind grace (forgiving everyone without thought to consequences), and those who combine the two and create a practical faith that actually translates.

"She's not going to be pin-curling for long," Ryan says. "I nearly got enough saved for ten more head of cattle. She's going to be the wife of a cattle baron one of these days." He rattles his eyebrows, and inwardly I wince. Ryan's a fabulous guy, but how realistic he is remains to be seen. He's not exactly good with the cattle. One of his small herd actually died, and though the truth has never come out, rumor has it he let it feed on ragwort (poisonous to bovines). And then there was the rifle accident when he mistook one of his dad's cows for a moose. So while I know that to be cattle is fatal by nature of the job, I think getting to the actual "beef" portion of their fate is more difficult in the hands of Ryan the rancher.

I smile at the thought of Kate in an apron, ringing a dinner bell. Naturally, she can't cook. Nor has she ever picked up a can of cleaning spray. But for Ryan, she'll try. She'll fail miserably, but she's so cute and such a "catch" for Sable that he'll just laugh about it and hire her a maid. And a cook. And probably a nanny, too, when the time comes.

She'll be one of those women who stays cute until she's in the grave. She has that kind of sparkle. You know—the kind of girl who's fifty and still flirting. Effectively. Kate will try to be the perfect wife until she gets bored with the role, and then she'll have to do something more. She'll lead up the town's library fund-raiser or organize one thousand frozen turkeys being sent to the poverty stricken. Whatever it is, she'll come out the hero, even if she is a complete failure at being a housewife.

Need I mention Kate lives a charmed life?

Opening the paper bag from Ryan, and sighting the fluttering cash within, I see the town probably agrees with me that it's time to move on. *Don't let the Sable door kick you in the butt on the way out.* And for once I'm grateful, and I hold the bag up as though it's a first-place trophy.

"Thank you, everyone!"

I look up at Ryan. "I feel like Kate for a minute." A look of horror crosses his face. "That wasn't a pass, Ryan. I meant my life is charmed for the moment."

"No, I know that." But it's clear his star quarterback days aren't far behind him—he still thinks he's the envy of every girl within fifty miles. He needn't worry; even if he wasn't Kate's beau, he's not of interest to me. I like them smart, and God love him, Ryan's sweet as pie, but the gate doesn't quite latch all the way.

Speaking of which, my mother takes this moment to slowly open the front door, scanning the yard and the crowd as if we can't see her. Naturally, all movement stops. My mother is sort of like the haunted house up on Cooley Mountain—she holds an enticing fascination for the conservative town because she does whatever she pleases. There's both a disgust and a bit of envy when it comes to her.

Janey Winowski has lived a hard life and, I'm sorry to say, it shows. Though she's only forty-three—having had me at the tender age of seventeen—her skin is singed red with broken blood vessels, and her store-bought, stringy blonde hair (with deep black and gray roots) resembles a "before" shot for any hair salon. I think it's her way of telling the world she won't acknowledge my single talent.

That my mother would have the worst hair in town is a shame she makes me bear daily.

But when I'm doing Reese Witherspoon's hair, it's going to be her who's embarrassed.

"You're going to clean all this up," she shouts, as though I'm a child. "The yard looks like a pigsty."

The yard always looks like a pigsty (I don't think the lawn's been mowed since 1973), but I'll give her that it doesn't look any better with all my crap out here. Still, it's not like we were in the running for HGTV to begin with.

"I'll clean it up, Mom, as soon as the yard sale is over."

This must be the magic signal, because people start to scramble for their cars. And now I'm left with fourteen bottles of shampoo.

I sigh. Someday, somewhere, I'm going to matter. I'm going to walk this earth and people are going to care! Someday soon. Perhaps hairstyling isn't a divine calling, but I'm good at it, and so I'm going to a place where looks mean something: I'm going to shallow, impressionable California, where good, chunky highlights *add value.*

"It's going to be all right," Mrs. Gentry says, patting my wrist. "She's going to miss you. It's her way of making her presence known and that she's still your mother."

"I'll miss her, too, believe it or not." I look into Mrs. Gentry's warm blue eyes. "It may be completely dysfunctional, but it's *our* dysfunction."

"She did her best, Sarah Claire. We all do our best."

I'm sure she did do her best, but she didn't exactly reach for the stars either. I just nod, rather than risk answering and sounding ungrateful. It is what it is, I suppose. But I'm ready for a transformation, and what better place than Hollywood! A place that made Norma Jean Baker into Marilyn Monroe and Archie Leach into Cary Grant. Why not Sarah Claire Winowski into "hairstylist to the stars"? Stranger things have happened. Paris Hilton happened.

"I've been having dreams of styling hair, Mrs. Gentry. I heard on a doctor show that the surgeons practice the surgery in their minds the night before. That's exactly what I do with my styles. I can see my success, taste it. Maybe that sounds ridiculous to you, but I feel like I'm called there, like God has some kind of plan for me laid out in Hollywood."

"Why wouldn't He?"

She's probably placating me, but since she's all the support I've got, I'll take it. "I guess maybe because I'm Sarah Claire Winowski, and where things can go wrong, they tend to explode fantastically. If there's a cow patty in the middle of a football field, it's my shoe that will find it."

She laughs and pats my wrist again. "Without a vision, you'd just end up like us here, who never left the town. Which is fine for us. Enough for us. But you always were a special little girl, always dreaming of some magical gateway into a strange land."

"I think I want the magical gateway *out* of the strange land, actually. Even if things do blow up miserably, I'll be in shorts at the beach and I won't care as much. I won't have to have that fake orange Wyoming tan from *Tantastic*. I can go for the real thing."

"Maybe you'll have a beach wedding and invite all us old ladies to wrap the candied almonds in netting. Was that ever one of your dreams all those times you drifted off from us?" She smoothes my cheek.

"Bless your heart, Mrs. Gentry. You're the only one who thinks a Winowski will marry anyone. And on the beach, no less."

"Not only do I see you married and breaking the family curse—" she raises an eyebrow to tell me what she thinks of my beliefs, "—I see you marrying someone who makes your heart go pitter-patter and treats you like the princess you are. Just like in those books and old movies we use to lose you to."

Mrs. Gentry was the town librarian. If anyone knew about my strange romantic fetishes, it was her.

I smile. "Pitter-patter like Mr. Gentry did for you?"

Her smile dissipates. "I hope for much better for you."

"That's cryptic. You two were always the envy of this town. Maybe you've forgotten that now because he's been gone so long?" I ask this hopefully, because if Mrs. Gentry wasn't the peak of marital bliss, then it just doesn't happen.

She smiles slightly. "You never know what goes on in people's homes, Sarah Claire. Mr. Gentry worked a great deal when he was alive, and since we didn't have children to come home to, he didn't really see the need to spend much time at home. That's why I liked to see you in the library at night. I knew you were safe when your mother worked, and I had some company while reshelving books."

"I think the library was open later than 7-Eleven sometimes."

"Don't misunderstand me, Sarah Claire. It was a good life; I'm not complaining. But it was lonely for both of us for so many years because we misunderstood each other. You have the chance to start fresh, and I want you to do it right. I don't want you to settle for anything less than the best."

What is doing it right? As much as I've read about great passion, no one has ever told me they loved me, or even that I was beautiful. It's sort of hard to fathom I'm going to wake up one day and get it. Once romantically challenged, probably forever that way.

Of course, once a guy in my mother's bar told me that I was hot. But with slurred speech, it came out as "shot" and completely lost all effect. Being beautiful to a middle-aged drunk is hardly a life accomplishment. Well, maybe in this forsaken town it is, but not in Hollywood.

"I can't imagine you lonely, Mrs. Gentry. I've never seen you without your posse." I look over to her giggling friends as they try one of my old cowboy hats on for show.

"I have my faith, Sarah Claire, and you have yours. Don't forget it in California when the men are lining up for a date."

California has a lot more men; therefore, statistically speaking, my odds may improve on romance. But keep in mind I work with hair, and men who are willing to come into a froufrou salon like I'll be working at . . . ? Well, most likely, they're not interested in what I have to offer. In any case, I'm going to hold off on thoughts of romance and get down to the business of becoming the hottest stylist in Beverly Hills.

"Right now, I'm only focused on doing my job, Mrs. Gentry."

I'm not anyone's girlfriend. And truthfully, I can't even say with complete certainty that I'm anyone's daughter—my mother's been a little vague on the subject. Well, I'm God's daughter, but it's not the same, is it? So I've retreated to the life of dreams, created by books and the stirrings of the old movies where life happens like it should.

Life just looks better after a Cary Grant movie.

"Did you hear me, Sarah Claire? You answer your mother!" my mother screeches like a great horned owl vying for its dinner.

"I'll clean it up, Mom." Sheesh, I will always be twelve

despite my twenty-six years here on earth. I want to shrink up and wither away like a salted snail.

Sometimes I wonder, *Why didn't she ever leave?* She seems to have nothing here; yet she clings to the town and this house like a life preserver. And it's going down.

She suddenly retreats inside the house and closes the door. Behind me, I hear the familiar sputter of a diesel pickup. It's the familiar red dualie, chrome running boards and hubcaps. It announces Sable's most prominent resident as sure as any trumpets.

There's a hush at the sight of Mr. Simmons, the town mayor and patriarch—long reputed to be my father. That's the weird thing about a small town. Everyone knows everyone's secrets, but no one ever talks about them. Bud Simmons has never even addressed me, unless it's to ask about my mother. (And if he is my father, may I just say thank goodness I didn't get that nose!)

The party is definitely over. All of the little old ladies give me bear hugs, each with a word of advice before departing as I keep my eye on the truck.

"We love you, Sarah Claire."

"If you need anything, you'll write." Mrs. Rampas barks. "Not on that dratted Internet either. You'll write a real letter like a lady would have done. Do you think Grace Kelly would use e-mail in place of fine, linen stationery?"

"No, ma'am."

"Don't get into any trouble, and don't go home with strangers," Mrs. Townsend says.

"Tell that cousin of yours to come home. He owes this town a visit," Mrs. Piper implores. "And don't follow him into trouble like you used to do. He's a fine boy with a bad habit for finding trouble, so you mind what you've been taught."

"By us," Mrs. Townsend reminds me. *Not your mother* is implied.

Finally, Mrs. Gentry envelops me in her giant, bone-crushing hug. She has tears in her eyes when she pulls away. "We'll take care of your mother, sweetheart. You go ahead and live your own life. It's time now."

I can only nod because her words make me wish things were different. That I could go back in time and fix things. Maybe if this had all happened in the forties, my mother would never have been a "bad girl" and my father would have married her and gone off to war to be the hero. We might have met him at the station for his triumphant return and listened to Glenn Miller as we praised God for bringing him home to us safely. But yeah. As it is, my father is a weenie of a man who can't speak to my mother directly for fear his wife will bat him over the head, and my mother torments herself with drink and unemployed men. *Strike up the band!*

"I love you, sweetheart. God go with you. I'll be praying every morning for you. We'll all be praying. You don't go alone. Don't forget that," Mrs. Gentry says.

I stand up straighter and peer into the future, all the while watching my so-called father amble out of his truck. "I'm going to matter. I promise you that much."

"You always have, Sarah Claire. This is just your chance to prove it to yourself."

The ladies climb into Mrs. Piper's Suburban and wave as they drive onto the highway, leaving a trail of dust. I can hear their hearty laughter through the brown dust as they head down the road with their trinkets from the sale in tow, and I can't help but wonder if they're stopping off at the dump on the way home or if they'll keep the things as reminders to pray for me.

Ryan stands guard behind me as Mr. Simmons approaches, the nose arriving well before the man. "It's all right, Ryan. I want to hear if he has anything to say." Granted, I'm not expecting any drawn-out, tearful goodbye, but you know, maybe he'll tell me he's thankful I didn't inherit his nose. It's the least he can do.

Ryan whispers in my ear, "If he wants to pay you in cattle for all the lost years, I'll take care of them for you." He grins. "The sooner I can get started, the sooner I can bring Kate home where she belongs."

"And I'd give those cattle to you. But get real—I'll be lucky if he has a leather keychain for me. I don't think guilt or conscience is part of his makeup." Actually, I don't think emotion is part of his makeup—but that's the embittered Sarah Claire talking, and I'm done with her for now.

Bud Simmons walks up to the picnic table, displaying all my costume jewelry and kitchen utensils. I notice he never meets my eyes, and he keeps the table between us. He'd probably rather face down a bull in heat than his as yet unclaimed illegitimate daughter. It makes me want to sing and dance like an old Shirley Temple movie and show him what he's missing. But with my luck, he'd think all he was missing was the bill from the psych ward at Sable General.

He picks up a wire whisk from the table and studies it. "Won't your mother need this when you go?"

"She generally likes to eat breakfast out." I can't help myself. "With handsome men."

Across the road, Mrs. Simmons sits in the truck, watching me as if I'm about to devour her husband. *Listen, honey. You're about the only one in this town who thinks this man is worth a lick. You and that . . . that daughter of yours.*

Spawn might be a better word. I know a Christian

shouldn't use words like *spawn* to describe their half-sisters, but whatever. She's spawn.

"Doesn't your wife want to come look? Lots of good stuff here. A lifetime of memories and treasures, yours for a song. It's all got to go. I'm leaving tomorrow."

"Evelyn's fine in the truck. She has everything she needs."

Then maybe you should just mount her beside the longhorn hood ornament.

"So she's staying, then, your mother?" he asks the wire whisk.

"As far as I know." I watch him look up at the house, and I notice the longing in his eyes. "I'll probably bring her to California when I'm settled. When the big money comes in, you know? I'm going to work at Yoshi's in Beverly Hills."

He flinches slightly. I've never doubted he's always loved my mother. He's just too much of a wimp to ever make a decent woman out of her. He was that way before he married Mrs. Simmons, and twenty-six years later not a thing has changed. Only he's older and craggier (and I think my mother is a little wiser—albeit maybe a little drunker as well). He finds his manhood in big trucks, cattle drives, his blooming bank account, and treating the women in his life like an accessory.

If that doesn't give you an indication as to why I veer toward the golden Hollywood age for my sense of heroism, I don't know what will. I simply can't imagine Cary Grant having an affair with a woman like my mother, falling in love, and then deciding she wasn't good enough to marry. And, worse yet, marrying the angry young Evelyn Weathers when his mother told him to. Maybe life needs a good director for the Hollywood ending.

Bud touches the string of his bolo tie and clears his throat. "You'll tell her I wish her the best without you? She gave up everything for you to have the life you did." He says this like I'm living the dream or something.

"You're going to buy the whisk?" I ask him.

"Fifty cents, huh? I'll give you a quarter for it."

"Deal."

He hands me the quarter, and I slide it in my front pocket. *Heartwarming.* Something to remember my father by.

Without another word, he takes his whisk, waits for a truck to pass by on the highway, and jogs to his waiting dualie and wife.

Ryan comes up behind me. "Do you think he's really my father?" I ask. "I sure don't see any family resemblance." I look up at Ryan. "And you better not either."

"Oh, yeah, he's your dad. No doubt. Did you see the way he watched for your mother the whole time?"

"My mother had bad taste."

"The worst," he agrees.

"I hope I didn't inherit it."

"Your mother wouldn't have looked twice at Cary Grant or Humphrey Bogart."

This makes me laugh out loud. "I love you, Ryan. You're perfect for Kate."

"No, she definitely deserves better than me. But I hope to spend every day thanking her for lowering herself to my level."

"I'll be home for the wedding." I give him a big hug.

"We'll be in California for yours. As soon as you round up the new Cary, whoever that might be." He laughs and starts picking up all the remnants of the yard sale (pretty much everything I tried to sell) and shoving it into the back of his old pickup.

"At least take a twenty for the dump fees." I hold up a bill.

He snorts. "Dump fees? I'm sweeping out my truck at the end of your daddy's property. It's about time he cleaned up some of his own mess."

"Well, I'm going to finish packing. You take care."

With a last wave, I take the front steps two at a time and open the squeaky screen door. My house is not what you'd expect. It's spotless, with the distinct odor of bleach most of the day and lines from the vacuum cleaner in the aged, orange carpet. We have that linoleum from decades gone by that doesn't wear but instead gets uglier as the designs appear to get bigger and darker over the years. It's a nice complement to the wall made out of mirrored tiles with gold squiggle decorations.

Spotless and yet still disgusting—now that takes talent. It makes you want to get drunk just so it makes some sort of sense. Everything has its place. Not the least of which is the alcohol. Mom alphabetizes the bottles along the mirrored bar wall and has always claimed she'd know if I took any. As if. Not even our decor would lead me to the booze. And trust me, if something was going to, it would definitely be the 1970s decor in my living room.

I vowed I'd never drink. Not out of piety or any religious conviction, but because having a mother like mine turned me into a control freak early on, and I would never allow something as mundane as alcohol to take what little power I had. I could vacuum, read, lose myself in old movies, and stay sober. That was pretty much it, so that's where I took my control.

"What did he want?" My mother is staring out the front window, which despite the dust outside, is sparkling clean (thanks to white vinegar and newspaper).

"He wanted to know if you were coming with me."

"What did you tell him?"

"I told him as soon as I could arrange for it."

She purses her lips. "You know I'll never leave here." But she pauses a moment, so I know at least she's thinking about the idea, pondering what life might be like.

"I know that. But he doesn't. You ought to make him suffer just a little bit. Don't you have the slightest desire to have him hurt just a little?" I pick up the suitcase I bought at Wal-Mart and unzip it. "This thing looked bigger in the store."

"You need to iron those jeans," she says as I fold a pair out of the laundry basket.

"You don't need to iron jeans." I receive her disapproving look. "I'll iron them in California."

She takes them from me and folds them brusquely into the suitcase. "You tell those old busybodies to mind their own business. I'm not going to church, and I don't need anyone checking on me or bringing me cookies to make me fat, you got it? Those women think they know my story, but they don't know anything and neither do you, so don't go thinking things will be so different in California. Life wears you down, Sarah Claire. You try to fight it, but it wears you down, and those women did their part."

"Mom, they're not like that. The women who are like that don't talk to me. I'm not worthy, you know?"

"They always thumbed their noses at us. You think you can make it different, but you can't make it any different, Sarah Claire. Their minds were made up a long time ago, whether they converted you or not."

I know better than to argue. "Don't forget to show up for your hearing, Mom. I put a thousand dollars down saying you'd be there."

"A thousand dollars. What does that judge think I did that's worth ten thousand dollars' bail?"

"Drunk driving is serious these days." She's looking the other way, so I roll my eyes and mouth a big *Duh*, if for nothing else than my own sanity. "It's not like twenty years ago when no one was on these roads. You could have killed someone besides yourself."

"Don't lecture me! I wasn't drunk. I don't care what his little walk-on-the-white-line test told him. I'm old. You try walking straight when you get to be my age."

"You're forty-three, Mom. That's not old."

"It's too old to walk straight on a white line at midnight, I'll tell you that." She holds up one of my shirts to indicate that it, too, needs to be ironed. "I'll get your precious money back. I only had to borrow because the mortgage was due. I assumed you wanted a roof over your head."

My mother is refolding everything I put into the suitcase from the laundry basket, and suddenly I'm just not in the mood. "You know, I need a nap; I think I'll pack later."

ॐ

In my room I plop onto my bed, gazing up at my ceiling and my poster of Cary Grant as he stares off into the distance, his cleft chin resting on his gentle hands.

"Everyone wants to be Cary Grant," he famously said. "Even I want to be Cary Grant."

"I do too, Cary. I want to be Audrey Hepburn and Deborah Kerr and everything old Hollywood has to offer. I want to live the dream." I smile, thinking tomorrow I'm really going to be doing it.

Back when I put that poster up, I was too young to realize it (and too old even then for posters on my ceiling), but subconsciously I saw something in that photo that gave me hope. I always believed God had more for me than this aged yet immaculate house, and for some reason, that poster—those sultry, deep, brown eyes—kept the dream alive. Long enough for me to save up the money to get out.

God didn't give me an overly active imagination and a friend in the library—with extensive access to VHS movies from times gone by—for nothing. It was my escape. I saw myself as part of something bigger. Even in school when the wealthy ranchers' kids called me white trash, I waited with anticipation for my life to change, for the right moment to embrace my fantabulous destiny. I imagined a hero (who may or may not have looked like Cary) who would love me intensely. He would travel across the Tetons to pluck me from my average existence and take me to my destiny and a life of romance and adventure. Just like Cary did in *North by Northwest.*

I wanted chivalry, pure and simple. And to be a part of Hollywood's history—and its future.

My active imagination is probably brought on by some form of psychosis, but it's there nonetheless. I read once that sometimes psychosis is healthy because it allows you to escape a poor reality. So I'm just waiting for the time continuum to shift, and I am on my way out of my unhealthy reality! Totally healthy.

But it's not particularly practical. In a nutshell, what I currently possess is my men-in-fedoras dream, a talent for hair, and a single quarter from my father for my troubles. If that isn't God telling me something . . .

God spoke to me. Oh, I know that's a hallmark for crazy people, but I was watching Cary Grant and Ingrid Bergman in *Notorious* and He spoke. When Cary swooped

Ingrid up in his arms to keep her from being poisoned, even though she had a past and a reputation and wasn't the kind of girl you bring home to mother, I realized there wasn't anyone to sweep me up. There never had been and there was no sense waiting for it to happen. I realized the only person who could change anything about my life was me. So I did. I called my cousin and made arrangements for California and my dream of becoming more than I could be here in Sable. Not just a hairdresser but the best of the best.

I decided to matter. Without the help of a man. I mean, after all, with the number of Christian men in Sable, minus the ones whose mamas wouldn't let them within twenty feet of me, I've had about as much chance of pairing up as a third hermaphrodite gorilla on the ark.

Ingrid's grand escape in Cary's outstretched arms was my sign from God.

I hear the doorbell and then my mother's bedroom door slamming, which is my signal that it's for me. Kate is standing at the window, waving at me. She opens the door and sticks her head in. "How was the yard sale?"

"I sold everything." Then I shake my head. "No, really, the ladies of Bell Baptist paid me for nothing, and your fiancé took the rest to the dump."

"Stellar. Mrs. Ball said good-bye. She was in today for a perm. She said she'd miss you quoting the stars' hair colors, and she still wants to know Betty Grable's."

"I told her, I can't find anything but a black-and-white photo. I *can* tell her it wasn't blue, and most likely it was a ten. Perfectly platinum."

"Ah, to have your color talent. It's a pity you didn't get much practice here. Hollywood is going to be perfect for you. People are really willing to try new things there. I read in the *Enquirer* that everyone in Hollywood colors their hair, even the guys! With highlights and everything. Even the men own hair products like flat irons. Can you imagine if one of our cowboys came in for highlights?"

"I tried to get Ryan to let me practice. He told me only one woman touches his hair. I think he thought I was trying to pick him up." I don't mention he always thinks that.

"He said that?" Kate plops onto the couch, letting her eyes rest on the mirrored wall. She's heavenly beautiful with sweeping curls of blonde hair and an inherent innocence in her bright blue eyes. Her sweet looks belie her sarcastic, Siamese personality, but I'm not sure that anyone but me sees the "quipping Kate." That side of her is reserved for me alone. Everyone else gets the sweet-country-girl-next-door. I get Roseanne Barr.

"He did. He said only you touch his hair, that it's an intimate act for him."

Her expression is dubious. "You're scaring me. He did not say that."

"He did. It was right before graduation from beauty college. I asked if he'd let me try a Ryan Seacrest on him. Kate, what's the matter? Are you mad at me?"

"Do you think Ryan and I are right for each other?"

"Um, yeah. The whole town does."

"I know what the town thinks. I'm asking you." Kate gets up and paces the room, fiddling with various knick-knacks.

"If a guy like Ryan would ask me to marry him, I'd have no reason to move, Kate."

She rolls her eyes. "That's what you think, huh? You do live in a dream world. So have you been studying the stars' hair colors for Yoshi?"

I nod. "I've been watching Yoshi's color videos. I want

to be an artist in my own right."

"That is definitely you. Too bad I'm the only one who's ever let you practice. You're too cutting-edge for Sable."

"I am not cutting edge."

"For Sable you are."

"For Hollywood, I'm probably a step above a Clampett. Can't you hear the banjo now?"

"Stop it. Don't bother going if you're going to take that woe-is-me attitude. Stay here and be a loser."

"I am not a loser!"

"Of course you aren't. I'm not friends with losers. I'm not saying this should go to your head or anything, but you do have to cop a little attitude or you won't make it. Repeat after me: José Eber can eat my dust!"

"José Eber can eat my dust!"

"Men in cowboy hats with mullets should not be designing hair."

I laugh. "Men in cowboy hats with mullets should not be designing hair."

"I am not a Clampett. I am a Faith Hill, ready to find my star."

"I am not a Clampett. I am Faith Hill, ready to find my star."

"And snag a Tim McGraw in the process!"

"Now there is a cowboy worthy of Hollywood status."

"A moment of silence for Tim McGraw's worthiness."

We both break into giggles, and I feel a renewed surge of adrenaline. "Girl, I am going to Hollywood!"

"I don't mean to be a downer, but you think your mom's going to be all right?" Kate nods toward her door. As if reading our thoughts, my mother comes out of her room, grabs a bottle of scotch out of the bar, and heads back into her lair, slamming the door behind her.

I shrug. "Will it make any difference if I'm here or not?"

"Probably not." Kate kicks her feet up on the coffee table. "One day I hope this whole town realizes what they've lost. Especially that sniveling Cindy Simmons, who for some reason I can't bring myself to color right. My hand just slips every time I'm mixing."

"You better watch that; she might have Daddy sue you."

"Let her sue me. Then she can go over to the Snippy Curl and get it done."

I laugh. "If I get famous, I wonder if my father will ever claim he's my father."

"I wonder why your mom doesn't make it public. I would have brought the scoundrel down a long time ago."

"I think she secretly hopes one day he'll come back to her."

"You can't be serious."

"Why else would she stay in this house and keep it like June Cleaver lives here, until the next drunken binge. It doesn't make any sense. *She* doesn't make any sense."

"That would be so romantic if he came for her—except for the whole leaving-his-family thing. That's not very Christian."

"Romantic? You think? The thought grosses me out. You need to sit and watch *An Affair to Remember* with me again. A true hero crosses barriers for love. Bud Simmons wouldn't cross the street for someone else. My mother can do better than him."

"And she has done better than him. Many times," Kate quips.

"Just never mind."

"I hope you keep your head on straight when you get to California. As I keep reminding you, *An Affair* is a movie. And Cary Grant was married how many times in real life?"

"I'll keep my head on straight, but *An Affair to Remember* is not just a movie. It's a beautiful dream. He doesn't love her because she's beautiful or because they met on a luxurious ocean liner. No. He loves her for who she is, for what they are together." I sigh wistfully, mostly for Kate's benefit. The elderly set gets it; why doesn't she?

"*Kate & Leopold* is more for me. If Hugh Jackman in Victorian garb so much as crosses a T for me, I'm there."

"Ah, yes. I spent many a night watching that one too. Mostly because I wanted to figure out what happened to Meg Ryan's lips."

"You spent many a night watching everything, reading everything, hanging out at the library with the widowed set —have I mentioned you have no life? I hope you find your life in California."

"Many times, and really, did you have to? If I had a boyfriend like yours, I'd have a life too, Kate. Did you ever think of that?"

"Now's your chance to actually live a little, not just as a couch potato to fake men in Victorian suits and fedoras. The only time I ever saw a real man in a suit was at a funeral."

"I'm just thrilled you finally get what a fedora is."

"It's a hat. For Johnny Depp wannabes and men who saw Indiana Jones one too many times. The Maltese Falcon has been located, so in actuality there is no reason to don a fedora in this day and age." Kate stares at me like I might be getting an idea. She has that way of telling my fantasy life to cool it just by staring at me. "That goes for men in suits too."

"I doubt Beverly Hills is like that. Dr. Rey wears suits all the time on *Dr. 90210*."

"You don't want a man in a suit, Sarah Claire. He's most likely an undertaker."

"No one dies in Beverly Hills. Duh. It's all the hair dye. It preserves them. They just get more skin pulled back and keep going."

"Whatever. You ready to hit the airport? I'll pick you up first thing in the morning."

I look at my half-empty suitcase. "I'm not packed yet. My mother was on ironing patrol."

"Well, she's going to be ironed to the sheets in a few minutes. Just wait until she's passed out."

I exhale, feeling my exhaustion to the core. "I should say good-bye before she's too numb to remember that I did."

"Better you than me. This is her chance, too, so lose the guilt. I'll see you in the morning."

With a wave, she's gone.

I think about what she said. There's no sympathy for the town drunk, except maybe at the bar. One thing I have to say for the drinking establishments of America is they take in most anybody. They accept you come-as-you-are with no effort whatsoever. My mother walks in with her roots showing three months of growth and wearing a halter top, and she'll still find a sympathetic ear. Someone willing to commiserate with her, have a drink with her, meet her where she is.

When I first became a Christian, I was naïve enough to believe the church would do this for her and she wouldn't have to drink anymore. I was fresh off the conversion high, and practicality didn't enter into my equation. Well, let me just say I learned the hard way there's a difference between God's grace and the church's.

Before entering my mother's room, I pause, wondering

what exactly I might get behind door number one. Will it be Mom number 1, the sorrowful woman who's crushed I'm leaving and needs to sniffle on my shoulder? Will it be Mom number 2, who hands me bleach and wants me to scour something before I leave. Or Mom number 3, who is no longer with us. I knock on the door, and when there's no answer, I open it.

"Don't go, baby."

Mom number 1 it is.

"We're a team. We've always been a team." She uses the back of her hand to wipe her moist cheeks.

I go in and sit down. "Mom, do you know how hard it is to get into this program? It's like we've won the lottery. I want life to change for us, don't you?"

"Not if it means you're leaving."

I take the bottle from her hands. "This will change things, Mom. You've got your entire life before you."

She nods as if she really wants to believe me while I stare at the bottle and her tears and wonder if anything will ever really change. What if my destiny is to be alone like her? To clean up after her?

"I love you, baby. You have to try this. I understand." But it's clear she doesn't. "You don't let them give you any crap, you hear me?"

"I won't, Mom. I love you." I kiss her on the cheek. "Thank you for working so hard for me. Now it's my turn."

I take the bottle to put back on the shelf on my way out. "You always were a selfish girl," she slurs and falls back onto the bed.

Lifting the bottle, I can see it's nearly gone. "A record," I say to my already snoring mother. "I have to be selfish, Mom, because the plastic people need me." I cup my ear.

"I hear them calling, *'Sarah Claire, where are you? Rescue me with perfect highlights and a shaped cut!'*"

Some people go to college. Others of us have a higher calling in foils and highlights. There's only one road to success in Sable, Wyoming, and it leads directly out of town.

chapter 2

*I pretended to be somebody I wanted
to be until finally I became that person.
Or he became me.*
~ Cary Grant

As the plane touches down, my stomach swirls with both anticipation and abject fear. I keep hearing my mother's nagging voice taunt me on my future failure: *"You'll never make it in the land of those fruits and nuts!"*

As opposed to the fruits and nuts at home, I'm guessing she meant. Maybe some of them here won't be dried and cured, at the very least.

The plane taxis the runway and pulls into its slot. When I look out the window and see the smog-filled air and graying buildings, I see only opportunity awaiting me. No one knows me here. There will be no looks or snickers. No one waiting to call me "white trash." No whispers of my father. *In fact,* I think with satisfaction, *I can say he's dead.*

Exploding with anticipation for the life awaiting me, I practically burst from the airplane, pushing past slow cowboys and sluggish vacation travelers. "Excuse me, excuse me." *New life starting here. Outta my way.*

෧

Okay, so I didn't expect my new life to be quite so smoggy. The choking scent of diesel—and probably two parts carbon monoxide—fill my lungs, and I put my hand over my nose to breathe. There's a sea of slow-moving cars outside the airport, men with whistles in orange moving them along, and the occasional screech of brakes. I look at my watch again. Scott's late.

What else is new? He never allows for enough time to finish anything properly, but he makes life so fun, no one cares. People love to be near him, and he can pretty much do whatever he likes and get away with it. Just for one day, I'd like to have that power and know the people attracted to me are not all over seventy years of age with the distinct need to mother me. (Even if I do need it.)

I park myself at the curb, listening to the security warnings replay again and again. Taxis and foreign makes vie for curb frontage, and I drink in the sights of sheiks in headwraps, Indians, businessmen in suits, and elegant women coordinated from head to toe, including their luggage. Some even carrying matching dogs. A new wave of passengers fills the curb, and I search for Scott's car. My first day in California and already my luck is starting. I'm abandoned in the bowels of LAX and I get to see that even dogs here have a place in this world.

Finally, a horn honks. Scott squeals up to the curb in a fancy, electric-blue coupe, flashing a magnetic smile from behind the windshield. It's *that* noticeably white. If the boys back home knew he wasn't driving a truck, he'd never hear the end of it. But as far as painting his teeth? I'm not sure I'd want to be there when they discovered that. As Britney Spears would say, "We're country."

Scott is a lean, graceful man, and I feel my stomach swirl in anticipation at the sight of him. I feel like I'm about to embark on the adventure of a lifetime, and—like when we were kids—Scott will lead the way. Oh, we'll probably get in trouble for it, but it will be worth it!

"Little Sarah Claire, look at you!" Scotty slams his door shut, opening his trunk before wrapping me in a hug. "I can't believe you came! I thought for sure you'd chicken out or your mother would tell you what a ridiculous idea it was and you'd slink home to your old movies and even older ladies."

"So rude. You're still rude."

"I'm in California. I'm supposed to be rude."

"I'm here, and I have no intention of being rude."

"Give it time. You'll be rude too."

"I'm going to be the best in my field, just like you, Scott. Only nice."

"I have no doubt you'll do your best, but just be warned: there are a thousand others just like you, and rudeness will help."

"There are none like me."

"That's my girl. Cop the attitude; you're going to need it."

"Speaking of cops, did you see that guy in handcuffs against the wall?"

He laughs at me. "You'll be seeing that often, except when you're at the salon. Beverly Hills doesn't have crime, at least not of the blue-collar sort. I think they arrest homeless there."

"They do not."

"They don't roll out the red carpet like San Francisco does, that's for certain."

"Think, Scott, you *have* homeless! It's too dang cold to have them in Wyoming."

"Which is why they have bar flies instead." He smoothes his hair.

"You look . . . you look shiny." *What's he using on his skin? Vaseline? That is definitely worth a butt-whooping back home.*

"This all you brought?" He picks up my suitcase, which now looks paltry beside his long torso. "Where'd you get this piece?" His disdain is evident.

"Again with the rude, Scott. I'm in the land of shopping. I figured I could get what I needed here." Granted, I don't have any actual money, but like Scarlett, I'll think about that tomorrow.

"What did your mother say about you coming here?"

"She wasn't exactly thrilled I was staying with you. She says you're a bad influence."

He laughs out loud. "She left you home alone with a book every night until three a.m. when you were a kid, but I'm a bad influence. Gotta love Janey Winowski. She's not responsible for a dang thing, is she?"

"She gave me stuff to clean while she was gone at night."

"Well, that makes her mother of the year, doesn't it, Sarah Claire? She may have withheld her love and nurturing, but she gave you bleach. Love in a Clorox bottle." He wipes his eyes. "It brings tears to a man's soul, it really does."

Obviously, there's no love lost between my cousin and my mother. "Mrs. Gentry told me before I left that my mother did the best she could."

"I'm sure she did for someone looking at the world though a bottle of scotch."

"I told her I'd had a dream where Cary Grant said I should move to California."

"Really? Cary Grant? Nice touch."

"You'd be proud. I'm not enabling anymore. I'm taking my life into my own hands."

"Do what you have to Sara Claire. I'm sure after a few more swigs, it made perfect sense to her."

"What she said is, 'Life is about living, not wishing all the time. In case you ain't noticed, Prince Charming ain't coming to rescue us.'"

"That sounds like your mom."

"I didn't back down though, Scott. I was so proud of myself. I asked her what was life without a dream."

"And?"

"'Reality, darlin'.'" I say in her twang. "'The longer you live in that dream world, the more disappointed with life you'll be. There ain't nothing in California you haven't got here.'"

"And you said?"

"'There's the ocean,' I said. 'You got lakes here,'" she answered."

"So what did it really take to break out from her spell, Sarah Claire?"

"I told her I'd get a job and send real money."

"Ah." Scott slams the trunk. "That's the auntie I know and love. 'Who's going to supply me with my next drink and post bail? I know, I'll get my daughter to do it.'"

"Scott, come on. I want to respect her. I need to respect her, but not her actions."

"That's just bull—"

"Never mind. I'm here."

"You may be here physically, but until you can lose the guilt, I'm afraid you'll run right back at her first frantic phone call."

"I won't. I made you a promise."

It wasn't like Mom could talk me out of the move; I am an adult, after all. But I also know she's a master manipulator, and I had to brace for it. She struggled like an upside-down beetle to undermine me with all her passive-aggressive reasons I shouldn't go.

"They'll never accept you there, Sarah Claire." As though I'd been the pinnacle of popularity in Sable. Dateless since high school is not exactly bordering on accepted, am I right?

If Scott hadn't sent me airfare, I would have fallen victim to the guilt, just like I always do. Being here, actually seeing more people than I knew existed—and this just at the airport—has changed something in me. This is my chance to be something different, to be my own person with a real career. I'm not going back unless I'm taken kicking and screaming. I have fingernails and sharp shears, and I know how to use them.

Scott opens the door to the little blue coupe for me, and I crawl inside to the supple leather seats in front of the shiny wood console. He jogs around the car, climbs into the driver's seat, and stops to look me over. "Little Sarah Claire come to California. I can't believe it."

My breath sucks in all the diesel the airport has to offer as Scott races toward the exit and the hazy sunshine, where my mouth drops at the concrete jungle and traffic before us. "I can't believe it either, Scott. I feel like my life starts today."

Sable, Wyoming can eat my dust. Except for all the sweet people I left. But that makes me want to cry, so I stick with the first thought: *Sable, Wyoming can eat my dust.*

I never liked the name Eldred.
Since nobody knew me in New York,
I just changed to my middle name.
~ Gregory Peck

"We're going right to the salon." Scott stares at me. "After we get you a pair of jeans. What are you thinking? You're not walking into Yoshi dressed in knockoffs." He shakes his head. "And not even good knockoffs, Sarah Claire."

"You told me not to wear Lee's, so I got these."

"You're trying to tell me the whole of Wyoming wears Lee's?"

"Of course not. I'm just saying I don't have many options in Sable, and I ordered these off the Internet."

"Right there, okay, that's what we have to work on. If you're going to order fakes, go to eBay and buy some real fakes. You're not even trying here."

I slink into my seat. "They're jeans, Scott. Denim is denim."

"You can't really believe that. If you believe that, you're in the wrong line of work. The beauty industry is not one where you walk into the salon in knockoffs and think no one notices. Is dye-at-home hair color the same thing as perfected highlights by a master?"

"Of course not, but—"

"But nothing. If it's not the same in your business, it's not the same in mine. Clothes matter here."

"I wasn't going to pay over one hundred dollars for jeans. That's ridiculous."

He scratches his forehead. "Okay, we're going to start at the beginning. This is a town where image is everything. If you thought Cindy Simmons made your life miserable in high school, you are about to encounter every popular girl who ever made girls' lives miserable across the country. They all came here with the hopes of being actresses and making the country's life miserable. The popularity contest only got bigger. Only now they all want to be on TV and on the cover of *People* and make your life miserable, all right?"

"I want to change people's lives who always thought they were nothing because of those girls."

"Then I'll get you a job in the valley."

My face is heating up so I break off the conversation and look around our vehicle. "I only see three types of cars here. What are those ugly bubble things everyone's driving?"

"They're hybrids."

"Why does everyone drive them?"

"They save on fuel, you get to drive in the commuter lane, and they're politically correct."

"Do they have another style? Or just that ugly one?"

"That's the most popular. Sarah Claire, we're talking about jeans. Quit changing the subject."

"Why is that the most popular? It's vicious ugly."

"They just are. It's a way of making a statement you care about the environment. Many of my clients drive them."

"Because they want to?"

"It makes a statement."

"Hey, I'm a country gal; I'm all for the environment. But I would rather commute with a friend than drive one of those things."

"No one's going your way here. You'll figure it out. You need a car and good jeans."

"Fine, but I'm not driving what everyone says I should. Until they make a hybrid that doesn't look like that, I'm a guzzler. Besides, don't their private jets sort of ruin the point of that?"

"Never mind. You don't have to drive a hybrid, all right? I'm not driving one."

"What's the point of having anything if you have to bow to expectation? Everyone has the money to drive what they want, but the culture says they have to buy a hybrid? I mean, great for the environment and all, but it's like being in high school all over again, only with a hypocritical point. Get a bicycle."

"You can't drive a bicycle in LA. You'd be dead in a week."

We pull up alongside a red hybrid at the stoplight. "Look at that, Scott. They're in cloth seats."

"Of course they are. Leather is bad for actors. PETA would get after them. Not that everyone's an actor, but they set a precedent here."

"So basically you're fine if you do everything that's acceptable according to the unspoken rules?" *Just like church.*

"It's not that bad; it's just not the era to drive a Hummer, all right?"

"I've just moved three states to live in a perpetual hazing from the popular table? Is that what you're telling me?"

"I'm telling you that your cheap jeans will not cut it in Beverly Hills. If you want to turn it into a battle over the environment, that's your issue."

"I'm not arguing the environment, but I lived in the country, Scott. I have yet to see something not covered with cement, so it strikes me as slightly hypocritical that you drive a small vehicle and suddenly you're John Muir." I raise my hands. "All I'm saying."

"Stop avoiding the clothing issue," Scott says, clamping his hands around the wheel until his knuckles are white. *Now he knows how I feel!* "You want to work with the best, you have to dress like the best."

"Okay, I've got you. The jeans are not kosher. I won't wear them to work."

"You won't wear them anywhere. This is not a job where you leave your image at the salon."

"Scott, I'm going to cut hair not broker world peace. Could you get a grip?"

"Where'd you get those things anyway? They have a seam on the back of the knee. Do you know that? Right across your knees is a line where some cheap two-bit company sewed your jeans together and ran out of fabric in the middle of it. You're supposed to be from New York City, and right now you look like you got dressed in a third-world country."

"I'm supposed to be from where?" Instinctively, I grab my jeans at the knees and realize he's right. I feel the lines across them, and suddenly making fun of the ugly-car-driving lemmings seems futile. Here I was thinking I'm runway material—okay, with the wrong squiggle—but instead I'm wearing quilted jeans. *I'm like a walking denim patchwork.*

"New York. It's a big city on the east coast. You know it?"

"I know it, but I don't think anyone will buy it. I'm not exactly Manhattan chic, you know?"

"No, you're not."

Now I know my cousin is a stylist. I know he's put his reputation on the line for me. But I can't believe in any world my jean choice could make this kind of impact. And if it does, that's just frightening.

"I'll buy new jeans tomorrow," I promise.

"Life doesn't mosey along here like back home. Everything is ramped up. Think of LA as a nickname for Life on Amphetamines. Got it? You've got to throw away the tomorrow's-just-as-good way of thinking. You'll die here." He pulls his hands off the wheel and snaps his fingers. "Like this, or die, got it?"

I hang on to the dashboard, thinking his driving is going to kill us and I'll be a footnote in his obituary. *Stylist to the stars Scott Weston died in a horrendous car wreck with an unknown woman dressed in sorry knockoffs at his side. Authorities say it may have been a homeless woman he helped off the street.*

"You haven't been to Wyoming in a long time, Scott. It's not backwoods like you remember."

He raises an eyebrow. "Sarah Claire, if you're here to tell me Sable isn't backwoods, you don't stand a snowball's chance in Malibu. You can just get back on the plane."

"I blew it on the jeans. Can we move on?"

He shrugs and goes back to driving, and I take a moment to study him. In contrast to his country-bumpkin cousin, Scott's the epitome of sophistication. He makes it look like he doesn't have to work on it—although if I know him, about an hour of thought went into every detail before he laid it out the previous night. Growing up around a lot of booze, we are nothing if not anal.

Scott's suit is impeccable: gray striped with an open pink-collared shirt. He screams new and fresh, like a newborn in the hospital. I am stained with stale air and greasy-chip essence, and probably a whiff of hard liquor from my nearest seatmate. I am Courtney Love without a stylist. Queen Esther before the beauty treatments. I am raw. A complete clod beside a Brooks Brothers' mannequin.

"I'm sufficiently humbled, all right?"

He loosens his grip on the steering wheel. "I'm sorry, Sarah Claire."

"You don't want me to embarrass you. I understand. I don't want to embarrass you either, Scott."

"It's not tagging along to one of my friend's parties, Sarah Claire. This is serious. No one knows where I'm from, and I don't want them to. Just please do what I ask of you. I brought you out here."

My cousin's facade of steel melts in his anxious expression. The same one he'd use before his father belted him one across the face. With dread, I realize his fears are all still there. And here I thought he had it all together. If he doesn't have it all together, there's no hope for me.

"You won't mess up. We can't afford it. This is not a nuclear disaster. You bought cheap jeans, a natural amateur mistake. We just need to work on image before we let you loose in Beverly Hills, all right?"

"Shouldn't it be natural to me if I'm going to do this? Like how I cut hair?"

He sees my lower lip trembling, and his tone reverts to the big-brother cousin I know. The one who is trustworthy and not completely mental about jeans. "There's just a few secret ingredients necessary to stir the pot of image. The main course is confidence. If you can wear a sack with confidence, it can become the latest rage tomorrow."

I nod, sucking on my wobbly lip. If I was looking to my cousin for mental stability, I think I've sorely underestimated the situation. My family gene pool is looking more like the cesspool I've known all along. Only in a better outfit.

"Thank you for getting me out, Scott." *Even if you are as mentally unstable as my mother. I can do crazy. I know crazy.*

"I promised you."

"When you were twelve you promised me. I never expected you to keep it. I'm just nervous about meeting Yoshi."

"He's fantastic. A true artist. You won't have any trouble bowing to his greatness. I wouldn't have done this if I didn't trust you, but you've got to trust your instincts a little bit."

But my own instincts told me to buy third-world jeans, so for now I have to learn to distrust my instincts. And to vow that my goal in life is not to drive a hybrid—and that my vehicle will sport leather. Real leather.

I throw my shoulders back. "If I can suck a pollywog up a rubber tube for biology, I can do this."

"Sarah Claire, I forbid you to ever mention that again." His gag reflex kicks in, and he makes a horrible retching sound.

I crumble into laughter. "You always were an incredible wuss."

"Who's making an incredible salary because of it, so don't knock it. If I'd been good at dirt things, I wouldn't have left home." He holds up a manicured hand. "So remember, you're from the Upper West Side in New York. Didn't I mention this in my e-mails?"

"I thought you were kidding. You don't want me to lie. Trust me on this: I'm terrible at it, and I'll make fools out of both of us."

In case it's not obvious, Scott has a strange relationship with truth. If he believes it in his own mind, it is truth, and any information to the contrary doesn't enter into his equation. Therefore, if Scott believes I'm from the Upper West Side, so will everyone else—that is, until I enter the picture. *I* feel guilty lying to a telemarketer.

Not to mention that it goes against my faith, but Scott is not exactly open to the idea of God. And I imagine my "dream" about Cary Grant hasn't helped him see his way clearly back to the truth.

"Do they really look like knockoffs?" I ask, incredulous that anyone would look that closely at such a utilitarian piece of clothing. "Or are you just being snotty?"

He raises his eyebrows, "They *scream* knockoff. Quality jeans are soft, Sarah Claire. Those things look like the old Sears Toughskins my dad used to make me wear." He shakes his head. "Painful. They had to stitch it together behind the legs? It reminds me of those old rabbit-fur jackets they pieced together in the seventies."

So a complete waste of thirty-nine dollars plus shipping. "I liked Toughskins, you know? They lasted forever and they were different from the Lee's that everybody wore. They made me unique."

"They really didn't. They made you look like you couldn't afford Lee's, which was, in fact, the case. First rule of thumb: we do not pick our clothes based on their half-life." Scott continues to stare at me, even though he's driving about eighty miles an hour a mere five feet behind the car in front of him. I grip the armrest, digging my nails into the leather. "Listen, if you think Yoshi is going to hire some girl from Wyoming—worse yet, the Hideway Bar & Grill slash Hair Salon—you've had too much happy punch on the plane."

"The bar was next door; it wasn't part of the salon."

"Was it in the same building?"

"Well, yeah, but a totally different space."

"Did you share the same parking lot?"

"Yeah, but we weren't open at night. So technically, no, we didn't."

"Sarah Claire."

"Yes," I answer, crossing my arms.

"It doesn't really matter that the bar and dart house were only open at night, all right? You're missing my point."

"Oh, I've got your point, Scott. You want to beat my past out of me."

"With a ball-peen hammer, if necessary."

"Lovely. I thought you were on my side. You wouldn't have recommended me if you didn't think I could do this, right?"

He looks toward the traffic.

"Right, Scott?"

He exhales savagely, like he used to do when I was about to tattle. "Sarah Claire, this job is not about talent. I'm not saying you don't have any, I'm just saying it's important to know the truth going in."

I laugh. "What do you mean it's not about talent? I'm on my way to Beverly Hills to learn from one of the very best."

"This job is about image, Sarah Claire."

"What are you saying?"

"I'm saying you got hired because you're hot, Sarah Claire. You look like Angelina Jolie, you're a size 4, and you're hot, all right? Yoshi can teach a monkey to cut hair, but he can't make a monkey something people want to emulate. People want to look like you."

This silences me. "I sent him videos of the cuts, photographs, and all the awards I won at the hair shows."

"I sent him an eight-by-ten glossy. That's why you have the job."

"I got this job because of the way I look?" I don't know why this gives me chills, but it does.

"The way you look after Photoshop in good clothes with an elegant salon in the background, yes."

All the fire has left me. I wish I could go right back where I came from and none of this had ever happened. But then I think about Cary. *"I pretended to be somebody I wanted to be until finally I became that person. Or he became me."*

"What did you say?"

"Nothing. Let's get this over with." Cary Grant could look like Angelina Jolie with Photoshop, if I'm honest. I've got dark hair and dark eyes, but as far as lips go, definitely not Angelina. As far as my bust goes, definitely not Angelina. But with a little practice—and maybe some wadded-up toilet paper—who knows? If my cousin can do it, then so can I, right?

My cousin gives the impression of being effeminate. On purpose. He walks with swaying, long strides in expensive slacks, and his hair is flat-ironed into the latest style while his wrist boasts an expensive European watch. In Sable, Wyoming, his manhood would be completely questioned by his amount of time spent on grooming alone.

He's not, in fact, gay. He simply works hard to create an aura of the unattainable. In Sable, he was known for being quite the womanizer. Apparently, that's not a good thing for a male stylist.

But if he were back in Sable, he wouldn't act or look like he does now. Scott's a chameleon who can easily shift into whatever persona he needs for the moment. If he came home, I'm sure he'd appear more rugged than even the toughest member of the professional bull-riding circuit. But we'll never know, since he hasn't been back home in the six years he left.

"I'm jet-lagged. I hope this goes well. Fifth Avenue. New York City."

"Is it possible to be jet-lagged from just Wyoming to California? Anyway, you know I think you're gorgeous, Sarah Claire. If you weren't my cousin, I might even date you."

"Be still my heart."

"I am like an artist." Again he moves his hands with no regard for the steering wheel. "I see the rough marble and the beauty within. You just need a little refining, that's all. It's what I do."

I love my cousin. I appreciate all he's doing for me. But he clearly has some seriously narcissistic tendencies that might need to be molded themselves. "Considering how rough I am, isn't that reason enough for a complete overhaul before seeing the infamous man himself?" I ask.

"No, you need an immediate peek before your interview tomorrow. You need to get a sense of the place. I want you to feel his vibe. He'll understand you've been traveling. He travels all the time himself. And he has to know I won't let you show up in knockoffs for work. He knows my work at least that well." He sneaks another look at my jeans. "But let's run by my place and get you a pair of jeans out of my client stuff. I'll lend you my credit card tomorrow."

I suck in a deep breath, hearing the words of little Cindy Simmons (aka Spawn) taunting me about my tattered clothes in school. Remembering the day she stood in sparkly jeans and perfect pigtails with matching hairclips and told everyone I wore the clothes she used to wear after her mommy donated them to the Salvation Army. I can recall that day as if it were yesterday: "*If I could have one thing in my life, God, besides my mom not drinking, I would want to look like someone cared enough to dress me in matching clothes and hair ornaments.*"

Now, here Scott is, ready and willing with a credit card, and I don't want a thing to do with it. It makes me feel as cheap as wearing Cindy's castoffs did, if you want to know the truth.

As if she's in the car with me, I hear Cindy's screechy voice taunting me: "*Who's yer daddy tonight, Sarah Claire? Can't he buy you some new clothes?*"

Back then, I used to stick my tongue out, jamming two fingers in my ears. "*Nyah, nyah. Sticks and stones will break my bones . . .*" (Although I never finished the taunt, everyone knows that adage isn't true.) But what I wouldn't have given to tell her my daddy was hers.

I decided to be a hairdresser because of Cindy. I wanted *everyone* to feel beautiful, no matter what kind of clothes they wore. I never wanted to make any woman feel the way she made me feel. *Like I was nothing.*

"Tell me about the two-hundred-dollar haircut." I close my eyes, thinking about being that good. About a day when I will be able share my expertise and command some financial attention for it. "What kind of people pay that for a haircut?"

Given the notion that it's seeing through my dream or going back to the Hideaway Salon, I'll dress any way I have to, even if it means donning a clown getup each morning to cut celebrity kids' hair. Heck, I'll even dress like a pork chop and cut their dog's hair if it keeps me from going home and admitting defeat to my mother or Cindy.

Scott pulls a credit card out of his shirt pocket.

"Here. Use this for whatever you need, but don't buy anything you can't take back, in case it's wrong."

No pressure there.

"So tell me, what's with the single names? The eyebrow lady named Anastasia you gushed about over the phone, now Yoshi. Is this supposed to be like Cher?"

"You earn the right of the single name. If I didn't have such a simplistic, backwoods name like Scott, I wouldn't have to use my last name either. By the way, your new last name is Winston."

My eyes widen. "You want me to lie about my name too?"

"There's no ethnicity in a name here unless it's Asian or something exotic. Winowski is not exotic; it makes me want to pop open a can of Schlitz."

I, who never drink, currently want to pop open a can of Schlitz. "So I'm basically lying that I'm from New York, lying about my name, lying about my résumé—"

"Look at it this way: at least you don't have to lie about your weight."

"Scott . . ." I shake my head. "I don't think I can do this. Remember that time I tried to lie to Mrs. Eagleston about my dog eating the homework?"

"Well, that was just stupid. Everyone in town knew you didn't have a dog. You can lie about a dog here."

"I don't want to lie."

"It's not lying. Think of it as morphing your image to the Yoshi standards."

Cary Grant did it, I tell myself.

My mouth is bone dry just thinking about how I'm going to get away with so many untruths and not get struck by a bolt of lightning in the process. I can practically hear Mrs. Gentry's sweet voice as my conscience.

"People come here every day and create the persona they want to be, fulfill their childhood dreams. That's all I'm asking you to do. You want a better life? This is part of it. Become the part. Think of it as method acting."

Think of Cary.

"You can take the girl out of the country, but can you take the country out of the girl and make her look like she's worth a two-hundred-dollar haircut?" I can't fathom what makes any haircut worth that. Unless I give it naked—and I do believe that's illegal, besides being completely unpalatable.

"We'll borrow from the designers while we're getting you started on your wardrobe. I know the perfect pieces, and you'll be fabulous. Yoshi will make you worth two hundred bucks. You just have to dress the part and learn from our tutelage. That's all there is. For you, this is like paint-by-number."

"*Borrow* doesn't work for me. *Borrow* in Winowski-speak usually means it fell off the back of the truck—or was 'removed,' ever so lightly, with help."

"*Borrow* means to use something with permission and return it," Scott clarifies. "In *Winston* speak." He emphasizes the word to remind me of my new name. "It means to dress the part. You have to invest in any new business; this is your investment. You are the product, so shine it up like your mother polishes a shot glass."

"Very funny."

"Just one of the reasons you must think of yourself as Sarah Claire Winston from here on out. Besides, your mother's already used your name. The last thing people want to see on their hairdresser's credentials is a rap sheet."

After an eternity on the freeway, we arrive at Scott's condo. He's letting me brush my teeth. I knew he still had a heart. He pulls underground to the parking. It's an odd feeling—the garage is dark and eerie but filled with highly expensive cars. After entering, it goes into lockdown and a giant metal gate crashes down behind us as if we've been eaten by the great car monster.

"This is creepy."

"It's no creepier than having your car not be here when you come out in the morning."

"Touché."

Scott exits the car and presses a button, and his car chirps. He halts. "There's one more thing before we go up."

"Don't worry, Scott. I'm finding an apartment as soon as I get the job. If you think I want to live with you and your revolving door of girlfriends, you're sorely mistaken."

He shakes his head. "No, it's not that."

"You aren't even going to try and deny it? Please have the decency to deny it. Those are someone's daughters, someone's sisters."

"It's every guy's dream; why would I deny it? But that's not it anyway. I told a girl that you were coming from New York and moving in with me."

"Without explaining that I'm your cousin and you're like my big brother, I'm assuming."

"Correct."

"Okay, so I've changed my name, I'll be changing my clothes, I'm living with my boyfriend, and I'm from New York City and not Wyoming. Am I forgetting anything?" *My faith*, I think to myself. *And my self respect—check it at the door.*

"That's pretty much it." He starts walking again and pushes the elevator button. "Oh, and I have a friend living with me while he gets his kitchen remodeled. He won't bother you, though. Think of him as Lurch on *The Addams Family*. He creeps about quietly and doesn't offer much in the way of conversation. Always has his head in a big fat book of no interest."

"Great. Just the kind of man I want to live with."

"He's harmless."

"I want my pets to be 'harmless,' not my roommates. That word makes me thing of the Bates Motel. Is he gay?"

"No, he's not gay! Why would you ask that? Why would I be living with a gay man?"

"I'm just asking. I wondered if 'harmless' was LA speak for gay."

"You know, you just might want to not talk for awhile. Your ignorance is showing."

"My ignorance is all I have left."

We walk into the elevator and Scott uses a key to push his floor at the top of the building.

"He'll be good practice. I told him you were from New York as well. But you're really my cousin with him. Your last name is still Winston, though, not Winowski. I have a pair of jeans that should fit you, and we'll be out of here to the salon. Brush your teeth and wash your face. Wear foundation, all right? Ready?"

"As if I have a choice."

Step into the shoes of yet another persona and live to fight another day.

*If a face like Ingrid Bergman's looks at you
as though you're adorable, everybody does.
You don't have to act very much.*
~ Humphrey Bogart

The elevator door opens to a sprawling, loft-style apartment with wide views of the city—the line of brown smog embracing us in its choking grip. It's the first wave of homesickness I have. I miss the mountains and the expansive blue back home.

"It's the air, isn't it? You didn't even look at the loft."

"Am I that transparent?"

"No." Scott laughs. "It was the first thing that struck me, too, when I came. I felt claustrophobic at first."

Scott's loft exudes fresh money with restraint. Its color scheme is rich, dark chocolate and black. It employs every schmaltzy, carefully placed (by someone else) hallmark of a bachelor pad. The modern equivalent to Rock Hudson's place in *Pillow Talk*, and I can't help but wonder if the bed pops out. For one thing, it's entirely too clean for a guy's place. I'm certain he employs a team of people to keep it looking as it does.

I wander in and take in all of its design details. "The kitchen is cherry."

"Stained nearly black. It's gorgeous, isn't it?"

I nod. "I can't believe you did this in six years, Scott. I

am just so proud. Is this really all yours?"

"All three thousand square feet," he boasts. Not in his typical bravado, but in that quiet, human side of him that shows his humble upbringing.

I wander around the room, shocked at all his space. I never thought we'd see the inside of a place like this, much less that it would belong to Scott. "I should have known when you were able to buy yourself the Camaro, you'd accomplish whatever you wanted."

He smiles at me. "Your room is back there down the hallway. Let me get the jeans. You're a 4?"

"I'm a 5," I say with confidence.

"Designers don't use Montgomery Ward sizing, all right? You're a 2 or a 4, if asked. Four if asked by a woman, 2 if asked by a man in front of a woman."

"Do I want to know?"

"Four makes a woman feel more at ease."

"Why?"

"Because it's more real-woman-sized than a zero or a 2, and it will put women at ease with you, make them think you're their friend. A 2 in front of a man, though, lets them know you plan to compete and says you're armed to do so."

I roll my eyes. "I don't plan to compete for that type of shallow man, and where on earth is a 4 real-woman-sized? Besides starving countries in Africa?"

"Look, you can't be judging the way things are here."

"Why not? You know, the rest of the world judges, and it's not like Hollywood doesn't put itself on display for that very thing. Heck, I bet every ten-year-old in America is capable of copying the Paris Hilton pose. Besides, America thinks that sickly skinny look is disgusting. We want to hand those girls a hamburger and an oxygen mask so they can think clearly."

"This is not the rest of the world. This is LA."

I know I brought this on myself, but it's like getting accepted at a Washington think tank on the basis of image. Except without the Washington or the think part.

"I'm not stupid, you know? I know about misses sizing." Quite frankly, I don't agree that LA is all that much more sophisticated if everyone's lying about who they are. That's no better than your average bar in Sable. Of course, *there* everyone knows your business and knows you're lying. But they allow you to go on anyway out of respect for how shamefully boring your life really is.

"I never said you were stupid," Scott yells from the other room.

"My first priority will be to find a church." *It sounds like I'm going to need one. Mrs. Gentry and gang are probably praying for my soul at this very moment.*

"Whatever. You want to try Kaballah with me?" he yells.

"That's not really Kaballah, what you have here, and, no, I don't. Christianity actually works for me, and I don't have to buy any red strings."

Scott sticks his head in. "Scientology?"

"I'm not looking for a new religion, all right?"

"Jesus is so yesterday."

"Can we talk about something else? I'll go to church alone, all right?"

"Suit yourself." He goes back into the bedroom.

The elevator doors open, and I turn to look.

Wow.

I blink a few times, rubbing my eyes, but when I look back the image is still there, etched into my mind as though I've walked into 1940. Like out of a time-traveling machine—or in this case the elevator—steps a man from a far more romantic era. He's tall and angular and wearing a fedora, just like Humphrey Bogart.

"'Here's looking at you, kid,'" I blather.

"Pardon me?" he asks, pulling his hat off to reveal deep brown eyes and a forehead that's creased in confusion.

"Your hat. It reminds me of Humphrey Bogart in *Casablanca*. I thought maybe—" No, we're not going to go there. No need for him to think I'm crazy in the first five minutes. There will be plenty of time for that.

He walks toward me and slides the fedora atop my head. "Finally, a woman who didn't think I was trying for Indiana Jones. I think I'm in love." He lifts an eyebrow in the most self-assured and entrancing way and smiles sideways. Actually, not unlike Harrison Ford, so I see why people think of him instead of Humphrey.

"It's not the hat. You smile like Harrison. There's more warmth in your eyes than Humphrey had." I grin up at him, cocking the hat to the side the way Ingrid Bergman used to wear it in her promo shots. The hat *smells* good— like expensive cologne—and it's still warm from his head. I close my eyes and drink the moment in, as this is probably the closest I'm going to get to my Hollywood moment.

"'I remember every detail. The Germans wore gray. You wore blue,'" he says in a deep, Bogart baritone.

My eyes pop open and I meet his gaze. "I wanted one good Hollywood scene, and you made my dreams come true all on my very first day. Now what will I have to look forward to?" I fall into the chair against the wall and he walks closer.

"A Hollywood moment? You're here to be an actress, I suppose," he says disappointment.

"I can't act, and I currently weigh more than eighty-nine pounds and like to eat, so no, not an actress."

"*Actor*," Scott corrects me as he returns. "They don't call themselves *actresses*. They want to be taken seriously."

Shut up, Scott. You're ruining my moment. "Who might you be, so I know who to send a thank-you note to for my Hollywood moment?"

"Such formality, and I gave you my hat." He pulls the fedora from my head, and I get another straight shot into his searing brown eyes. *Yummy.*

From the corner of my eye I can see Scott staring at me, and I wish I could shoo him away as he used to do with me when he wanted to be alone with a girl. I give him my best "Go away" look.

"So you've met each other," he says.

"Ilsa, is it?" my stranger says, referring to the movie.

Now, I'm a practical girl. Yes, I have my Hollywood visions, but unlike my mother, I have never expected a man to rescue me from anything. It's a great idea in theory, but I've sobered my mother up too many times to think it was possible.

Suddenly, I think it's possible, and I'm giving my mother a tiny bit more grace.

"Sarah Claire." I reach out my hand as I stand up. We're still awkwardly close, so I step back to shake his hand properly.

"Dane Weston," he replies.

Dane Weston. Dane Weston. Sarah Claire Weston.

"It's perfect!"

"What's perfect?"

"Your name. It suits you." *It suits me.*

"I was going to tell you we all call him Lurch. Lurch, this is my cousin Sarah Claire. She's from New York City," Scott says with confidence, even though probably a good eighty percent of the sentence was a lie.

I'm still holding Dane's hand. There's a pulse shooting up my arm, and quite frankly, I'm not inclined to give it up any sooner than I have to. There are some moments you'll remember forever. If I never see Dane Weston again, I will remember holding his hand, staring into his incredible brown eyes, and smelling the scent of his hat. *Here's looking at you.*

"New York?" Dane asks, looking quite confused, as I'm sure I look about as New York as a Wyoming mule deer.

"By way of Wyoming," I counter. *Let's talk about you!*

"Stopping at the airport is not by way of Wyoming, Sarah Claire."

I may not be LA-sophisticated, but I'm not sure anyone is going to fall for the necessary stopover in Wyoming. Lucky for me, Dane chooses to ignore the obvious, and I take the hat from his left hand again, not relinquishing my grip.

"You're not Scott's roommate?" I ask in a mere whisper. Exactly the voice I used to ask Steve Harris to the Sadie Hawkins dance in high school. He turned me down cold in front of the school cafeteria, so I choose a stronger voice now and try again. "Because I'd pictured you more . . . well, more like Scott."

"Likewise," he says. "You are his blood. I was expecting you to have three cell phones on your person, at least. And I never expected the blue eyes."

"I don't own a cell phone." I laugh coquettishly. I'd like to be Ingrid Bergman-smooth, but I'm more Shelly Winters-forward. Screw Steve Harris and the silly Sadie Hawkins Dance. Steve now shovels cow manure for a living, and I am staring into the deepest brown eyes I have ever seen.

"Sarah Claire?" Dane squeezes my hand, and I swallow hard.

"I'm sorry. I was just thinking about my interview at the salon. I'd better get dressed for it." I pull my hand away, wondering if Dane sees what Steve saw. Does he see a swine in pearls, or has Scott done a better job of covering up my past?

God, if ever someone saw me as I want to be, let it be Dane Weston.

"I'm pleasantly surprised you're not more like your cousin." Dane grins. "He's far too full of himself."

"Isn't he, though?"

"Excuse me!" Scott tosses a pair of jeans my way. "Get into these and quit your whining. Save that attitude for Yoshi's. Did you want to see the rest of the place?"

I pull myself away from Dane. "Not right now. Just point me to my room." Because I really want to be alone. I want to replay this moment in my head so that I never forget it and how I felt like a starring role for one moment in time.

He points to a hallway. "At the end, turn right."

I wander into the back room, where it hits me. *I'm going to be living with this, my very own Humphrey Bogart.* Me, who hasn't been around men my entire life—except for Scott, and he doesn't count. Now, I became a Christian at thirteen. I made my vow of chastity at fourteen (not that there were a lot of suitors at that point, but it was heartfelt), and yet for the first time in my life, I can imagine how my mother fell victim to men. *It wasn't that I'm better than her, it was that I have better taste than her!* Dane could point his little finger and I'm afraid I'd follow where he led.

I stick my head back out the hallway and look in Dane's direction just to see if I didn't make him more handsome than he really is, but he sees me and lifts that sexy eyebrow. "Did you forget something?"

I shake my head in double-time and slam the door. "Nope. Definitely didn't imagine it." Ah, to be dignified and elegant like him, rather than the bumbling, colt-like fool I am. Isn't it just my luck I finally meet the man of my dreams and I'm going to be rooming with him? I mean, there is no way I can pretend all the time. I'm not that good of an actress. *Actor.* For once I see what I want in life, only to have it plucked from my world.

"Dane Weston," he said in his beautiful, eloquent way. I allow the name to ferment in my brain. I know this is so eighth grade, but I can't help repeating the name with my own.

I scan the back pocket of the jeans Scott threw at me. Naturally, they're stitched with an emblem I don't recognize and ripped randomly in small patches. If these were dropped off at the Sable Salvation Army, I would think their condition had rendered them rag material. Here, that random shredding is worth money, according to the tags.

Who cares about jeans? For that matter, who cares about hair?

There's a knock at the door, and I zip myself into the curve-hugging denim. They are comfortable, but as I look into the mirror, they're not exactly keeping any secrets either.

I open the door, hiding my bottom half behind the door. "They're Chip & Pepper jeans," Scott says. "In case you're asking."

"My t-shirt is from Kmart," I say, sticking my tongue out ever so slightly.

"Is this your way of holding out for an Armani blouse? It's in the closet behind you, along with a pair of Chanel heels. But don't put heavy wear on them; I have them saved for a big client. I put everything I thought might work for you in the closet before you got here. We'll see how you do after today."

"Is he married, Scott?"

"Is who married? Yoshi? Yeah, to his business."

"Not Yoshi. Dane."

"Sarah." Scott shakes his head. "You're here for a career, am I right? Let's focus on the image."

I pretend to refocus, but inwardly I'm thinking how I can get my answer without him. "Hey, I read *People*. Mixing expensive pieces with cheap ones is very chic."

"You can pave the way all you want once you're set up at Yoshi's. For now, you play by my rules. Dane is perfect practice; use him to see what works. If you can get past him with a look, you're good. He has classic taste."

"Chip & Pepper is classic?"

Scott sighs again. I seem to make him just one big expulsion of air. "Now, your former salon was on Fifth."

"What kind of women does Dane date?"

"Dane is off-limits, Sarah Claire. Repeat after me: you worked for the Ted Gibson Salon on Fifth. They're an Aveda salon, so their organic background is perfect. They train stylists and offer spa treatments, as well. Yoshi is taking my word on this, so don't blow it. I told him you and Ted had creative differences."

"Why is Dane off-limits? I finally have a Hollywood moment and you want to rip it out from underneath me before I've fully digested it? That's just wrong."

"Focus, Sarah Claire."

But of course, I'm focused already. (Is *obsessed* too strong a word?) Granted, my chances with a man like Dane are like the odds of getting hit by lightning here in sunny SoCal, but if all those nights alone taught me anything, it's that even a lowly servant girl like Jane Eyre can find true love. Of course, her man was blind first, but whatever.

"Did a man ever rescue your mother, Sarah Claire?"

Like a slap to the face, Scott has my attention. "Salon on Fifth. Aveda. Organic. What else?"

"You were passed over for a promotion."

"I was passed over for a promotion, and it wasn't because of my talent. Politics got in the way."

"Very good add, Sarah Claire. You're getting it." Scott nods his head.

"And somewhere, like in the *Picture of Dorian Gray*, there's a painting getting very, very ugly with my lies." I hate to tell Scott that California is one of the hardest places to transfer one's license to, and Yoshi has to know good and well where I've been working.

"Yoshi is a genius with color. He's going to basically start from scratch with any trainee. He'll recognize your talent, but he'll want to erase most of how you've been programmed. There's one way at Yoshi: the Yoshi way. He knows one hundred times more than your instinct will tell you, so listen to everything he says."

"Please stop saying 'Yoshi.' I feel like if I hear that man's name once more, I will have to suffocate him on sight."

"*Tsk, tsk.* Unresolved anger, Sarah Claire. You need a jacket—a short one. Look in that closet and make sure everything is fitted. You want the pointed heels to elongate that leg." Scott runs his hand down my shin.

"Is Dane married, Scott? Did his wife throw him out?"

"I told you, he's remodeling. His wife? What, do you think she gave him a frying pan and plopped him on my doorstep? You've been watching Nick at Nite again, haven't you? He's not married, and I don't know how he ever will be. Just like you, he lives in a dream world, with his head in a book."

"Really?" I say brightly. "What kind of book?"

I pull my journal out of the suitcase pocket, and Scott grabs it. "No more of this. From here on out you live life; you don't dream it. That was always your problem, Sarah Claire. You need to face reality."

"Reality sucks. Do I need to point that out?"

"It *has* sucked. Put that in the past tense. From here on out it rocks."

"Does he have a girlfriend?"

"There's Armani makeup in that black box there." He points to the floor. "I got it in a sample pack from the Emmys this year, and my clients seem to like the products. Great highlighting features, especially the blush. Just gives your face a halo effect."

Scott is clearly avoiding my questions. "You know way too much about girl things. Where's the mystery anymore? Remember when you raced your Camaro and worked on cars for a living?"

"It's only going to get weirder. Brace yourself."

I think I'm ready to go back to the Hideaway, do a wash and set, and snuggle on the sofa with a movie. Just two days ago that felt like the perfect day. Unfortunately, now I really want to take one six-foot-something souvenir with me. That would certainly get the Sable tongues wagging for a reason. *And if I'm capable of having a reason, may he look like Dane Weston.*

What would Mrs. Gentry have to say about Dane? Could that sweet, genteel lady be capable of a low, guttural growl?

chapter 5

I've never sought success in order to get fame and money; it's the talent and the passion that count in success.
~ Ingrid Bergman

I'm still absorbing the fact that grown people pay to have someone dress them and that it's a competitive business. Isn't the whole point of success dressing the way you want to dress? Isn't that one of the first things you learn in preschool? It's horrifying to think of someone poking and prodding at me and sticking jelly boobs down my shirt.

I look into the mirror again, wondering what my new "image" says about me. Does it say "Steve Harris said yes to that Sadie Hawkins Dance"? *Would my life have been different if he had?*

What I'm trying to say is that I stole Dane's hat. I'm not proud of it. But it was there sitting on the hook on my way out, and I thought, you know, it would just give me that added edge—the confidence Scott spoke of. But now I'm feeling sort of guilty. Like what if Dane was having a really bad hair day and I stole his cover-up? And I borrowed it like a Winowski borrows things, which does nothing for my confidence level. And as a Christian I'm ashamed to admit my superstition was stronger than my morals.

LA is the strangest place. Everyone drives, though I'm seeing a slow jog would get you where you needed to be much faster. Santa Monica Boulevard, which we take into Beverly Hills, is really just an excuse to wait at ridiculously long stoplights and stare at the people beside you, generally inside their BMW or Prius. There doesn't seem to be much else around. Oh wait, there's a Jaguar. I stand corrected.

Unlike the airport, there doesn't seem to be much culture here. It's about as white-bread as Wyoming. I feel like I've been zapped and I'm now living in a Barbie townhouse. It's only a matter of time before Barbie's driving a hybrid. Trust me on this.

"How come there're no bikes? It seems like it would be faster," I say as we sit at another eternal stoplight. "How do you stand this? Going thirty feet to wait another five minutes?"

"What good is faster if you're dead? Trust me, you don't want to be riding a bike here unless you've got a death wish. You just deal with it, all right? A lot of people means traffic."

I look out the window, my eyes resting on a gym lit up inside so we can all amuse ourselves with other peoples' perfect bodies—Lycra-wrapped entertainment for this particular stoplight.

"Look at those people. Why don't they just run to work?"

"Sarah Claire, people here aren't necessarily outdoors-men, all right? You can't wear an iPod and jog. You'd end up dead. Besides, it's illegal."

"No way! What do you mean, it's illegal? Besides, I'm just saying you don't have to be an outdoorsman to run in all this perfect weather. Jogging doesn't make you Paul Bunyan."

"People run, just not here, all right? They run up in the hills or on the beach. Not on Santa Monica Boulevard. It's illegal because you can't hear cars."

"Whatever."

"Take that stupid hat off; you look ridiculous."

I borrowed it fair and square. "It gives me confidence. You said I should be confident." *Besides, it smells good.*

"I said you should be confident, not look like Johnny Depp at a premiere."

"It's Humphrey Bogart."

"He's dead and a furniture collection at Thomasville. Is that the kind of success you're looking for?"

"He's timeless. So, yes."

"Take the hat off, or I'm telling Dane you have a thing about stealing people's clothing and not to leave anything around, especially his boxers."

I quickly pull off the fedora. "You have control issues, you know that?"

"This is the famous Rodeo Drive. That's Ro-day-o, country girl."

"You mean I can't buy me a saddle there no more?" I give it my best twang, but inside my stomach is doing Olympic gymnastics. *I'm here. I'm really here.*

Finally, we're thrust into a line of cars that leads to a parking garage. After a parking fiasco where someone in a Prius called us a not-very-environmental name, we walk to the pristine alley that houses Yoshi's. I wish I had a camera. I'd love to send Kate a picture of me arriving at my destiny.

From the street—which is within the confines of what Scott called the Beverly Hills Golden Triangle—the salon looks like an exclusive Japanese tea house. I think it's been modeled after Charlie's Chocolate Factory—*No one ever goes in, no one ever comes out*—because it's incredibly quiet here. Free of the hustle-bustle just two blocks over. Hollywood royalty is always beautiful, but the price of getting there is never shown. Apparently, it's held in secret silence. The Pentagon should have such intelligence.

"What do you think?" Scott asks.

"It looks secret. Where's the name of it?"

"Trust me, people know it's there. I meant of Rodeo Drive, before we parked."

"It was what I expected, only cleaner." It's weird to see all those names I read in the magazines on shops: Michael Kors, Armani, Stuart Weitzman . . . José Eber, Frederick Fekkai. Seeing the hair salons, I realize that off-Rodeo is akin to off-Broadway in New York. "Like the whitewashed buildings of Greece."

I refrain from adding it was like Greece with more bling—tacky gold doorframes, designer names, and people who looked like they dressed for New York's fashion week. It reminded me of a period film in Bath, England—the elite walking about just to be seen in the latest fashions. There was one couple of overweight tourists in bad shorts; otherwise, it was one scurrilously low-riding pair of jeans after another. Crack is more than a drug here.

My heart is in my throat as I try to remember everything I've been told. Luckily, I'm so nervous I don't remember my name as it is. So if I flub anything, I can plead unadulterated fear and public schools.

"You're on your own from here," Scott says on the sidewalk. His cell phone buzzes and he looks down. "I've got to take this. You'll be fine."

"Aren't you going to at least introduce me?"

He shakes his head, talking into the cell phone, and I'm left staring at the impenetrable walls of Yoshi's. Granted, there's a door right in front of me, but it seems like the type of place you need an engraved invitation to enter. I keep picturing that scene in *Pretty Woman* where Julia Roberts tries to buy clothes in a boutique and is told she's not welcome. I'm thinking there's not going to be any Richard Gere to get me out of this mess.

I brush my fingers through my hairstyle, suck in a deep breath, turn the handle, and push open the door. Inside, a fountain trickles gently into a koi pond. A labyrinth of sweet-scented plants (jasmine) lines the pathway to the jade granite receptionist station. In my head runs that very annoying song about eating the dishes. Curse that Willy Wonka; he's ruining my moment!

But it's beautiful. It's everything I expected—and much less. Not too fancy. Not too plain. Just right. My eyes wander to the ceilings, painted in a modern, murky green, and I feel like I belong. I know I shouldn't. Or don't. But this doesn't feel like Sable where I was always the third wheel; this feels like home.

I stand at the receptionist desk staring into the shop. Compared to the gardenlike spa entrance, the salon itself is very stark—but in a good, make-yourself-at-home way. Simple black leather chairs, white laminate shelves, and bamboo hardwood floors (rejuvenating and environmentally sound, according to Scott). It's a very clean modern look. Bleached. I don't know what I was expecting—perhaps gold or marble wash sinks?—but I love it. See, that's the thing about the rich: they do things cheap and people think it's the epitome of chic. When I'm rich, I'm going to put on my white canvas Keds and tell everyone they're the new black.

"May I help you?" A young Asian woman with magnificent, jet-black straightened hair and a cropped shirt that shows off her belly button ring greets me. I don't know if she was sitting there the whole time or magically appeared. *You can even eat the dishes!*

"I'm Sarah Claire." I pause. "Sarah Claire Winston. I'm

going to work for Yoshi."

"Did you bring a head?"

"I didn't. I didn't know how to get it on the plane." Heads are personal in this business. You're assigned a head with real hair at the beginning of beauty school. You make up stories about it, what it needs, what its goals and ambitions are—then you usually pass it on to some poorer stiff than you in beauty school. Not me. I kept Vanilla. Her natural-red straight hair was the key to my future. She's back in Wyoming. Hey, I'm practical, and I wasn't toting a head in these high-security times.

"Yoshi's teaching via satellite, Miss Winston, but he is expecting you and he'll be done shortly."

"He is? I mean, I'm not due until tomorrow."

"I know," she says mystically.

He knows. She knows. Am I the only clueless one here? Did I leave my psychic abilities back in the cowboy state? Or in the car with Dane's fedora maybe? "Do you mind if I look around a little?"

"Scott Baker called this morning and announced your arrival. Feel free. Just stay out of Yoshi's way. He's in back teaching."

"Oh. Does everyone work on Monday?"

"Yoshi works seven days a week. He uses the sinks for teaching during off hours and struggling actors as his heads. This is not a nine-to-five, if that's what you were thinking."

"No, no. I wasn't thinking that. I was just curious."

"You might want to say good-bye to your social life if you hope to show Yoshi you're serious."

Why am I suddenly feeling like an intern on *Grey's Anatomy?*

"Do you have a boyfriend?"

"No, why? Is it obvious?" I start to pat my jeans, but

it's clear whatever she was asking me, it isn't my clothes.

She tosses a white clipboard on the countertop, and I feel like I'm at the starting gate waiting for her to say go. I want to explore. I want to discover what it's like to feel like a stylist in Yoshi's Beverly Hills.

"Yoshi asks that all applicants read our manual and fill out this application so that he can refer to it when speaking with you. You can wait in the back room while you write." She looks me up and down. "Out of clients' view. Even though it's only a teaching model, Yoshi has a strict policy about the appearance of his stylists," she says, as if to make sure I get her message. "*Yes, you look like dog meat. To the dungeon with you!*"

I look down. The Chip & Pepper jeans are not enough to overcome the rest, I guess. "My cousin dressed me," I say, thrusting my shoulders back. I grab the clipboard and head toward the salon.

"Yeah, you look great," she calls after me. "It's just that Yoshi doesn't allow skinny jeans in the shop. No denim at all, actually." She crosses her arms. "We think it looks tacky and lazy."

This from someone who's forcing me to gaze at her belly button.

"No skinny jeans, but midriffs are okay?" I ask innocently. Really, there's not a catty sound attached to it.

She yanks down her shirt. "No, but I have plans after work today."

I don't even want to know. "You look darling. I was just clarifying for myself." I start to gaze at the walls and the gorgeous pictures from magazines and autographed glossies of the Hollywood elite.

"Renee Zellweger has been here?" My eyes zoom to the next photo. "Faith Hill? Oh my gosh, McDreamy? I love him. I totally love him!" I look back at the receptionist. "Have you met all these people?"

"Just a few of them. You're going to save the starstruck routine for me, right?"

"Oh, absolutely! It's just so weird to think I have a shot of one day working on Hollywood royalty, you know? My hairstyles might be seen all over the world."

"I know. It's big, but you have to play down that you care an iota."

I giggle my excitement. "I'm sorry. Of course, I know you're right. No starstruck."

"Fill out the paperwork first. It will get you in a serious mood to meet Yoshi."

My eyes go right to the forms and the glaring empty spaces marked Previous Experience. Lying is bad enough. Lying on paper is illegal. She's right. I'm definitely out of the giddy mood. "My cosmetology license is—it's in another state," I say to the girl. "I've already had my state review, but I'm still not approved to work here."

"As long as you're in the application process, that's fine. California is one of the states that makes it hard to transfer. Yoshi knows that. You don't need a license to sweep hair."

No, I don't. But what is that supposed to mean? "But I need a license to wash hair," I say hopefully.

"If Yoshi finds your work satisfactory, he'll make sure you get what you need for California's extra hours. You won't be cutting hair for a long time, so I wouldn't worry about it."

"Right. I'm a long way from working on Hollywood royalty—that's what you're saying to me?"

"Don't be discouraged; just be realistic. So, what's Scott like?" This is said with a hint of friendliness. "Is he as cool as he seems? Have you known him long?"

I'm worrying about how long it's going to be before I touch hair again. I should have brought Vanilla. I could have snipped her hair and blow-dried it. She could have kept me company.

But back to Scott. I can't remember if he's my boyfriend or cousin at the salon. She asked about a boyfriend. Is that what she meant? "Yes, we've been close for a long time." *Always avoid answering directly.* That may become my new mantra. Just like *Don't ask, don't tell* at home.

"I'd kill for his job. Do you get to wear the clothes all the time? He's genius. His work on *You Are My Life* . . . classic. He's like a stylist for real people, you know? He's not dressing people up to look ridiculous for photo shoots. He avoided that whole ugly legging thing that cost so many stylists their job. I hear he's the prince of prosthetics, too, and considering his own line of products. That is so hot."

Oh yeah, my cousin's line of jelly boobs. Now there's a pinnacle of success to take home to Sable. Not.

"He's very artistic, and he's a perfectionist. I guess it shows in his work." *Relationally? That's another story.*

I look down at my jeans. Heaven forbid she asks me what they are, because I don't remember as of two seconds ago. *Salt and pepper, chili pepper, something food-oriented. Overpriced is all I remember.* "I get to wear the clothes. At least for a little while. I just moved here, so I'm going to be building my wardrobe." *Duh, like I didn't have a wardrobe in New York City?*

She leans in toward me. "Yoshi is really excited you're here. He's so anxious for some of Scott's bigger clients. They always come to Yoshi in an emergency, but not regularly, and he's so competitive, he can't stand them going elsewhere. It's like every client at another salon is a dagger to his heart; he takes it personally." She shakes her head.

"Yoshi's better than all of the others combined. A true artist. But he's not very relational. You know when Jennifer Aniston's marriage broke up? Chris McMillan was there for her. That's what people want from their hair people these days: relationship. Yoshi's just got the talent, not really the emotional pull. He does have Kelly Winkler. You know her? From *Lilly Minder, MD*? The show on Cable 54? She's in here all the time."

"I'm not familiar with it, no." *Cable 54?* Apparently, there are a few more TV options here in lala land.

"Oh, girl, you have to watch it. TiVo it; it's on Tuesday nights. It's all the buzz here. Kelly is hot, hot, hot. She's got a movie going this summer when *Lilly* stops filming, and so Yoshi knows she's ready to break out. That's why he took her personally."

"So are the stars nice? Do they expect a lot?"

"You came from Ted Gibson. Didn't you have some there? So many people are bicoastal these days."

I should just shut up now. I'm bicoastal. Which sounds like a disease, but it's apparently an affluent way to live.

"Now that Kelly Winkler's on board, Yoshi's getting some of the other stars of the show, because they all think they're going to break out as well. They won't, but it's good for appearances. Yoshi's focused on the movie stars because then he'll get screen credit, and that should help the product line immensely. That's the ticket here in town. Product. Royalty streams. Your cousin seems to get that." She stands up. "Scott has a lot of film stars. I can see the family resemblance."

Ah, so he is my cousin.

"I'm Jenna." She holds out her sleek, graceful hand. "While you're getting the run of the place, just come ask me any questions. I'm the office manager, so if it's happening, I'm aware of it."

I love it. In Wyoming, we'd be lucky to have a receptionist. Here, we've got an office manager!

"Just for future reference? No skinny pants or denim. It's policy. If you appear smaller than the clientele, they don't come back. We joked that we should print on the mirrors, 'Objects standing behind you in the mirror are bigger and more tank-like than they appear.'" She laughs melodically. "Yoshi wants his clients to sizzle and his stylists to be hot enough to be inviting but classic enough to be couture."

Whatever that means. "Seriously?"

"It's our motto."

"It doesn't make any sense." I mean, I know I'm a country girl, but that doesn't make any sense. How can it be a motto?

Jenna's jaw twitches. "Look, just fill out the forms. It isn't exactly your place to be telling Yoshi what makes sense." She thumps her hand on the granite, and I realize I've failed the one piece of education I brought with me: I ticked off the receptionist. Worse yet, I ticked off the office manager, and this I managed in the first five minutes!

A door opens and I snap back to attention. A tall, Asian man with gold highlights in his black hair approaches me and looks to Jenna. "This her?" he says, as though I'm not standing right there. I wonder how he can tell I'm not a client, and my mind immediately goes to my boots. The only clothing of mine that I'm wearing.

Yoshi is clean. Unconscionably so. I half expect his teeth to glisten when he smiles, but of course, he never does.

Jenna nods subtly, thoroughly disgusted with me.

"Come in the back, please," Yoshi orders. "Jenna told you no skinny pants?"

I can hear the rushing of my heartbeat. "Yes, sir."

As I'm led through the salon, I'm a bit starstruck as I imagine myself bent over the simplistic yet elegant wash sinks. Maybe I'll be leaning over Lilly Minder—or hey, maybe even the next Cary Grant or Dr. McDreamy—one day!

There are magazine covers lining the hallway to Yoshi's office, and they are all current. "The salon is in so many magazines."

"Of course it is. You were expecting . . . ?"

"Just that, sir."

"We're currently doing makeover shows for *Wake Up, LA!* and the E! network. There is no shortage of opportunities here."

"I brought in my portfolio," I say, holding out my book as he enters his office. He just waves it off and sits behind a desk filled with trophies and pictures of him with famous people. I keep the application clipboard, my heart pounding at how I'll get out of this. *God help me. I can't lie to him.*

Yoshi doesn't look at me. He looks right behind me into a mirror and watches himself. I want to turn around and see what he's saying to himself, but I imagine that's just as rude as what he's doing, so I keep forward, trying to pretend he's not looking right through me. He kicks the door shut with his leg. "Sit down. You're making me nervous."

I sit.

Yoshi crosses his leg over his knee. "Let's get a few things out of the way. I know you're from Wyoming, so don't bother filling that out." He finally looks at me over my portfolio. "It's better for both of us if you don't lie on paper. I know you've never stepped foot in New York. I called the salon Scott said you worked for and they'd never heard of you. And your license is from Wyoming, so I should assume you were working in New York . . . why?"

"I—I—" *But what can I say, really?* "I'm good, Yoshi. And I will listen to everything you have to teach me. I'm better than if I was from New York because I come with absolutely no attitude. None whatsoever." Except that slightest bit of old Hollywood royalty fantasies, but I'm totally willing to squelch that.

"Listen, I know what my training is worth. I know why people will lie to get it. I know Scott Baker would lie to his own grandmother to get what he wanted." He pauses and pulls his glasses down to stare directly into my eyes. "I would too, though, so I don't hold it against him. Or you. You're a survivor. I like that. But you lie to me again and this is over, all right? I don't care who your cousin is."

"I'm not a liar, sir. But I need this. I want to be the best I can be at my job. It's not about the money or even meeting the stars—though I'm more Hollywood-struck than I thought I'd be. It's just, I often see the image I want to make on a customer, but I don't have the ability yet. I have the foresight but not the skill. You can give me that skill, and that's why I'm here."

He nods. "It's good you understand that. I get so many of you thinking you're the next Yoshi straight out of beauty school." He laughs. It's creepy; it reminds me of the old snickering Peter Lorre.

"Your cousin may have a talent for dressing, but it's clear he hasn't a clue of how hairstylists get licensed," he mumbles. "It's my license at stake if I don't check out your references. California has very strict standards. Sure, people can buy licenses, but I'm glad you didn't go that far. I'd rather see this."

I nod. "I'm so sorry about the misunderstanding."

He looks straight at me with his piercing black eyes. "It was intentional, no?"

"It was intentional," I admit. I mean, I didn't stop Scott.

"Have you studied? The bigger the outfit—"

"The smaller the hair."

He nods. "Very good. Headbands?"

"Perfect for today's sleek look. Used widely in the New York shows this year and making a distinct comeback."

Again he nods, and I can't help but think my *Vogue* subscription was worth every penny, because it's not like I've ever had use for this stuff.

"You don't get into my academy unless I want you in my academy. Your credentials matter not an iota. I can teach anyone to cut hair, but do they have the image I want for Yoshi? That is what matters to me."

He's keeping himself locked on his own image in the mirror. "There are four levels here. You'll be starting out at level one, where I will teach you to wash hair again. A good shampoo is why people come back. You get water all over them, they're gone. If you leave them relaxed, with a good head massage, they are putty in your hands."

"Yes, sir."

"Level two, I'll be teaching you to cut again, and color properly—the Yoshi way. For the first year, you will be mixing my color to my exact specifications. We have a color room, and you'd do well to get acquainted with it and listen and learn from my color mixing. See where the patrons start. Where they end. Color has its own advanced training, which you'll be taking later. I'll be quizzing you on the mixes by the end of the week, but you'll be concentrating on shampooing. We practice that on real people. No heads. Do you have a head?"

"Vanilla. I left her at home."

"Good. I don't want you attached to an old head and your own ways. You'll get a new head this afternoon."

"Yes, sir." I feel as though I'm betraying Vanilla, the beloved head that loved me when I was poor and badly trained. Yes, I do realize that borders on psychotic, but you know, Vanilla is one of the few who misses my presence.

"You never mix until you're instructed to do so by one of our colorists, and only then to their exact specifications. People will stop our clientele on the streets and ask about their color because it's natural, but it has much more of a wow than they can get at any other salon."

"Should I be writing this down?" I ask.

"You should be writing everything I say down. It's gold. Pay special attention to the techniques used in washing hair; it's your first entrance onto the salon floor working with customers. I cannot stand to see someone sit still. If something needs to be done, do it. Do not wait for someone to tell you to jump into action."

"No, sir."

"There should never be hair on the floor. When a stylist is cutting, and you see hair drop, get the broom immediately. But do not make the customer feel as though you're hovering or that they're creating a mess, no matter how bushy they are. It's an art, do you understand?"

Not in the least. "Of course."

"We offer all our customers a menu. Wine, champagne, espresso, mineral water, diet soda. It is all available to them while they relax. It's your job to make sure their glass is full and they're happy during their experience here."

"You offer champagne?"

"Coming to Yoshi's is a celebration," he answers, deadpan.

"I don't mean to be forward, but when will I be cutting hair, exactly? It's my passion; I'm not quite sure I can live without it for so long."

"Eventually, you'll be doing the rinses and washes, giving hand massages in your free time. But until I say so, you are not to be on the floor for any reason other than cleaning the floor or bringing beverages. Is that understood?"

"Wh—when do I get to learn?"

"Every moment is a learning opportunity. Classes are held daily before the salon opens and in the evenings on Tuesdays and Thursdays. We'll have special classes offered on Sundays for specifics, where representatives from hair companies will assist. Today we're teaching razor cuts. You missed a fabulous day. Any questions?"

"Did you ever meet Cary Grant?"

I did not just say that.

Yoshi's serious demeanor falls away and his eyes sparkle. "Are you really going to take this moment with one of hairstyling's greats to ask about a movie star?"

"It's just I had this poster and— 'A movie star'! Cary Grant was far more than a movie star!"

"Sophistication, my dear girl. Sophistication is everything. I can't have a teenybopper in here looking for autographs. You will meet stars daily—" He stops himself. "But, yes, I did meet Mr. Grant once, and he was everything you saw on the screen. He exuded charm and grace. Practice that skill and you will embrace that same sophistication."

I want to reach out and touch Yoshi. He met *the* Cary Grant. It's like in Exodus when Moses is warned he's walking on hallowed ground. Granted, I know this is not the same as that, but man, can I just touch him right now?

"I need a fresh start, Yoshi."

"Everyone needs a fresh start. That's what LA is all about." Again he peers over his glasses at me. "You have years of training ahead of you. Are you willing to do that? More than half your class will fall away before it's finished, but the ones who get Yoshi-trained can go anywhere in the world. You understand this?"

Anywhere in the world. Power. Control. The best in my field. I have to think long-term. One day I can send a Christmas card to Mrs. Gentry from Paris.

"There will be other pupils in your classes, but you're the only one on staff, which means all eyes—and they will be jealous eyes—will be on you for your position. You don't wear enough makeup."

I swallow. "I'll get some more."

"Naked lips, though. Don't come in here looking like an old Technicolor movie with the real Max Factor doing your makeup. Your coloring is good; just shine a little more. Do you have a bronzer? Tan is very in here."

"I'll get some."

He holds up a finger. "On second thought—" He pulls a business card from his desk. "You need a blue peel. This is Isabella. She offers the best blue peels in the city. Call her and arrange to have one done for yourself."

A blue peel? Another single name? It sounds expensive and quite possibly painful. I'm not fond of pain.

"Did you see Jenna's skin? Or even your cousin's?"

"The plastic look!"

"What?"

"The peel. That's what gives everyone the mannequin skin?"

"I haven't noticed that, but—"

"Sure. Sure, it looks like they're wearing Vaseline."

Yoshi sighs loudly. "It's a medium skin peel. Your skin

will glow afterwards, and I think that's going to help with your appearance overall."

"Actually, I'm more concerned about the money aspect. Right now, I mean—"

He slams his hand on his desk. "You're out here with nothing, aren't you?"

"Well, yeah. That's sort of why I came out." *Does he think I left the diamonds at home?*

He stares at me for a long time, saying nothing, only scanning my expression for some telltale sign—perhaps that I can forgo the peel. Ugh, when I hear that word, all I can think of is *What on earth will they peel off?* How much epidermis must be victim to my job choice? Will I look like an orange?

Yoshi looks back over my shoulder. "I'm taking a chance on you, Sarah," he says to his mirror. "I have no idea why, but I'm taking a chance. Your cousin will probably hijack my clients, and I'll regret this—"

"Yes, sir. I mean, no, sir. Scott wouldn't do that."

"Jenna!" After some rushed footsteps Jenna appears in the doorway. "Get Isabella's number, call her, and get an appointment for Sarah."

"It's Monday, Yoshi. No one works but you."

His eyes thin. "Your cousin working today?"

I nod. "Yes, sir."

"Would you stop saying that? Call her at home, Jenna. I can't have Sarah out too long."

"Out?"

"It hurts like a mother!" Jenna says. Then she perks up. "But you look great afterwards. Totally worth it."

I whimper. I'm not fond of pain. Have I mentioned that? And I really have no money. "Mr. Yoshi, sir. I really can't afford this right now. I know that sounds ridiculous, but I can't."

"There is no beauty without a price," Yoshi says. "But that's fine; we'll schedule you for next month. Who's on duty now? Sarah needs her hair cut."

I grab my head. "I do?"

"I have spoken."

And with those incredibly arrogant words, I am led off for a makeover of frightening proportions.

I have spent the greater part of my life
fluctuating between Archie Leach and Cary
Grant, unsure of each, suspecting each.
~ Cary Grant

I am shorn. The door slams behind me, and I stand abandoned on the pristine sidewalks of Beverly Hills in skinny jeans with a very bad shag cut deemed "edgy" by Johnny, my very gay and perfect-looking hairstylist-in-training. I will say he fit the Yoshi image to a T, but if indeed Yoshi can teach a monkey, that doesn't speak well for Johnny. My hair is . . . awful, to put it mildly. It's a boxy, shaggy bob that looks like what it is—a very bad razor cut by a trainee. He didn't even waste organic product on me, and if I'm not a poster child for styling paste, I don't know who is.

I was also shorn of my name. Scott didn't go far enough with the Winston, apparently, because instead of Sarah Claire, I am now Sarah Winston. So sophisticated. And if I didn't look like a labradoodle, I'd say it worked for me.

I pull out a compact, and even in that tiny little circular reflection, it's bad. I came across three states to get a bad haircut and an appointment with a scary, foreign woman who will take my skin and turn it into the plastic look of everyone else. Which, lucky for me, I can't afford yet. And rather than money in my pocket, I'm in more debt for the job requirements—along with a necessary four days off next month for pain and suffering! I have entered Stepford, and my transformation is nearly complete.

I look at my watch, wondering where on earth Scott went and if he has any plans to retrieve me. I'd call his cell, but wait—I don't have one.

Thankfully, he pulls up just then. He spends a moment cooing into yet another woman's ear before clicking shut his phone, which is far too small for the size of his head, and looking at me. "You're done?"

"You're disgusting, do you know that?" I climb into the car.

"I'm only paying the bills. How'd the interview go? You're starting tomorrow, I take it. Your hair is ghastly, by the way."

"Yeah, thanks. Love you too. I got the job, but only because he wants your clients." I cross my arms. It seems I'm destined to be defined by family members no matter where I go. "That's the only reason he's hiring me. When he cuts hair, someone shadows him at all times, and I *may* get that privilege in six months or so. Until then, that's as close as I'm coming to a head of hair unless I take a trip home to Sable. Or buy a Barbie head at Toys"R"Us. My duties will include making sure the toilet seat is down after a male client goes to the bathroom, sweeping up hair, and making coffee concoctions with a steamer engine posing as an espresso machine."

My cousin starts to laugh.

"Not funny!" I tell him. "Not funny at all."

"It's a little funny. Who doesn't have to pay their dues in life, Sarah Claire? What makes you so special?"

"I have a skill," I say with my palm on my chest.

"To Yoshi, you have an eight-by-ten glossy and a skill

yet to be learned. Right now, you have only potential."

"Chauvinist—"

"Never mind. Certainly you didn't think you were going to have your hands on Ashton Kutcher in the first week."

"I'm scheduled for a blue peel next month before I'm let loose on the hallowed grounds of Yoshi's styling floor to sweep hair."

"Ouch."

Not what I wanted to hear. "It hurts?"

"Hair is such a personal thing. My clients go where they want, so don't let that stop you with Yoshi. Just appease him and you'll have your job. If you get good enough, he'll lose all power. Did he give you the Yoshi spiel?" His eyes roll. "You know, the '*You are Yoshi. You will eat Yoshi, sleep Yoshi*—'"

"It wasn't that bad."

"I guess he's trying not to scare you. He *is* that bad. He's a genius, but a crazy genius. Tom-Cruise-jumping-on-Oprah's-couch genius."

We squeal up the road until we're once again in traffic on Santa Monica Boulevard, the place to be while you sit in your overpriced car wasting gas on idling. His phone rings again, and he holds up a finger. "Scotty here."

Scotty?

Another distraught female voice comes over the speaker. "They're saying I'm not on the list, Scott!"

"Who's saying that, baby?"

"These thugs at the door! Big-necked losers. They have no idea what they're doing! Didn't you get me on the list? How could I not be on the list?"

"I'll be right there, Cassie. Just hang on."

"You're going to help me, baby, right?"

"I'm just the blackness in your universe, helping you shine."

Can I puke now?

He flips the car around and pulls to the side of the road, then reaches over me to open the passenger door, pushing it toward the dirty sidewalk. "I've got to get to work; this girl's on the verge of stardom. Get yourself home, all right?"

"Scott, you have got to be kidding." I cling to the seat. "I don't even know where you live yet. Just take me along. I'll help you be the blackness in her universe. Come on, I can suck up. Remember?"

"Can't do that." He scribbles on a pad that's mounted on his dash. "The address." He rips off the paper and pulls a twenty from his ashtray. "Go get yourself some dinner, and go home and prepare for tomorrow. Read that manual from cover to cover. And lose the furrowed brow; you're going to need Botox before you're thirty. You want to look like your mother?"

"Please, Scott." I try to keep the desperate pleading from my voice, but to no avail. "Can't you just take me home first? Or I can go with you. You'll never know I'm there."

"I'll never make it with traffic, and I'm not showing up to work with a woman on my arm. I have enough needy women in my life where that isn't smart business."

"Fine. Maybe if you had fewer women on your arm, your problems might be fewer. Did you ever think of that?"

He pushes the door wider. "Go shopping before you get home, Sarah. I'm not going to baby-sit you, and I hardly think you need me to dress you. You've had a subscription to *Vogue*, I'm assuming, and this is your business too. Show me you know what you're doing."

"Yes, but the magazine is the only part of it I can afford. Unless you count rubbing the perfume-sample pages on my wrists."

"Go vintage, Sarah. There's a shop up the street. Do your best and accentuate your tiny waist and your booty. Hollywood loves a good booty."

"Somehow, that doesn't provide me with any motivation."

"Booty sells in Hollywood."

Why do I suddenly feel like something ordered at Kentucky Fried Chicken? "What is wrong with you?"

"Go. Before I lose this client."

I slink out of the car, and he quickly pulls the door shut and peels away from the curb amid a few annoyed honks.

I can't even be the blackness in someone's universe.

I asked for this. I have to remind myself this is not Scott's fault. Enjoy the moment, right? I'm in Hollywood, California. Swimming pools. Movie stars. And currently, I'm as Clampett as they come—without the bank account but certainly rivaling Ellie May with my new 'do. I wish I *had* enough hair for pigtails.

It's a mind-clarifying thing, being dumped on a bustling city street. I almost feel invisible, and it's actually sort of freeing. No one's expecting me. No one will get drunker if I don't show up when I'm supposed to. I could break out into dance, and not one person would care. Sure, they might stare a bit, but not one person would call the church and tattle on me. I don't even have a church yet!

"Cary Grant's star is at Hollywood and Vine!" I say out loud. Two guys in jeans and tight t-shirts stare me down, but they just keep moving. See? Being crazy here is no big deal. I am invincible!

"Hollywood and Vine!" I yell after them. "I'm going to see greatness!"

They just shake their heads at me. I feel powerful and mighty. I can be anything I want to be here! I feel like seeing Cary Grant's star, Clark Gable's, William Holden's!

"Excuse me," I ask a passerby, a woman of about fifty. "Do you know where Hollywood Boulevard is?"

"To the left up there. Toward the hills. Take North Highlands until you reach the Boulevard." She clicks her tongue. "Tourists."

My heart starts to pound in my ears as I get closer to the infamous Walk of Fame. Sure, I know it's just a bunch of stars' names on a sidewalk, but to me it represents hundreds of dreams coming true. To me, it's proof that Archibald Leach truly became Cary Grant. At least in the eyes of the world.

Even at the height of ski season, Wyoming didn't have this many people. Everything is gray here, except the hills in the background, with their dilapidated fifties-era homes. I'm sure they're worth a fortune, but wow, are they a blight on the land or what? For this place to be concerned with the environment really is the epitome of irony.

Although it seems we only just left Beverly Hills, I'm rapidly discovering Hollywood is a different cup of tea. It's . . . um . . . scary, actually. The pristine streets and well-dressed patrons are long gone. The shops are selling fast food—or things I've never seen before that, let's just say, don't seem necessary in my life. There's a lot of cheap lingerie and tools for heaven knows what. Certainly nothing in my future. I'm sure they must be illegal in the state of Wyoming.

There are more people *lying* on the sidewalk than actually walking on it. Each one of them holds a sign:

"Veteran. Need help." "Homeless. Need work." Some of them wave them at me. Some of them just prop them in front of their sleeping selves. *All* of them unnerve me.

I kick off my heels and start to walk a little faster along the filthy concrete, knowing I'm probably subjecting myself to multiple bacterial infections but needing to feel like I'm moving. As evening is closing in (granted, not for a few hours, but it's a concern since I'm alone here, with only my address on a scrap of paper), I'm suddenly seeing my life story on Lifetime. I can see the trailer now: *"She came to give Hollywood body. Instead, it took hers."*

I shiver. A web of my own imagination traps me until I'm holding my breath and praying there's a church to run into. But then I remember how in *The Sixth Sense* the kid went into a church and the dead guy came in there anyway! I shake the thought. It serves me right for getting theology from a ghost movie.

I speed up, walking as fast as I can without being obvious or breaking into a full run. No one's chasing me, but I feel those prickles on the back of my neck as though I'm being followed.

Then, almost before I'm aware of it, a familiar pink-and-brass glow on the sidewalk. I'm here.

Donna Reed. She's the first star I see. I stoop and run my hands over the brass letters. "You were one of my very favorite screen kisses, Miss Reed. You and Jimmy Stewart in *It's a Wonderful Life*—now that was romance."

I run to the next star. Preston Sturges. Okay, sorry, Preston, but I have absolutely no idea who you are. I'm sure you were a great addition to Hollywood.

Next. Rita Hayworth. Ooh, redhead for the ages. Alan Ladd. Eh. Not so moved. Henry Fonda. Oh, I loved him in *The Grapes of Wrath*.

Then I see it: John Wayne! Oh, my gosh, would my town go crazy. The ladies would be squealing with delight.

Shirley Temple. She was my favorite on a Saturday morning. Michael Landon. Loved *Little House on the Prairie*! Alistair Cooke. Loved *Masterpiece Theatre*.

When I spy the next one, I know I'm close to the Holy Grail of my Hollywood fetish: Clark Gable. "Frankly, my dear, I loved you!"

I know what's coming next. I've planned my exodus for too many years not to. The tears well up in my eyes as I look at his name.

Cary Grant.

I kneel next to the star and run my fingers over the letters. Does he have any idea what he's done in my life? Does he know how he kept this woman, younger than his own daughter, company? How he brought hope for a dream? My tears fall onto the star as I look up to the heavens. "Thank you, God. Thank you for seeing me this far. I never thought I'd see the day."

I don't know how long I sit here on this filthy sidewalk filled with hope, but I feel someone come up beside me, and that presence makes me look up.

"Are you all right, miss? Did you need something?"

"Who, me?" I ask. *Yeah, you—the one crying on Cary Grant's star.* See, this kind of behavior isn't even normal for LA.

"Is there something I can help you with?"

I stare up, blinking wearily. I have never seen this many muscles on one human being in my lifetime. I'm not the gawking sort, but this is like car-accident gawking. He's a living anatomy book, showing the muscles under the skin—except his actually bulge out from the skin. They're that defined and that obvious, and I'm trying desperately not to look. Really, I am.

"Where's your shirt?"

"Where are your shoes?" he asks me.

I hold up my boots in my hands.

"Back in the gym. I was jogging with a client and I saw you—"

"You jog here? My cousin says people don't jog here."

"People jog here. They pay me to jog with them." He holds out a hand. "Do you want to get up?"

"I was just looking at Cary Grant's star. He was here."

Gym Boy nods. "New to Hollywood?"

I smile up at him. "Was it the fawning over the star that gave me away?"

"It was the lack of shoes on a Hollywood sidewalk, actually."

"I could just be another homeless person."

"You're too cute to be homeless, so you must be a struggling actress. I suppose you could be both."

"The people here make Cindy Simmons look like dog meat."

"And Cindy Simmons is?"

"The most popular girl in Sable, Wyoming."

"They must make them pretty in Wyoming, too, if you're the second-most popular."

"Oh, I wasn't popular. I was a hairstylist."

He laughs heartily. "So, you look like you could use a beverage. Can I make you a power drink back at the gym? A whey shake, perhaps? Lots of protein to keep you going, give you the energy you need." He winks, and it's the first wave of warmth I've felt in hours. Granted, I'm sure there's a gym subscription behind his tenderness, but I can't afford to be picky now, can I?

The ripples of Gym Boy's six-pack make me lose my

train of thought. I am not the salivating type, but I have absolutely not seen this before, and quite frankly, I always thought it was the airbrush that did that. Nothing like having all the men prettier than you to destroy your self-esteem.

"You want me to follow you back to the gym?" I ask him.

"People generally pay me for the privilege of running behind them."

"What self-respecting girl would want you running behind them?" I mean, is it just me, or would that make any woman feel like she was carrying the caboose of a freight train?

"I encourage them."

"Well, I can tell you right now, that wouldn't encourage me." I dust off my bum with my free hand.

He raises his brows. "And what would encourage you, Miss—"

"Sarah Winston." I hold out my hand, but it's filthy from Cary's star, my tears, and my own shoes, so I drop it back to my side. "What do you eat?" I ask him. "Besides fruit smoothies."

"What?"

"You have no body fat to speak of. I wondered what you ate. It's a fair question."

He preens a little and curls a bicep. "It's all about protein and portions, little lady." He has a receding blond hairline and the prettiest blue-green eyes, like a tropical sea. He's way out of my league. Though I guess Dane and Cary are too, and that hasn't halted the dream.

"So you're a Cary Grant fan."

"Isn't everyone?"

"Are you going to take me up on my offer of a smoothie?

It's not everyone I offer a free power drink to. Just walk toward the light."

"The last time I went towards the light, I got this haircut, so I should know better."

He smiles broadly, showing good teeth. "You have the cheekbones to pull it off. Though you might want to rethink your stylist next time. Don't you have a friend or something? Isn't that what you do?" He shakes his head. "Yeah, that's not going to help business."

"Brutal honesty. I can't stand that in a person."

He laughs again. "Where are you from?"

"New York." Swallowing after my lie.

"So how are you familiar with the most popular girl from Wyoming?"

"Upstate New York." At his unconvinced look, I wince. I look down at my bare feet and then at the cheap boots in my hands. *Sigh.* "I'm from Wyoming, actually."

This makes him laugh out loud. "So you're here to be an actress? Because you're not very convincing." He smirks. "I've heard the hairstylist routine before, you understand."

I shake my head. "No, I really am here to be their hairstylist. I got a job training in a Beverly Hills salon."

"I think that's harder, actually. To be the stars' hairstylists. They're particular, and if it doesn't come out like they want . . ." He whistles. "I should know; I see it every day with actors who want six-packs but don't want to work out. I steer them down to the plastic surgeon's office because that's the only way they'll get them."

"I'm looking for the vintage shop." I look down at my feet again. "Well, but Cary Grant's star was my priority. Sue me."

"It's not open past six." A shrug flexes his muscles. "Besides, the best vintage shop is where the stars drop off their clothes. It's that way. They might not be open late either, though." He points back down the creepy street with the lumps of homeless folks I'm sure I should feel pity for—Christian compassion and all that—but on this day I only feel a little terror at passing them again. There's something unbearably weird about perfect weather and lumps in big coats along the sidewalks.

"I'd rather just go to the other one tomorrow. Thank you again." I start to walk up the street, and Mr. Beautiful follows behind me. Granted, he's giving my ego a fantastic boost, but the Wyoming girl in me just wants him to call it a day. *I just want to fix my hair and fixate on Cary's star again and getting there. Is that too much to ask?*

"You have no idea where you are, do you?"

"I'm heading that way. On the Walk of Fame."

"Would you come back here? I'm totally safe. Come ask someone in the gym how I can protect you if you don't believe me."

"But I have to go with you to do that, and I could be dead by then. Right here I have Cary to protect me."

He poses with his biceps flexed in all their glory. "I'm totally safe. If I was going to hurt you, would I be offering a fruit smoothie? Juice drinks and violence are opposing extremes."

"I'll give you that much."

"If anyone should be scared, I think it's me, because I'm allowing a woman to follow me who isn't wearing shoes on Vine and who is sobbing over Cary Grant's star."

"It was a few tears. I wasn't sobbing. That's a bit too much drama, but if you knew what it took to get me here . . ."

"The name is Nick Harper, trainer to the stars." He pats his bare chest. "I don't have a card on me, sorry."

"So, *this* is the best he could do?" A woman's voice tinged with a hint of crazy slices though our conversation.

I turn to see a lovely (as in gorgeous, but from her expression not exactly heart-filled) woman. She has that natural-colored auburn hair that every woman tries to recreate in a salon, only to look like they have wood polish glazed on their hair. She has icicle-blue eyes, the color of a glacier, and they feel just as cold as she gazes down on me. Now, I'm 5'6", average height, but this woman is monstrously tall. And at the moment much scarier than the homeless lumps up the street—her eyes are frosty and her venom seems meant for me. I step closer to Nick. Sort of a *He's with me* move.

"You don't know who I am," Amazon says to me. "I can't believe you have the audacity to not know who I am."

I don't, and trust me here: I wish I did, if only to protect myself.

"Xena, Warrior Princess?" Judging by her reaction, this was the wrong answer. "I'm new in town. I doubt very much that we know each other." Stepping ever closer to Muscle Man, I try to restart our conversation. "So they say William Holden's star—"

"I don't believe we were done speaking."

She must be mistaking me for someone else—perhaps the only other average girl in town with her own real, if slight, chest.

"You'll want to remember the face since you're shacking up with my fiancé."

My eyes wither shut. *Scott!* It's not enough he abandons me on the street; he has to send a stalker! I stumble to find words. "I'm not shacking up with anyone. I'm a Christian."

"Hey, no kidding, so am I," Nick says. "I knew you had that spark. It's not normal for me to follow someone down the street. Really out of my character—"

"Excuse me, nearly-naked man," Amazon says. "I hate to interrupt, but we have business to discuss. I'm Alexa Paul. Have you heard of me?"

"Are you in a show I should know? Because I don't watch very much TV, and in Wyoming we don't get all that many channels, and I didn't even know who Lily Minder was and—"

"I'm Scott's fiancée," she says flatly. "Maybe he's mentioned me?" She holds out her ring finger so I can see the sparkling dazzler, and my breath catches.

"Tiffany's. Very nice. Scott has good taste." Sometimes it's just better not to talk. Her icy blue eyes look like they want to shred me. If I tell her I'm not living with her boyfriend, she'll know I'm lying. As I said, I'm a terrible liar. I *am* living with her boyfriend. And say what you will about my cousin, he's currently the only option I have for a roof over my head. I've got to soldier on with this. Besides, if I can keep the alcohol lined up and in alphabetical order, I can mislead a beauty queen.

Of course, now I'm looking at my lovely Gym Boy, whose abs could speak if they wanted to, and he's going to think I'm not much of a Christian but rather the confused hoochie mama, if I admit to living with Amazon's boyfriend. So . . . as I said . . . sometimes better not to talk. I opt for the Fifth. That counts here in LA, right?

"It's a beautiful ring," Nick says brightly. *Don't hurt me* remains unspoken.

"Isn't it?" she asks him. "The only problem with my engagement is that my fiancé isn't answering my telephone calls, and next thing I hear, he's moving in with someone else. Shouldn't a guy break off an engagement before he moves in with someone else? I mean, am I crazy, or is that supposed to be normal?"

Nick shrugs and she turns back to me. So much for my hero.

"Do you want to explain that?" Alexa asks me. "Since Scott won't?"

Um, could it be the Psycho *music that starts when you come around? Just a random guess.*

I'm not an expert at love by any means, but something tells me when your boyfriend quits taking your calls, things don't look good. If I ever had a boyfriend, and he didn't return my calls, I'd hope I'd get the message. (But may I never have that kind of jerk in my life.) Didn't I witness enough of that in my childhood to make me smarter than your average girl? Now I know from experience that Scott always has a trail of angry women, so this is nothing new. But the engagement ring—that's an entirely different twist. I didn't think my cousin was capable of commitment, but there it is in Tiffany's platinum. Minus the commitment part, I guess.

"Scott Baker?" I ask, just to ensure I've got the right stalker. "Scott Baker asked you to marry him?"

"Yes, Scott Baker, the man whose car I saw you getting out of not ten minutes ago. Before you had a love affair with someone's star on Vine?" She shakes her head slightly. "Scott has interesting taste, I have to say. Look, I know you're staying with him."

"You're following me?" And here I was afraid of the homeless people, when I had my very own shadow tailing me.

"Not you, *him!* Until he turned around like a bat out of— Are you going to tell me you're not staying with Scott? That you didn't come into town yesterday?"

As I said, no expert at love here, but this girl's got issues. She's making my baggage look like carry-on. "It's not what you think." I look at Nick at this point. "Scott is—"

"My fiancé told a mutual friend the wedding was off because the woman he *truly* loved was coming to town and he wanted to try again. I assume that's you. Or is there a stack of women he truly loves?"

With Scott, no one truly knows.

"I'm just going to go back to work." Nick points up the street and quickly scrambles to leave. I guess my power shake is history.

"I thought you were done for the day."

"I just remembered something I had to do."

He runs. Cary Grant would never have run. I don't think even his alter ego of Archie Leach would be that weak.

"Alexa, do you know where Scott lives?" My voice is calm.

"Of course I do. Didn't you hear me say we were engaged?"

Yes, but we're talking my cousin here. Who knows? "I'm going out on a limb and appealing to your better nature. I could use a ride."

"You want me to drive you to my fiancé's house so you can stay there? Are you really asking me that?"

"It sounds stupid, doesn't it?" I try to laugh light-heartedly, but my heart is pounding. Scott is going to kill me, but it's his own fault for being a worm. "Maybe Scott will be home and we can talk to him." *If he doesn't kill me first. Either death by the warrior princess or my tactless cousin.*

One way or another, my Beverly Hills career is looking remarkably short—like my badly cut hair. It's really true that you can't escape your past. Leave it to me to come to California and get accused of my mother's sins. It's like she wrapped them up with a bow and sent them airmail to catch up with me.

But I touched Cary Grant's star so . . . whatever.

I was asked to act when I couldn't act.
I was asked to sing 'Funny Face' when I couldn't sing,
and dance with Fred Astaire when I couldn't dance—
and do all kinds of things I wasn't prepared for.
Then I tried like mad to cope with it.
~ Audrey Hepburn

"Hold the elevator!" I squeal, as I have just outrun a closing garage gate, but the man within just stares at me and reaches for the buttons. The doors close swiftly. "Jerk!" I shout just as the doors come together. "May you get a haircut just like mine! If you had hair, that is!"

That was below the belt, but it's been that kind of day. I punch the button, but I'm too late, and I have to wait for yet another selfish time-consumer to ride to his floor. So far, this state sucks! Bad stylists, beautiful stalkers, and six-pack-ab men that run at the sight of a catfight! And now waiting at the bottom of a condo garage because someone is too selfish to hold the door. The worst thing about having money is that you have to live by rich people. You'd be better off taking your money and investing than having to live in the "right" neighborhood with jerks like this. The worst part about me is I don't have money and I still have to live around rich jerks. *Hmmph. Give me white trash any day. White trash would hold the elevator.*

I've been buzzed up to Scott's expansive condominium via an intercom system, and I'm pacing the elevator, wondering how I'm going to tell Scott I met Alexa. That she's still wearing his ring. That he's an idiot. Not necessarily in that order.

The self-importance in this town really is unbelievable. I mean, first there's Yoshi, who treats his office like a sanctuary surrounded by his various awards and admirers. It's like I'm one of the Levite priests being allowed to enter the Holy of Holies. Then you've got people storing their cars behind automatic iron doors like they're priceless works of art. And finally, you have to get "let" up by a buzzer or punch in a secret code just to get home. It's all so *Mission Impossible*. I think Hollywood has been subjected to one too many Tom Cruise movies. Success here apparently means *How many hoops does someone have to jump through to get to you?* Even Scott's supposed fiancée doesn't have access to him. Now that's textbook trouble with intimacy.

I pace the entire ten square feet of the elevator like a lion huntress, livid at my cousin for making me endure Alexa's pain and at myself for not relieving some of it for her.

The doors open. My cousin is in the kitchen. Clearly he thought nothing of dumping me on the street. I'm about to get downright shrewish when I spot Dane and soften immediately at the sight of him. Even if he is out of my league, I don't need to go proving it outright. I touch his hat on the hook as I enter the room and flinch as I see Scott notice.

"Your fiancée drove me home." I drop my boots near the entry.

"What the heck happened to your hair?"

Dane looks up from his *Business Week* at this and quickly goes back to it. I'm assuming it's because he has the manners to not notice how bad my cut is.

"Yoshi had someone he considered 'edgy' cut it."

"With what? A lawn mower?"

"Look, I'm going to fix it. Let's move on to you. Did you hear what I said?"

My cousin just stares at me with a gaping hole in his face.

"About your fiancée, I mean?"

Why does the human heart long for things that aren't good for it? After driving with Alexa, I had an epiphany. We women always want to meet the competition; we always think it's about someone being prettier than us. But it's never about that. If it was, supermodels would have long-term marriages and fat housewives from Sable would be lonely. But it's just the opposite, from what little I've seen here.

Betrayal changes who we are inside. Once the essence of trust dissipates, all else is up for grabs, and when someone you thought you knew shuts down and eliminates you from their life, there's nothing you can do about it. The powerlessness kills me. I know it well. I watched my mother waste her life on it.

"My fiancée?" my cousin finally chokes out.

"She drove me home after we had a nice chat over dinner. She even paid for it."

Scott's mouth is still agape. And for once, he's not nearly as cool as he pretends to be. "Alexa?" he coughs again, as though he's never heard the name.

"I saw the ring, Scott. It was over-the-top tacky in size, straight from Tiffany's, and had your name written all over it." As I watch him shrug, I give him more proof. "She showed me your initials inside the band."

His jaw tightens. "Sarah Claire, just stay out of it."

"Like I had a choice to stay out of it. I do believe it was you who dumped me on the street, making me easy prey for people following you. If you're going to ditch me on the street, at least have the courtesy to slow down long enough for your stalker to catch up with you, huh?"

"She was following us?"

He's opening Styrofoam containers in the kitchen. The room is decorated in a very commercial and sterile style, the kind where you have to do a Google search for the refrigerator. My cousin's scooping take-out, and it spoils the pristine image to see food take its place among the barren nothingness. He punches buttons on the microwave as though he's not interested in what I have to say about his fiancée. "I see you found your way home. I told you you could do it. You're going to be dashing about the city on your own in no time. What better way to get your feet wet?"

"Than to be dumped on a city street while you slow the car, you mean? Yeah, I can't imagine a better way. It's just so reminiscent of my Sable dates when I wouldn't put out. Thanks for bringing up the warm cozy for me. I'm feeling the love."

At this, Dane drops his magazine. "You let her out on the street? Dude, what's wrong with you?"

"Listen, it was her idea to come out here. I came on my own. At least she's got the apartment and the job prospect. It's more than I had."

Dane shakes his head and picks up his magazine again. "You're cold, man."

"So you're not going to mention Alexa?" I ask.

"I assume you told her you were my cousin." He slams the spoon down on the stainless-steel countertop.

"Careful, you'll scratch that."

"I never could count on you, Sarah Claire. You always were a tattletale. The minute you thought you'd get in trouble, you'd go running to tattle."

Um, because I'd have the marks of a wooden spoon if I didn't.

"I wanted to, and right now you make me wish I'd spilled the whole sordid truth. Enough of this passive-aggressive garbage. Deal with her like a man, Scott!"

Scott raises his eyebrows and Dane drops his magazine again. "So." Dane smiles. "You do have claws. I wondered how a cousin of Scott's could be so sweet. It's nice to see a little bite in you."

"She's as tough as nails, Dane. Don't let the country girl in bad jeans fool you. She stole your hat this morning."

"Shhh!"

"She probably planned that whole fiasco to get into my wardrobe closet and make me feel guilty."

"I'm not manipulative, Scott, and I never have been." I look back toward Dane. "I stole—" I clear my throat. "—borrowed your hat because for some reason I thought it would bring me good luck."

"Did it?" he asks.

"I have the job, so I guess so." *But maybe tomorrow I could steal you and we'd be set!*

"Don't feel for Alexa. She's all venom—a snake coiled up in a magnificent skin."

"She brought me home tonight, and she bought me something to eat. I have to believe there's some kind of decency in her. Something you've missed. I'm going to write an e-mail and watch a movie on the computer."

Dane stands up. "You can watch a movie out here. I'll leave."

I smile at his thoughtfulness. At this moment, I need that kind of sweetness. "I'll be more comfortable in bed. Good night."

"Did she look good?" Scott asks me suddenly. "Alexa. Did she look good? Did she look happy?"

"She looked magnificent. I was absolutely invisible beside her."

"That probably had something to do with that haircut."

"She's a sweet girl. Maybe a little on the psychotic side, but then you're not exactly Prince Charming either. If it's not her, what exactly are you looking for? Who would you sweep into your arms and take to safety?"

Dane looks up again at this and raises an eyebrow.

"Ignore her—she has this weird, antichristian fantasy about Cary Grant rescuing her." Scott points to his head and spins his finger. "I think she watched *Notorious* one too many Saturday nights. The result of being dateless in high school."

"How do you know it's antichristian?" I ask. "You, who used to cut Sunday school?"

"Isn't it?"

"Just never mind. In the old movies they closed the door on any of that business." I stick my tongue out at him. *Some things never change.*

"You were dateless in high school?" Dane asks, shaking his head. "What is wrong with the boys in Wyoming?"

I take a moment to smile at Dane. Again. He's going to think I have some sort of facial tick. Always smiling and grinning at him.

"She had the restaurant staff eating out of her hand. Men buying her drinks at will. I told her to take the ring off, but she said it actually helps her get more attention."

Scott's face flinches, and for the briefest of seconds I see the remnant of the man I knew in Wyoming. "What did you talk about at dinner?"

"Los Angeles. Beverly Hills. How to make things work for me here. She was very helpful. She came here from Texas and had a lot of advice on how to present myself well. She thinks two-button jackets are the right look for me."

At this, Scott's jaw clenches as he bites down. He obviously doesn't like sharing the stylist spotlight.

"It's the cut that matters, not how many buttons there are."

"Oh, she said that too."

Naturally, we talked about Scott. But that is exactly what he's looking for, so I choose a more circuitous route—my own turn at being passive-aggressive. Men—let me rephrase that: the men I know—are like trapped animals when it comes to commitment. If they think they're going to be caught in the snare, they retreat like moles into a dark corner. Or in this case, a bachelor-pad loft. Talking with Alexa, my mission had become clear to me. Getting Scott married off would be like breaking the family curse, so I intended to do my best to see that it happened.

For some reason, Alexa thinks my cousin is the bee's knees. I'm the first to admit he can con a queen bee into honey. I'm mean, come on: *"I'm the blackness in your universe helping you shine"*? No woman on earth is dumb enough to fall for that line. Unless she *wants* to fall for it.

The scent from Scott's carton of garlic noodles is overpowering. He shoves a forkful into his mouth. "You don't know the whole story, Sarah," he says around the food.

"Gross, would you close your mouth? I—" I pat my chest. "I plan to be the one to break our reign of isolation." I have confidence. "When I get my mother into rehab and she's safely in a new line of work, things will change for me. Yoshi will ask me for advice, stars of stage and screen will ask me for an autograph—that kind of thing."

"I think you have more chance of the Cary Grant reincarnation happening. And I know you don't even believe in that sort of thing. That's how ridiculously optimistic I find your thinking."

"My mom just needs a change of scenery. In Sable, our family is the black sheep, the other woman, the barkeep. What if she came here and found a new title for herself? What if she was the infamous Sarah Winston's mother? It worked for Stallone's mom."

"Uh-huh. Sure it did."

"What if my mom came out here and went to college? She's smart, you know."

"She's not *that* smart. She's been in jail more times than I've got fingers. Smart people generally stay out of the pokey and they aren't on a first-name basis with their bail bondsman."

"It's time for my movie." I lower my voice. "Dane, thanks for offering me the television out here."

"Dane." My cousin's falsetto mimics me. "Can I steal your hat for the movie? It makes me . . ." He lowers his voice to a Marilyn Monroe purr. "It makes me feel so . . . Well, you know, some like it hot."

"Grow up." I'm an angry nine-year-old. All that's lacking is the foot stomp. I look to Dane, but he says nothing. He just gets up and walks toward his room.

I have an amazing ability to repel men I find attractive. Dane has just joined the ranks.

"Thanks a lot. Don't make me act like that."

"I cannot help the way you act. Unlike you, Sarah Claire, I don't take on responsibility for other people's garbage. I have enough of my own."

"Like I don't."

"So your plan is to have this husband-to-be arrive from the past, I take it." Scott laughs at this. "Because you are aware there will probably have to be a great paradigm shift of time for this to happen. For your mother to get a new line of work, I mean. Face it, that bar is her shell."

"What did I say to Dane?"

"You're avoiding the subject. I believe we were talking about breaking the family marital curse."

I am talking about breaking the family curse. "There's got to be a man in the greater LA basin searching for a practical yet ambitious career-minded Christian girl, and I intend to find him."

Dane opens his door and comes searching for his magazine.

"Maybe you should do one of those prison programs. You know, write-to-the-convict. They're always looking for upwardly mobile people with fear-of-intimacy issues. What do you think, Dane?"

"You found someone willing to marry you, my friend. I doubt your cousin will have to make such an effort. Those skinny jeans are good for at least one commitment." Dane winks at me.

He winked at me! *He did notice.* "Thank you, Dane." I step forward, hoping to continue our conversation, and I can see it in his eyes that he wants to. But something stops him, and he stashes the magazine under his arm, looking back at Scott.

"Men don't think all that clearly when they see a pretty face like hers in jeans."

"It isn't a pretty face that gets noticed," Scott says.

I watch the exchange take place between my cousin and Dane. "What's going on here?"

"Nothing," Dane says.

"Hey, if I'm going to live in a bachelor's crib, I deserve a few details." I try to keep my voice lighthearted, but it's pounding in my chest.

Dane starts to chuckle. "Does this look like a crib, Sarah?"

I look around the spotless room, where Scott's noodles and Dane's *U.S. News & World Report* are the only sign of humanity.

"Looks can be deceiving," I tell him, thinking back to my filthy, bleach-induced youth.

Dane walks closer to me, his eyes unwavering, until he stands right in front me. Slowly he reaches around me with his arm, and I feel his wrist at my waist. His touch brings my body to life as his face nears my own, and for a moment I think he's about to kiss me. Then he . . . pulls a piece of mail from the counter and steps back. "Looks *can* be deceiving."

What . . . I blink, trying to regain composure as my face flames. I'd thought . . . *Oh*.

"Don't you have a glass carriage waiting to take you to 1940 or something?" Scott asks.

"I said that when I was twelve, Scott. I've grown up a little since then." *Barely, but still*. "Deep down in our hearts, who doesn't wish for the kind of love that comes from a different time?" Still trying to recover from my humiliation, I refuse to look over at Dane.

"People who live in reality, Sarah Claire, that's who."

"Reality bites. I need a shower. Besides picking up a little LA sidewalk bacteria—excuse me, Hollywood bacteria—I just feel grimy, and I have a haircut to fix." I pull my portfolio close to my chest. But who am I kidding—I know I'm going straight for the TV. I need a good dose of Cary, is what I need. I look back at Scott. "If you have anything for me to wear, I could use one more day of nice clothes. If not, I'll mix and match with my fake Laundry pants. It seems skinny jeans are out."

"Jeans with seams at the back of the knee are always out. There're a few things in your closet. Help yourself. They're all last season, but on your salary, one can't expect much more than that."

I walk down the hallway. But as I'm about to enter the doorway, I notice Dane is behind me. I turn and am faced once again with his piercing sable eyes. My mind immediately goes to prayer. *Lord, You did good on this one.* (I didn't say it was a good prayer!)

I know everyone says that about the piercing eyes. But his really are intense—in a sexy way, not that creepy, Christopher Walken way. I wonder momentarily if they're contacts. But no one would bother with fake brown eyes. Would they? Then again, this is LA—one never knows what's real and what isn't. I read last year alone America had 270,000 boob jobs. That's a half a million fake things right there.

"I'm sure Alexa never meant to frighten you," he says. "She's very territorial when it comes to Scott."

"Thanks," I say, a little more dramatically than I'm feeling. I'll take attention where I can get it, especially when I get to see Dane close up. Even if he did just fake me out.

He is deep. Intense. In a way that I can't get close to but feel as though I'm meant to. I feel like I've known him all my life. *"Of all the gin joints in all the world . . ."*

He clears his throat as though he's about to say something important. "I don't think it's a good idea for you to be walking the streets of Hollywood alone."

"That's something we can agree on."

He steps closer to me, and I can feel my heart pounding at his proximity. I want to close my eyes and have a real Hollywood moment. Right here in Hollywood. If I closed my eyes and tilted my chin, puckered my lips ever so slightly, would he kiss me?

I pray he can't hear my heart pounding, for it's so pathetic. Leaning up against the door, I drink in his gaze, then scramble to refocus on the wall behind him rather than allow my mind to wander to bad World War II fantasies. I hear the scratchy sounds of "I Love You for Sentimental Reasons." It's as though he's floated across the foggy tarmac for me, calling out my name, rather than the mundane truth of walking up the hallway to warn me of my own lack of common sense.

I can't remember when someone ever looked at me like Dane is. I'm completely powerless under his intensity. I feel parched and isolated from everything I know, and I can't trust myself to behave as I always have because Dane is the epitome of all I imagined. He's the human form of the hero I've daydreamed about for so many years, though I never saw his face in my dreams—except when I opened my eyes and saw Cary's poster.

But it wasn't Cary's looks, it was his brain and capacity for the different that attracted me. *What if Dane's none of those things? What if this magnetism I feel is totally one-sided?*

I pull away from the wall and stand up straight, reminding myself this is exactly how my mother would come home when she was certain she'd met "the one." Two weeks later she'd describe the same man as Satan himself.

But looking up at Dane, it's easy to see why I haven't given up on the idea of romance. I keep trying to stare at the wall, but his gaze wins out consistently. Which isn't good—when your longings and dream life are as strong as mine, it's easy to see everything you want in a gaze. *And it's a lie*, I remind myself.

I try to *will* his expression to show me the truth of his feelings for me. Although, what am I expecting? I've only known him a day. "It's only been a day."

"What?" He furrows his brow.

I clear my throat. "I'm glad Alexa was following my cousin, or I might never have found my way here again. I didn't see a lot of taxis in town."

"Your cousin told me you might be interested in going with me to church on Sunday."

I nod, a little too frantically.

"I have a great little church that meets in Hollywood. It has Baptist roots, but it's a community church."

"Mrs. Gentry would be pleased."

"Who?"

"She's my adopted grandmother back home. She was very worried about me coming to the big city alone."

"Well, you had your cousin out here."

"Actually, she knows Scott. I think that made her more nervous."

The corner of his mouth lifts. "Scott told me you were a Christian. And don't worry, he also explained you're off limits. So I have no plans to hit on you."

"Did he say why I was off-limits?" I ask, hoping he'll explain the earlier exchange between him and my cousin.

"I assumed it was because he acts like your big brother, but I told him not to worry, I had no intention of making a play for his precious Sarah Claire."

"Right."

"Wait." He disappears into his room for a second, then returns. "Here's my business card." He hands it to me after writing his cell number on the back. "Don't walk again, at least not until you know the neighborhoods. Please call me when you need a ride; my schedule is flexible, and I can get you anytime." He pauses. "I meant that I *had* no intentions, but that was before I met you."

Gulp.

"Call day or night, Sarah. I'm a light sleeper."

I feel my mind start to wander into places it shouldn't. I hold the card up. "Thank you, Dane."

He comes closer to me, and I focus on the cleft in his chin rather than the sable eyes that seem to hypnotize me at will. There's a current running between the two of us, and my stomach surges with the warmth. I wish I could just fall into his arms. *Honestly.* I wish I didn't know better. It's as though we can't separate, and I close my eyes and drink in this moment. It's lovely and toxic all at once.

Nothing makes a woman more beautiful
than the belief that she is beautiful.
~ Sophia Loren

I've read through Yoshi's manual a few times. The gist of it is this: be a doormat and like it. Luckily, I'm well-prepared for that. I study the labels on all the clothes Scott threw at me and check the Internet to decipher a few. May I just say, anyone who buys clothes simply because of a label needs to go live in a third-world country for a while—even a small town in America. Well, okay, maybe that's harsh. Designers need to make a living too, I suppose. But do they have to fuel the inadequacies of women to do it? I do notice the stitching and cut are nice, but when you get into couture, it's just ridiculously expensive as far as I'm concerned. And I'm worried about impressing people . . . why?

When I log on, there's an e-mail from Kate. *Ah, normal Sable style.*

TO: *SCSable@frontiercomm.com*
From: *KateBFF@frontiercomm.com*
Subject: *Men stink*

So after you left, Ryan decides to get his panties in a bunch because he feels like now that you're gone, I'll spend all my time with him. I mean, I love the man and all, but please! A girl needs her space, you know? I spend all day twirling pin curls and coloring old ladies' hair various shades of Easter egg. I want to relax. He wants me to listen to his mother so she can tell me all about being a rancher's wife and how to cook properly. Hello? Am I not a hairdresser? Do I want to be nothing but a rancher's wife? Maybe raise a Cindy Simmons of my own?

Speaking of which, the new rumor is that it was Ryan who got you pregnant, so we're not friends anymore. Ah, the *National Enquirer* Sable style. We really need a movie theater here. Any empty chairs there at Yoshi?

Luv ya, miss you already. Me.

P.S. Did you see the ocean yet?

To: KateBFF@frontiercomm.com
From: SCSable@frontiercomm.com
Subject: Men do not stink—especially Ryan

Chill, girlfriend. You have a fabulous catch in Ryan, and don't go thinking the grass is greener like I did. Sable is your town, girl, you own it! I'm here in California and the men are all prettier than me. Probably skinnier too. I was good with that until I met a personal trainer today at Cary Grant's star. AAAAHHH, can you stand it? I saw it!!! Had a moment. Anyway, met a trainer, whose bulging pecs actually made his chest bigger than mine (he wasn't wearing a shirt—don't ask!) Anyway, that was a little disconcerting. I can handle being smaller than the plastic chicks, but sheesh, muscle men? That's just wrong.

Scott was engaged! Do not pass that on—he'll kill me, and he's already looking to throw me out. Not really, but I am annoying him. We're annoying each other. His fiancée is so beautiful, but they're not getting married. Not sure why yet, but I think he's an idiot. Of course, I guess I always did.

Next month I get a blue peel. Not sure what that is, but it sounds painful, and soon my skin should look like Barbie's. (Everyone's skin here looks like they applied Vaseline. Apparently, being shiny and completely void of pores is a good thing—so much for our Noxema days!)

Scott has a roommate. *To-die-for hot—wears a Bogey hat!* I want to bear his children. Do you know what it's like to live down the hall from that kind of gorgeous? He's a Christian too. Invited me to his church this week, but he doesn't talk much. Can't say I need him to; as long as I can gaze longingly, I'm good. It would be great if he was blind and I could just stare unencumbered. Oh, and you'll never guess. He wears a suit. Don't know what he does yet; his business card is weird. (Oh, he gave me his card so I could call him for a ride. Isn't that sweet?)

The salon is fancy and weird. No one talks to each other without sneaking around, and today wasn't even a "working" day. It was a teaching day. It's a "team salon," meaning basically that it's communism with Yoshi as our fearless leader. Too warped, but if I get to cut hair like him, it will all be worth it. The stylists make good money, though they spend a lot on upkeep for themselves (clothes, accessories, apartments), and any one of them is better than what we saw at the hair show that time (except the guy who cut my hair—think that was a test). Gotta run. Kiss Ryan for me, you loser.

Love, Me.

P.S. Saw the ocean from the plane, that's it. More later.

❦

The good mood is not to last. The next morning as we exit the elevator, Alexa is standing there in long, lean jeans and a flowing shirt in aqua, which only makes her eyes seem that much more hypnotic. She locks onto Scott and her eyes turn pleading. I think about pushing the Close elevator button and just disappearing from the scene, but if I know my cousin, he'd just leave me here to find my way to Yoshi's. To teach me another lesson.

"Please, Scott, just hear me out." She tries to take his hand, but he won't touch her. "We can talk about this."

Scott won't look at her and tries to walk around her as if she is a mere figment of his imagination. She stands in front of him, placing her hands on his elbows, and tries to force his gaze to her, but he doesn't relent.

"Go away, Alexa."

"You owe me at least a good-bye, don't you think? Even if you can't forgive me."

"I don't owe you anything and you know it." Again he tries to get past her, and she fumbles to retain control of him. He finally gets around her, thankfully, before he pushes her. I'm numb with culture shock. I feel like I'm in the middle of a *Dynasty* rerun, and with a dash of guilt, I see that such scenes are anything but entertaining.

"Scott, if you want to call this off, be a man and say so! Take your ring back. Make a stand!" Alexa screeches, and I can see this hits Scott between the eyes. At the rise in her voice, I'm not sure where to run. Scott's car is locked, or I'd gladly hide from the turmoil, but the truth is neither one seems to care that I'm here.

"You want me to be a man, Alexa? You never gave me the chance, did you? Just decided you always knew what I wanted without ever asking me."

"I made a mistake, Scott. People make mistakes!"

He stops and looks back at her, his eyes steely and cold as ice. "You're right, Alexa, people do make mistakes. And if I could forgive you, I would."

He chirps his car open and I run for it.

"This is it, Scott. I'm not waiting around for you forever. If this is the way you choose to end this, it's something you have to live with." She's got her fists on her hips with one long leg outstretched. She means it. Everything about her body language says so.

"I'm good with that." Scott gets into the car, and Alexa stands in front of it, somehow looking both sexy and pathetic. That's an art. Scott opens the window to her. "Before you go placing the blame on me, I think you might want to do some soul-searching about who really said good-bye." Then he pushes the button to roll the window up, shutting her words out one at a time.

"Scott, can't you just talk to her? Hear her out?"

"Never mind, Sarah Claire."

My heart is pounding, and I can't bear to leave Alexa here like this, broken. "Why did you make her think you'd marry her if you wouldn't? No woman wants to be a man's courtesan forever. You've turned into one of my mother's men!" I cross my arms and close my eyes rather than look at Alexa's broken spirit.

"I *did* ask her to marry me! You said you saw the ring."

"What are you so afraid of, Scott? She loves you, and it's obvious you're not over her. Do you want to end up like my mom and your dad? Who even came to your dad's funeral, Scott? Is that how you want to end up? With no one to love you or look after you when you get old? Not ever having someone you can trust?"

His current coldhearted, distant demeanor aside, I know Scott has a heart. He was always the one who took care of me when Cindy picked on me, or when the kids made fun of my shoddy clothes. Now he looks at me with the first true emotion I've seen from him since I've been in California, and it's hard to watch.

"I've always been loyal to you, Sarah Claire." His voice breaks slightly. "Can't you give me the same respect?"

I feel my eyes sting. Scott turns the ignition, and slowly Alexa steps out of the way and begins to walk backward, never taking her eyes off of Scott (and never looking remotely disheveled). It makes me sick to my stomach, watching her stand there, her arms hanging at her side, long and lifeless, like a rag doll's. There's not a woman alive who hasn't felt like she does right now, and her beauty didn't protect her.

We drive out of the garage. I look back to see Alexa get into her Mercedes and slam the door, and I hear myself let out a small sob for her. No one deserves that kind of treatment. No one.

But Scott is biting his lower lip, and to his credit, it's trembling. He is not heartless.

I wish for Alexa's sake I could give her back her future with Scott, and most of all the part of her heart that Scott will always have. I pray silently for both of them, wondering if there's anything more I could have done. We ride in complete silence until we're at Yoshi's doorstep.

"Don't be upset all day," Scott says as I open the door.

"Why can't you just break up with her, Scott? Take the ring back and put an end to it."

"It's complicated, Sarah. I owe her something."

"You owe letting her go."

He nods. "I probably do, but I can't do it. Not yet. There's some things I have to work through, all right?"

"Please come with me to find a church this weekend."

He laughs. "You and Dane, you think your God is going to solve everything, don't you? I took Dane's advice once before. I asked Alexa to marry me, and look where it got me." He snorts and rubs his fingers and thumb together. "Money you can always count on. An invisible God, not so much. I'll call you at six and let you know if I can pick you up."

"Dane told you to marry her?"

"Go. You're going to be late."

I shut the door, feeling as though I've lived an entire day already. But I refocus. I have to. Right now, a man named Yoshi holds my future in his sought-after fingers.

Getting ahead in a difficult profession requires avid faith in yourself. That is why some people with mediocre talent, but with great inner drive, go so much further than people with vastly superior talent.
~ Sophia Loren

Two weeks. Eight hundred and forty-nine dollars in clothing. And I still have yet to touch a head of real hair. Unless you count "Strawberry," my new best friend and head from the Yoshi School of Beauty. Luckily, we start shampooing today, so I'll have real contact with something besides the espresso machine. Yoshi sort of fudged the truth with shampooing being the first order of business. It's actually "accounting," as in keeping a careful accounting of all the Yoshi product you sell and learning how to make clients feel as though their hair will wither away without it.

To sum it up, I am a grunt. As in *"Grunt: one who does routine unglamorous work—often used attributively <grunt work>."*

It's official. I have flown across three states and left my mother to fend for herself for the highly glamorous job of being a well-dressed coffee runner at a Beverly Hills salon. I can hear Cindy cackling now in her expansive digs. She's probably right now getting a pedicure, at the new salon that just opened up, and she's wondering what happened to little Sarah Claire who used to cut hair. She's laughing at her rhyme right now. I can hear it echoing across the Grand Tetons.

Today I'm currently walking into the local coffee shop because I'm going to find out what makes people drink this rotgut and why I must smell like java everyday. For this experiment, I refuse to make the coffee myself, because the service has to be a part of the experience.

Inside the Coffee Bean and Tea Leaf there seems to be some sort of system that I'm ignorant of. People are divided into distinct milling groups. A gal comes in behind me and heads straight for the proper line. I know I'm going to be one of those people who has to stare at the menu for an eternity. Like the people who tick me off at McDonald's: *Get the hamburger and fries and let's move on!* Back at the shop, I could suggest the appropriate drink for a person's mood, but I'm clueless as to what I'll actually order now that someone is going to serve me.

There's clearly a line for ordering and another more loosely connected line of people waiting until the coffee gal calls something out. Then they zap to life as though they've been hit with a stun gun.

"You in line?"

I turn around, and of all things, it's my one friend in California: Hollywood trainer to the stars and girl wimp, Nick Harper. Granted, he thinks I'm a crazy woman who sobs over Cary Grant's star and has a *Fatal Attraction* stalker, but then again, I think he's a muscular wuss, so I guess we're even.

I nod and smile. "I'm in line. I'm going to get a coffee." *Brilliant.*

"Sarah, right?"

"Yeah." I turn back around. He remembers my name.

"Did you get home all right? I was worried about you."

I could tell. I mean, running into the gym for safety—that just screams *"I'm so concerned about you."*

"I did. That was my cousin's fiancée. She thought . . . well, never mind. It was a misunderstanding. We worked it out and had dinner together."

"Your cousin," he says slowly, like he doesn't believe me. But soon after his eyes brighten, which seems to signal a renewed interest in our friendship. Albeit a little late. Although he's very good-looking, he's pretty-boy Hollywood good-looking, which does nothing for me. I like them intellectual, and call me odd, but men who are willing to use gel in their hair for that proper bed-head look turn me off. It doesn't help that I have to interact with my ideal every day. Or that said ideal has been called out of the country on business and I haven't seen him in a few days. And you know what they say about absence and the heart. No, none of that helps.

"I live with my cousin. Well, and his short-term room-mate, but there's nothing—" I slice my hand through the air. "—nothing going on."

He laughs. "Who are you trying to convince of that?"

I'm so obvious. "It's your turn." He points to the cash register, where a perky young woman is ready to help me. Shoot, I didn't study the menu. Nick distracted me!

"Good morning. What can we make for you today?"

All I can think about is Nick standing behind me, ready and willing to judge me by said order. Just like that poor girl who hired him to run behind her. "I'd like a good starter coffee. Espresso, I mean." I lower my voice. "Something for people who don't really drink it. Um, let me think . . ." I put a finger to my chin.

"How about one of our Carmel Ice Blended Drinks or an Extreme Ultimate Ice Blended Mocha Drink?"

I make the mistake of turning around and seeing Nick shake his head.

"Way too much fat."

"But I like fat, and I don't hire people to run behind me."

"Everyone likes fat until they have to work with me to get rid of it. It's painful. Are those fat calories worth the pain of burning it off? Are they worth visible panty lines?"

"Ew. But no." I'm a 4. And I feel fat here, so I'm going to give Nick the benefit of the doubt on this one, but only because he's here. I'm not getting into the eating-disorder-of-the-week club.

The sighs from behind me are becoming apparent and it's clear the patience for the espresso-impaired is extremely low before the first morning cup of java. Mental note: experiment with new things apart from rush hour.

"I'll just wait," I say and pull away from the counter only to see the line is now ten people long. I know I didn't take *that* long.

"You don't drink coffee?" Nick asks me.

I shrug. "Never got started on it. Not the hard stuff anyway. Someone told me to try—oh, there it is! A vanilla latte, please."

"Sugar-free, non-fat," Nick corrects. The gal rings it up as though it is not my cash paying for it, and I want sugar and fat.

"Iced or hot?"

Another momentary brain malfunction. "Iced." I mean, it's not like it's twenty-below here in Southern California. Ever.

She then calls out a string of words that I suppose is my order. The really sad thing is that I could name most any alcoholic beverage without thinking twice about the ingredients. Not that we don't have Starbucks in Wyoming.

It's just that they are where the tourists go—not Sable. The locals in Sable all go to Milly's if they want coffee, disdaining corporate coffee and the tourists. If they want to pay three dollars or more for a drink, they go to the Hideaway and made sure they take away a buzz for their troubles.

My drink is ready quickly, as I think I held up the line.

"A tall, black coffee, no room," Nick says.

"It was good to see you," I call to him with a wave at the door.

"Wait a minute." He pulls a few bills out of his wallet and tosses them at the cashier. "Keep the change." He jogs over to me. "You can't keep me in suspense. I want to be here for the big moment when you get your first taste." He watches me intently.

I place a straw in the cup. Well, I try. I have trouble finding the hole and lose a good portion of my drink onto the top of the cup. I finally start to take a swig, but Nick pulls the cup out of my hand.

"What are you doing?"

He puts both cups on a nearby table and points down. "You're wearing it." Taking a napkin, he starts to pat at my thigh, where a drizzle has fallen onto the slacks Scott lent me.

Um, excuse me. I step away from him and his probing napkin. Then I look down. *Shoot!* I grab the napkin myself and start dabbing. Scott's going to kill me. Luckily, the pants are black. But still . . . *Good grief, I just want to cut hair.*

Finally, I give up and sigh. "I have to go back to work. Nice to see you, Nick."

"I'm still waiting for you to drink that." He nods toward my icy cup as though I'm about to have an out-of-body experience.

Grabbing the cup, I sip then nod my head, disgusted by the bitter taste. "It's strong."

"It's straight fake sugar. Stick with the coffee. Want to try the real stuff?" He holds his coffee out toward me. "No calories as long as you don't add cream and sugar."

"Thanks, but I have to get back to the salon. I just wanted to see what I've been serving . . . I mean missing."

"No, really, I don't mind."

I take a swig so he'll go away. "Mmm, yes. Still disgusting."

"You have shoes on today. Your hygiene looks pretty good. I'd lay real odds you actually took a shower since I've seen you. Are there any more stars on the Hollywood Walk of Fame you've become attracted to? You know, people volunteer to keep them clean. Maybe you should volunteer for Cary's."

"I'll keep that in mind, thanks." I'm sure Nick is charming in some form. "Good to run into you. I don't think I'll be doing so in the future, since I'm going to stick with Diet Coke."

"It's an acquired taste," Nick says. "You'll be hooked in no time."

"As in acquiring a complete lack of functioning taste buds? I think that stuff must kill them, like sniffing too much weed killer, you know?"

"So I won't see you here tomorrow is what you're saying?"

I shake my head. "I'm thinking not."

"Then I guess this is my one shot to ask you out. I would have done so when we first met, but the whole living-with-a-guy, psycho-ex-girlfriend thing just seemed like something I didn't want to take on. I may be in shape, but I don't have a death wish either. Today, it's a different story."

Okay, but to me, the story today is that you ran like a little girl into your bat cave, and I'm looking for a man who will cross time for me. I'm used to guys who have ridden bulls or at least broken a horse or two, so a guy who leaves me on the street with a psycho woman so he won't get his hands dirty . . . ? Not exactly on my list of sexiest men alive.

"So, dinner?" he asks again. "How's Friday night?"

No. Just say no. No need to be nice. You'll never see him again.

"Sure, that would be great," I hear myself say. *I am so lame.*

"Great. You want to meet me at the gym around seven? I have a business card today."

No, I don't want to meet you at the gym. I want you to come get me, like a proper date. Does he want me to come take a look at his abs before we go?

"You know, I'd better call you that afternoon, just to make sure things are going well at work. I'm still not sure about my schedule at this point, and I really have no way to get to your gym."

"So you want me to pick you up?"

"Isn't that generally how it's done?"

"Oh, of course. I just thought it was convenient for you. It's just two miles up the road."

"How is that convenient, exactly?"

"Right, you've been on your feet all day. My mistake. Usually women sit at desks all day and the walk does them good."

"Are you going to critique what I eat? Because the coffee-fat-content thing doesn't really do anything for me." It pains me how much I sound like my mother.

He purses his lips and is silent for a moment. "I will try really hard not to, but do me a favor—don't order the prime rib, all right? Or lobster. Heavens, don't order the shellfish."

"I'll make it easy on you." *Are you going to wear more than a tank top?*

"So how's Friday sound? Is that okay for you?"

Frighteningly scary, that's how it sounds. Dane is due home on Saturday.

"Can we do it a little later just in case I don't get off early?"

"I understand. All those starlets want to look perfect for the weekend."

"And they'll want coffee while they do it," I mumble.

"Are you going to give me your phone number? Or do I have to beg."

"Oh, right." I'm mortified and finally make the admission. "I don't actually know my phone number yet. I'm working for Yoshi, but I'm not exactly in a position to get phone calls there." Or exist, quite frankly. "Why don't you give me yours?"

"There's something eerily suspicious about a woman without a phone number." He pulls a card out from his black Adidas' pants and smiles. The light gleams on his face. What are they doing to the men here to give them that sheen? Are they slathering Brylcreem on their face? Or am I the only one without a blue peel? Is there a significant beauty secret that has been left out of Wyoming editions of *InStyle.*

"If I give this to you—" He draws the business card toward his chest. "—how do I know it will not be lost, eaten by the dog, given to Ashlee Simspon, or sent to Wyoming to incite wild rages of jealously?" He downs the coffee in a giant gulp and crushes the cup in his free hand.

I grab the card and plop it in my purse. "I guess you're going to have to trust me."

"I'm always up for a challenge." He winks at me and heads out the door. As he starts to jog up the street, he turns around and gives me one last smile while he jogs backwards. He is the complete opposite of me: cool, comfortable in his own skin—he can run backward, for crying out loud—and I'd lay odds that he went to his high school prom.

I have a date. Go figure.

I am not a has-been. I am a will be.
~ Lauren Bacall

I toss my nasty-tasting, sugarless drink down one of the rinse sinks at the salon and spray the milk residue down the drain. Just the sound of spraying water makes me wish I got to cut hair. It's Pavlovian.

I now contain enough nervous energy to keep a hummingbird airborne for a month—without the aid of caffeine. I have two business cards in my pocket—Dane's, in case I need a ride home, and now Nick's. I don't even know if two men *had* business cards in Sable. Oh, wait, I know Bob the septic guy did, because it was stuck to our refrigerator.

Of course, one of the cards means more to me than the other. Dane's been in France, so it's not like I could call him for a ride, but I haven't left that business card home once. I've written him several e-mails. I sent him none of them.

While the salon is busy with action for the day, I sneak to the back room and call Kate at the Hideaway. I miss her, and I haven't had a date in years, so it's not like I don't have something to say.

I close the door to the mixing closet and dial the number.

131

"The Hideaway Hair Salon."

"Kate?"

"Sarah Claire!" I hear her squeal and then the regulars calling my name in the background.

"Is that my girls?"

"I told them you saw Cary Grant's star. They want a picture. Hang on, I have to put Mrs. Rampas under the dryer." She drops the phone, and I hear the familiar whirl of the dryer and Kate's footsteps. "I'm back."

"I have a date."

"With Dane?"

"No, the trainer I met at Cary Grant's star."

"The one with bigger boobs than you?"

"Pecs. And yes."

"Whatever. Is he smart? Seems to me he's not that smart. You have to find a smart one, Sarah Claire. Are there any smart ones out there?"

"Of course there are. Dane said he'd introduce me around when he got back from France. At his church, I mean."

"You haven't been to church since you got out there?"

"I've been reading the Bible. Quit making me sound like some kind of heathen."

"You don't have to wait for Dane to go to his church, do you?"

"Do you want to hear about my date?"

"Yes, what's Muscle Boy's name."

"Nick Harper."

"Does he have that skin you keep talking about? The skin-peel kind."

"Yes."

"Ew."

"It's still a date," I remind her.

A date is something I haven't been able to accomplish in the last three years of living in Wyoming, not because there aren't men, but because my singles' group consisted of guys I grew up with. Guys I remembered eating paste in kindergarten and who ran the nude relays in the snow to celebrate a football win. It's hard to be led in prayer by someone who ran the highway with little more than athletic shoes. To go so far as to think of creating children with a paste-eater is mentally impossible.

They've all turned into fine men, incidentally, but it's too late for me. Once you've known a guy to snack on Elmer's or taste someone's lip gloss in class, all romantic notions die forever.

"Well, let me know how it goes," Kate says flatly. "She's got a date," I hear her say to the posse. "Pretty boy."

I hear their groans.

"Dane isn't due back until Saturday," she tells them.

"Let me talk to her." I hear Mrs. Gentry's voice. "Sarah Claire, this is Eleanor Gentry."

"Hi, Mrs. Gentry," I say with the stinging of tears at the sound of her voice. "How are you?"

"It's lonely here without your spark. We all miss you greatly. Movie night isn't the same."

"I stood over his star. And I saw Clark Gable's for Mrs. Rampas."

"We're overjoyed, dear. Your mother is doing well. She said you haven't called, but I told her you must be busy."

Guilt. I hate guilt, but I guess I'm entitled to some here.

"I'll call her, Mrs. Gentry."

"Do you know the trainer's IQ?"

"What? Well, no, I'm not giving SAT tests or anything, but he seems knowledgeable enough. He wears a UCLA shirt, so he must have gone to college."

"Don't let any of those college boys let you feel less than you are, Sarah Claire. You're a very bright girl. I just wanted to remind you of that. Good-bye, dear."

"Hey." Kate comes back on the phone. "I was serious about Yoshi's having a chair," she whispers into the phone. "I think I need to leave here, Sarah Claire."

"What on earth? Kate!" There's a pounding on the door. "Kate, I have to run. I'll call you back tonight." I put the phone back in its cradle and open the door.

Jenna greets me nervously. "Where have you been? Yoshi was out here looking for you twice! If he knew you were in the coloring closet, he'd be arresting you for espionage for certain. He wants to see you before you go to Isabella's for your consultation."

"I'm sorry, Jenna. I ran into a friend at the coffee shop and then—never mind, I won't bore you with the details. Was I gone that long?"

"You just have to learn how to sneak in and out like a ghost. Be seen when you want to be seen—like when you're working overtime—but don't ever disappear. Get someone to cover for you. It's an art."

"Meaning you didn't cover for me?"

"No, I did. I told him you had gone outside to water the plants. You noticed they were looking parched."

"Sarah!" Yoshi bellows, and I realize how little my life has changed. Instead of an ungrateful, drunk mother, I now answer to a tall, angry Asian man, but it's still the same life.

"Yes, sir."

"My garbage can is full in my office. See that it's emptied before class starts."

"Certainly, sir."

I'm hoping it's a test, because I paid for a lot of advanced training in Wyoming to be packing up this guy's garbage and serving people coffee. Even if I do recognize their faces from *Us* magazine.

I rush to his office, where he is still yelling at someone in another language, and take out the trashcan lining and its contents. He stops abruptly and stares at me.

"Bring a new liner in; you don't just take the old one. Where am I going to throw my garbage while you're emptying the old one?"

"I'll be back in a jiff," I tell him.

He shakes his head. "No, we do things the Yoshi way. Go get a new liner first, take the old bag out, tie it, and then put the new liner in before you leave the office." While he's talking, he never takes his eyes off himself in the mirror. He even bobs around me when I get in the way. "Check the guest toilet. I may have left the seat up."

I exit and stand against the wall outside the office, which has the same energy levels as the lion cage before the meat gets thrown inside. I breathe in deeply. Ann, a stunning blonde who has been the one stylist to offer me the slightest hint of a smile here and again, is outside with a liner. "Don't worry, he does it to all of us. Just be calm. Once you learn the way he wants everything done, it's a no-brainer. I had to do about six weeks of garbage/espresso time before he let me wash. Here." She hands me a pair of rubber dye gloves.

"What are these for?"

In Sharpie pen is written, "Toilet gloves."

"I saved them to remind myself every day where I came from. They're yours if you want them."

I grab the edges of them. "Thanks for this."

"You'll get through it."

I take the garbage bag before entering the small jade

office again. The walls are covered with Hollywood stars' autographed pictures and prestigious hair awards I've only seen in trade magazines. I never tire of focusing in on one when I get the opportunity to enter the sacred office. The simple truth is this man is a genius in his craft, and he's earned the right to be a jerk, but if I ever get famous, I'm going to remember this and act accordingly.

Do you hear that, God? I'm ready for my close-up.

Yoshi slams the phone down, and I'm in his office with nowhere to turn, feeling like a complete idiot with the garbage sack only half-fastened to the receptacle, the full bag of trash underneath me in my awkward pose. I'm not quite sure how to do this job with flair, but I can certainly tell you I'm not accomplishing it.

"Aren't you through with that yet? This job should take you thirty seconds and no more. I've timed it." He pats his forefinger to his watch.

"I'm sorry, sir. I got sidetracked by all these awards and photographs. It's like coming backstage to the Oscars for an actor." I'm backing out of the office when he holds his palm up.

"Stop." He looks directly at me. "Why come out here and live in the most competitive market in the country?" This is the most attention he's paid me in the two weeks and 120 hours I've been here.

Of course, the paying-for-mom's-bail story, or even the electric bill, is probably not going to charm him. To show up Cindy Simmons is stupid; even I know that. And the fact that I had no life in Wyoming after twenty-six years is just pathetic, so I think of my other excuses. I have no shortage of them.

"I want to be the best at something, sir. This is the only thing I do well enough to try and accomplish that. I want to see how far I can take it; it's just something I have to try. Who knows, maybe you'll tell me I haven't an ounce of talent, and I'll be going home soon. I want to drink everything in while I can."

"You won't be going home," he says. "At least not yet."

"No?" Color me skeptical.

"Being the best is ninety percent attitude, but you have to *want* it, Sarah. You have to want it enough to devote your life to it, and it will cost you."

Is anyone else hearing "The Star-Spangled Banner"?

"There is no free meal, and paying your dues is mandatory. Every single one of those stylists out there has earned the right to be here. They swept hair, they emptied my garbage can. They wiped gum off the sidewalk if it was necessary. Being the best means being humble above all else and willing to learn. Have Ryan fix your hair before you go see Isabella. John's going through something."

I nod. "I studied your book on techniques, planning on trimming it myself, but I knew I couldn't go any farther without watching you. The slicing, the surface cutting—I want to do it the right way. I didn't dare try it without seeing the master first." I pause. "I know I sound like a complete suck-up, but I want you to know I'm grateful for this opportunity. Even if nepotism did play a small part in my destiny."

He sits back in his chair. "I came to this country with nothing. I didn't even know the language except what I had picked up through shaving businessmen at the airport. I had a family to support back in Japan, one pair of shears, and a comb. In my village I wasn't ever going to be more than a Main Street barber."

In my "village" I wasn't ever going to be anything more than my mother's daughter. India's caste system has nothing on Sable, Wyoming.

"I understand, sir."

"Make me a cappuccino," he says and lifts the phone.

Apparently, our moment of warmth is over.

Outside, Ann hands me a mop. "Yoshi wants you to mop and clean the bathrooms before the other students come. He hates the scent of bleach, so be sure and spray the lavender mist when you're done." She grins as though she's been there before.

"Aye-aye, matey," I say, thinking if I'm going to swab the poop deck, I might as well adopt the language.

"He'll want his cappuccino first, though."

I pull the mop behind me as we approach the great stainless-steel machine, where Californians seemingly worship. It's extremely complicated, with several buttons, levers, and directions. I'm not the technical type, and our Mr. Coffee had one button, so it was a full three days until I didn't feel at risk that it might blow up in my face and give me the cheap version of a blue peel. What I knew of coffee before this consisted of knowing, when Mom came in a little late, to throw four spoonfuls of Folger's in and press the button.

Jenna comes up to the machine. "There's a call for you, Sarah. Says it's urgent. We'll cover for you. Line two."

Confused, I head for the phone.

"Sarah Claire, what did you tell Kate?"

"Who is this?"

"It's Ryan. Who do you think is looking for Kate? Unless you know something I don't."

"Ryan, how did you find me?" *And what have you done with Baby Huey?*

"I read Kate's prayer journal. She's praying for your salon."

Nice detective work. "What do you mean, what did I tell her? Five minutes ago when I talked to her? I told her I had a date."

"No, on your e-mails. I know you two have been e-mailing each other."

"She's my best friend, Ryan. Is there a crime against that?"

"She says she's rethinking the wedding."

"When? When did she say that?" Okay, I know I shouldn't feel guilty, but I immediately feel guilty. Maybe my leaving inspired Kate, and no one can be inspired and stay in Sable. It's like a law of physics.

"She wants to follow her dream."

Uh-oh. "Kate has a dream?"

"Everyone has a dream."

"Yeah, but her dream is to marry you, Ryan."

"Apparently, it's not just that."

I swallow hard and see the girls are circling. I can only assume Yoshi is nearby. "I have to go, Ryan. Call me at Scott's later if you need to talk."

"Look, you know me, Sarah Claire. I don't get mad easily, but I don't want you filling her head with ideas. She's not like you."

If Kate has a dream, she's never shared it with me. I do know that in high school she once wore a St. Christopher's Medal around her neck and told Ryan it belonged to a guy in Montana. Just to make him jealous! Clearly, it worked. "Bye, Ryan." I hang up the phone and try to look busy at the espresso machine, but my mind is racing.

Kate inherited over ten thousand dollars from her grandmother. That was ten years ago, and she put it into Schwab. She could actually make a dream come true. I wonder if that's what scares Ryan. Maybe she said something to him.

She is so going down for not telling me.

The phone rings again. Jenna holds it out to me. "It's him again."

Yoshi has come out of his office and is glaring at me, but I just turn my back toward him. "Ryan, I'm sure it's nothing. When did Kate ever do anything crazy?"

"Exactly. Maybe she's seen there's more to life than being the wife of a cattle farmer. She's seeing just how boring her life with me is going to be."

"Don't jump to conclusions. I'll talk to her tonight. You'll talk to her tonight. Everything will be fine. I really have to go." I place the phone back in the cradle and meet Yoshi's gaze. "Sorry about that. A little emergency."

I can't help but wonder if Kate's left Wyoming. If, somehow, my leaving opened the floodgates and Sable's population is now going to dwindle.

I know I am right for Scarlett.
I can convince Mr. Selznick.
~ Vivien Leigh

Isabella's salon is little more than a closet—a very white, sterile-looking closet. I fill out paperwork stating my health issues—none, unless you count my genetic predisposition to drinking—and reasons for the visit.

"I'd like to keep my job at Yoshi's," I write. You can't fault me for honesty.

Isabella comes into the closet and pulls the clipboard from me. "I not do the blue peel on you," she says in an accent that makes me believe there's torture involved in her services and she doesn't necessarily hate it.

"What? Why not?" I want to shake her shoulders and scream that she has to do the blue peel on me. I want to look like I'm wearing Vaseline too!

"Yoshi will want you to work, and your skin—" She runs the backs of her fingers down my cheeks. "Your skin is so pure, so fresh. Yes, I believe a blue peel would make you look better. But I'm estimating it would be nine days or so before you looked better and you've already got that hairstyle to deal with."

I touch my hair. "I fixed it. It's growing out."

"Yes, of course. Who did that to you? Johnny?"

I nod. The infamous Johnny.

"Yoshi will want you back to work regardless, and I cannot have you going out ugly. That haircut—" She waves her arms around. "—is bad enough. It's nothing less than hazing, what goes on in that salon, and you can tell him I said so. You don't need a medium peel; the most I'd give you is a light peel."

"Will I look like Barbie?"

Isabella looks confused. "Do you want to look like Barbie?"

"I want that plastic skin."

"It is not plastic, no? It is poreless. It is . . . pure."

"It's a little freakish, but I totally want it. As long as it doesn't hurt." I clasp my eyes shut. "No, even if it hurts I want it."

"I can do a light peel and have you back at the salon in ninety minutes. My assistant can do that for you, but you can tell Yoshi from me that I will not do the blue peel on such innocent skin."

"I can wear makeup when I'm done?"

"You won't need to wear makeup. Your skin will be perfect."

"Perfect." I let the word play on my tongue. There's no such thing as perfect, I tell myself, but who am I kidding? I so want to try for perfect. "How much?"

"Four hundred fifty."

"Sold!" My eyes go wide. "I mean, yeah, that's okay."

"I give you discount. You're a working girl."

I'm hoping it doesn't mean the same thing in her native tongue. Going to give her the benefit of the doubt on this.

"If Yoshi give you any trouble, you tell him he shouldn't be worrying about your skin when your hair looks like that."

My hair is not that bad anymore. She's making me want to hang myself.

"Beauty has its price, dahlink, but you're beautiful enough naturally." Then she cackles. "As if that could be true in Hollywood. Run along with you and I'll get Millicent to help you."

I scamper out of the white closet and into a smaller white closet where I'm told in badly written English to undress and put on a white smock. I do and am taken into the "inner room," to use a phrase from my Bible study. Only there are no priests with pomegranates on their robes, just more white and a pristine terry cloth-covered dentist chair. At least, that's what it looks like to me. I climb into it, wondering if wearing nothing but a smock is necessary.

There's a small knock at the door. *Don't hurt me!*

Millicent's arms are like ham hocks, her hands big and beefy. Her skin and teeth are flawless, though. It's like someone took a Barbie head, ripped it off, and plopped it on their brother's GI Joe doll.

"I'm Millicent." She looks over my clipboard information and mumbles to herself like a doctor. "Very well, then, lay back. Here's a personal fan. If your face starts to burn, you just hold it up and cool your skin down."

I sit upright. "I'm only getting a light peel."

"Yes, it says so right here. Lay down."

"So do I still need the fan?"

She laughs. It's not a soothing laugh. "Oh, yes, you'll need the fan."

"What do I do if I can't take it?"

"You think about why you're here. If it's an engagement ring, you see the moment; an acting role, you see yourself in costume. You do what you have to do."

I do not have $450—well, not to spend freely on a chemical peel. But worse yet, I do not have the guts to follow through with this.

"You don't have any heart ailments, do you?"

That's it. "Millicent, I'm not sure I can go through with this. I'm just getting over a haircut and—"

"There is no beauty without pain. Sit. You are young and strong. I've seen less whining through a tummy tuck." She pushes me back down on the dentist chair, and I try to hum hymns as she cleans my skin with cotton pads and places a scalding washcloth on my face, followed by an ice-cold one.

Then I see her stirring a fan brush in a concoction. It makes me want to run, but I think about Cary. I think about how Vivien Leigh didn't give up on being a part of *Gone with the Wind.* She knew she was Scarlett. I know I'm Yoshi's girl.

She starts to paint on the chemicals, which has an orange acidic scent. "This isn't bad," I say bravely.

"It won't start to work for two minutes. Brace yourself."

"Brace yourself? I'm glad you're not a surgeon with that kind of bedside manner."

It starts to tingle. It starts to sting. It starts to . . . "Get it off, get it off!"

"Three more minutes. Count sheep if you must."

"Scarlett only had to put on that corset!" I call out. I start to count, and finally, as I get to the point of what feels like third-degree burns, she drops a cold cotton pad on my face and starts to streak off the acid. "Thank heavens!" I say viciously.

"Great. You're done with step one."

There are two more medieval torture rounds before

I'm finished, and I limp back into the dressing chamber to get my clothes. I move vaguely, hoping to not upset the angry pores any more than they already are. All I can say is if this is the light peel, strike me dead before I go medium.

But then I look into the full-length mirror at my skin, and there it is. Results. Already. I'm plastic! I'm Barbie's brunette friend: Malibu Sarah.

"Do not go anywhere without this sunscreen." I'm handed a small tube and sent packing, a naked mole rat, blinking miserably in the bright sunshine.

☙

I walk into the salon with my shoulders back. I am plastic! I want to shout, but sadly no one seems to notice a thing. Jenna doesn't even blink when I walk back in; she just comes behind me and starts pushing me toward the classroom. "You're here. Good, you'll get some hours in class. Hurry up."

"I got a peel," I tell her.

Jenna looks up at me and her eyes pop. "Sarah, what did you do?"

"I got a peel with Isabella."

She grabs me by the arm and yanks me to the product closet where she takes a mirror off the hook. "Look."

I gasp. Every single flaw, every single skin imperfection I've had since I was thirteen is apparent. Enhanced. "I had plastic skin! What happened?"

"It looks like you've had some type of reaction. I've seen this before."

I exhale, exhausted. "Why is it that every human being on the planet can get a skin peel, but I do it and I'm suddenly every adolescent's nightmare?"

Jenna shrugs. "Sometimes it happens. Everyone's not the same."

"No, no, in Hollywood everyone is the same. I was plastic five minutes ago, I swear it."

"Well, you're not now. I have some stage makeup under my desk. Wait here."

I lean up against the wall of soy shampoo and try to breathe deeply.

The door opens abruptly, and it's not Jenna, it's Yoshi. "This is how you keep yourself busy? Standing in my supply closet?"

"No, Yoshi, I—"

"I'm starting class. You're too good for class?"

"No, Yoshi, I—"

"Get out here."

I shake my head.

"I said, get out here."

"I can't—"

"Those words are never spoken in my salon. What are you doing in here?" He flicks on the light, gets a good look at me, and quickly shuts it off. "Oh."

"I've got pancake makeup," Jenna says as she rushes past him.

"You might want to check out the auto shop. She needs bondo." He closes the door and I hear his voice change to customer-friendly. "Mrs. Spelling, how are you, dear?" He sticks his head back in. "Sarah!"

I nearly jump out of my skin. "Yes, Yoshi."

"We're practicing thinning on the models for the reality show *Supermodel* today. I specifically want you to sit in."

"Yes, Yoshi, I've watched you in your videos with the razor cuts and the six-shear scissors. Amazing. I bought myself a pair after teaching myself on my best friend, Kate."

"Did I ask you to blather on?"

"No."

"Get a smock on and come into the classroom."

Jenna uses an oval-shaped sponge to pound makeup onto my face. "Look up," she says. She pounds more under my eyes. Then she gets a tub of powder. Industrial sized. "It's mineral powder. No one's going to know you're under there."

"She told me to wear sunscreen at all times." I roll my eyes.

"Girl, the sun is not going to find you under all this makeup, trust me." She holds up a mirror.

I'm orange. "I'm an Oompa Loompa."

"You have a different tone than me. You're more olive than I am."

"Not anymore."

"It's the best I can do, all right? Get into Yoshi's class. He's anxious to show off his skills."

"Jenna?"

"Yeah?"

"Thanks."

"*De nada.* You'll be beautiful tomorrow. It's only a day."

"But I'm orange."

She wrinkles her face. "Yeah, sorry about that."

I walk into the classroom and find a group of lanky, emaciated teenagers with good bone structure and a dream. Their fearless leader, who I assume is the producer of the show, is consulting with Jaime about what type of hairstyles they will have. I can only assume from what Yoshi's teaching today they will be thinned and shorn like sheep. I try to sneak into the back and be as nondescript as possible. For an orange. Sarah Claire, the new OC.

All of the girls are seated in chairs. "You are?" Yoshi asks.

A shaking Chihuahua of a girl says, "Minasa."

"Minasa, you will be shaved bald today. It will make a bold statement, and the camera will love to have full access to your bone structure."

Minasa starts to weep, fingering her full head of dark hair, complete with what I can only suppose are expensive weaves. They look good on her, and though she does have fabulous bone structure, she doesn't want to be bald. I don't care what kind of genius Yoshi is. That's cruel.

"You are?"

"Kreata."

There's one thing about Wyoming: no one names their kids things that look like a menu item. Maybe you get a Cheyenne here and again, but Kreata?

"Sarah, come here."

I walk toward Kreata—pronounced *create-ah*—like she's some type of building toy, and I look into her wet eyes. She's terrified of what we'll do to her, and I wish I could offer her solace. But this is Hollywood, and making a statement is how she'll get remembered. And I'm orange; it's not like I'm going to give her a lot of solace.

"Sarah, I want you to thin her hair out here on top using the thinning shears."

I open my mouth to remind Yoshi he said on his videos never to use the thinning shears, that they were for amateurs, but I can't find the words. "You're going to let me cut?"

This makes Kreata burst into tears. It's sort of like hearing you're getting the intern in surgery.

Yoshi ignores the emotion. He's quite good at that. "If I were to hold her hair up here—" Yoshi takes a long, blonde strand and holds it straight up about eighteen inches above her head. "If I were to ask you to thin her hair, where would you start with the thinning shears?"

"I wouldn't use the thinning shears. I would—"

"Who is teaching the class here, Sarah?"

"I would cut right here." I point to about two inches off the model's crown of her head.

He hands me the scissors. "Do so."

I snip . . . and all the hair Yoshi is holding comes free in his hand. My jaw drops and the room gasps.

"Kreata! Your hair!"

Yoshi's face gets red. "I told you we were cutting with thinning shears. Why do you have scissors?"

"That's what you handed me."

"How dare you blame your incompetence on me!"

The model has a tuft of hair sticking straight up like Alfalfa, and I don't remotely know how to comfort her. "I'm so sorry. I thought I had the thinning shears."

She buries her hands in her face. "Just fix it. Please fix it!"

I look at the tools gathered on the rolling table, and Yoshi pulls it away on its castors. "After you did this to her, you think I'm going to let you touch her again? Get the girls some coffee!"

"But I—"

"Now!" Yoshi bellows.

I can tell by his reaction that he didn't mean to do it; he screwed up. But he's definitely not going to admit it. It's my shame to bear, and it's a hard lesson learned about trusting. I walk out of the classroom unsure of what just happened but thoroughly convinced my job is over before it's begun. He hasn't even let me wash a real person; I should have known he wasn't really going to let me cut.

Slamming the door behind me, I leave the familiarity of Yoshi torture for dinner with my cousin's ex-girlfriend,

Alexa. I don't know why I agreed to this. I imagine it has something to do with Mrs. Simmons' face that night when she confronted my mother at the front door. Guilt is never a good motivator, but as it is, I'm a victim to it. Dinner with Alexa at seven-thirty and she's picking me up in her Mercedes. Just like a last meal of steak and sweet-potato pie, I get to go to the gallows in style.

Her silver coupe is outside when I enter into the alley. I feel as if I should pull my trench coat collar up over my nose. Alas, I don't have a trench coat. Or a collar, for that matter.

Alexa is propped up against her car, her long, lean legs crossed at the ankles and the familiar red sole of a Christian Louboutin heel facing me.

"Hi, Alexa."

"Thanks for meeting me, Sarah."

"No problem." *I'm scared, but that's not your concern.*

She wastes no time. "I knew you weren't involved with Scott. Before you told me, I mean." She opens my door.

"How did you know? Besides the fact that I look like a hillbilly next to you, I mean." I slink into the car.

"Because no woman is this stupid, I don't care where she's from." She slams the car door, shutting me into her vehicle. It echoes like a cell door.

I watch her walk around the front of the car, moving like a runway model with long, jolty coltlike steps. She doesn't look comfortable with her beauty, like she was gawky as a teenager and has only recently grown into this beautiful butterfly. I see the uncertainty in her eyes, and I can't help but feel for her. She's only a woman fighting for the truth. She deserves that much, and I want to give it to her. But the fact is I don't have it either. I can't imagine why Scott wouldn't take five minutes to give her some closure.

I remember Mrs. Simmons knocking on our door once, rubbing her tear-stained cheeks with her fist. My mother opened the door wildly, without a touch of compassion.

"What do you want?" my mother barked.

"Where is he?" Mrs. Simmons answered.

"How would I know? Can't you keep track of your own husband?"

"Not when there's women like you around. It's really easy to be the good-time girl, isn't it? No dinners on the table, no laundry to do. One job only, but he won't marry you. No man ever will!"

My mother slammed the door in her face, but not before Mrs. Simmons looked me straight in the eye. I'll never forget the look of desperation mingled with hatred in her eyes. The next day everyone in school was told by Cindy that my mother wasfree for the taking. We never recovered from that night. Our reputation was sealed in stone.

Alexa puts her right leg into the car first. It goes on forever. It's like she herself is never going to get into the car. Just her endless limb. While I wait, I ponder the fact I'm in her Mercedes with its supple gray leather interior and all the appointments. Just sitting in this car might be worth dying for. I mean, if you're going to go, you don't want to go in a Kia, know what I'm saying? At least Mom would think I'd made something of myself. "She died in a Mercedes" would be her mantra at the Hideaway. Who knows, maybe Mom has a secret insurance policy on me and her troubles would be over.

"You don't talk much, do you?" Alexa asks me. "You don't have to talk about Scott. I don't want to hear it anyway."

"I talk. I'm just not sure what to say to you."

"Why don't you tell me why you're here with Scott?"

"I've known him since I was a child. We grew up together in Wyoming."

"I should have known he'd go back to his hick roots. Is that what he wants out of life?" She looks over at me with her icy blue eyes. "No offense."

"None taken," I answer uncertainly.

"Are you hungry?"

"I am. Haven't eaten all day."

"It will be nice to have some girl time over dinner." Her tone is gentle and considerate, which both unnerves and relaxes me.

I meet her gaze. She is way too good for Scott. Although at this point my stomach is growling, and I would befriend Freddie Krueger if food was involved.

"Why are you following Scott?"

"You need to ask him that, Sarah. I wouldn't be following him if he'd just tell me good-bye. It's not too much to ask for the years I spent with him. I mean, sure I made a mistake, but it doesn't mean—" She stops and looks at me. "Your outfit isn't great for evening. You've got hair on you. I think we'll go somewhere casual."

"Casual would be good."

After a few stoplights, Alexa pulls up to a restaurant called Jody Maroni's Sausage Kingdom. Sausage I can do, though I can't imagine the lean beauty queen inhaling a link of meat.

The restaurant is . . . well, it's sort of tacky—bright, sunlight-yellow tile with red, white, and black accents. But I'm thinking a girl can get a decent meal here— none of those California portions they call dinner. I feel myself exhale, knowing our conversation will look better after a full stomach.

"You have to try the Venetian chicken with sun-dried tomatoes."

Complete word salad. "What?" I try to mask my ignorance, but the truth is Californians can't even eat a sausage normally. Sausage is pork parts and things you really don't discuss in mixed company. Sun-dried tomatoes? Come on.

"The Venetian chicken is to die for, and not bad in calories. Jody's is my guilty pleasure."

Did they drag my chicken in the canals of Venice? If so, that might be acceptable sausage.

We park her car in the lot with other luxury vehicles. Apparently sausage is big doings here in Century City. (I only know where I am because there was a city sign announcing our departure from Beverly Hills and West Hollywood.)

"Or they have this new one with pomegranates!" Alexa is very enthusiastic about her food. "I might try that one."

As she says this, I hear Dane's voice telling me Iran is the number one importer of pomegranates. He has facts like that all the time, and I think he's rubbing off on me.

Alexa slams the door, locks it with a beep, and steps quickly along the sidewalk. "This is my favorite place to eat. Scott likes being seen in all the right restaurants, but this is way more fun, and I'm actually full when I finish. I suppose when it comes to eating, I'm a country bumpkin too." She looks at me again. "No offense."

"You can say 'country bumpkin,' 'hick,' or 'cowgirl' without apologizing. I don't take it personally."

"You don't?"

"Why should I? Wyoming is beautiful country."

"Of course it is."

"Scott's from there," I say, the slightest edge in my voice.

"That's right," she remembers.

"How long have you two—"

"Been estranged?"

"Yeah."

"About a month. He told me there was someone else, and I suppose that was my clue, but I thought he just needed a break, you know? He asked me to get a few things out of his apartment that I'd left there, but he didn't tell me the engagement was off, or ask for the ring back. I thought he needed some space, but I haven't heard from him since. Dane moved in, and that was the end of it."

"Maybe he doesn't want the ring back," I say brightly. Although I'm sure we both know my cousin may be a lot of things, but generous with his cash is not one of them. I believe the word *skinflint* applies here.

She shrugs. "I keep hoping, but he's changed his cell phone, and Dane picks up all my calls to the house. I still have hope. I guess that's why I'm following him, but it's bordering on pathetic."

"Yeah, but men make women do crazy things."

"I should know better." She heaves a desperate sigh. "But I didn't bring you all the way to dinner to whine at you. I want your opinion."

"My opinion?"

"If Scott isn't coming back, why won't he ask me for the ring?"

"You're asking me to make sense of that? Oh, Alexa, I couldn't tell you why he can't face you in the first place. He's usually so confrontational. If there's anyone who enjoys confrontation—"

"See? I know, that's why I still have hope that he's

coming back."

"Maybe you need to play hard to get." I lift up my finger. "I know. Maybe you should put the engagement ring on eBay and forward him the URL? If he thinks you're getting the money for it—"

She starts to laugh so hard that she throws back her head. "I like your way of thinking, Sarah." She shakes her head, "But no, I can't do that."

"And I wouldn't suggest it." I clear my throat. "You know, as anything more than a joke."

Meeting her earlier on the street that night, I was convinced Alexa was psychotic. Now I wonder if she's saner than I am. Which doesn't really speak well of my Christian walk, but there it is. Getting dissed without closure is the ultimate female bonding issue.

"You were going to marry him, and he's not returning your calls?" I say this mostly for myself—unable to believe that my cousin would be capable of something I thought reserved for the likes of Bud Simmons.

She shrugs. "I can't force him to get married, can I?"

I'm taken aback at this answer. It seems so reasonable, and yet she is stalking the man. "So why are you following him again?"

"I only want closure. I only want him to tell me to my face what I've done is unforgivable. I want to hear him say it."

Unless he's the blackness in your universe, not sure that's going to happen. "I don't know what to say. He hasn't told me anything, Alexa."

She opens the door to the sausage king and all eyes go to her. She's still pretty in the greenish-hue of florescent lights. So wrong. Just for one day, I'd like to possess her kind of beauty. I'd go back to Cindy Simmons and give her an earful about true inner beauty.

We walk up to the counter, waiting our turn to shout at the guy behind the cash register.

"I thought Scott liked the flashy types, but maybe that was wishful thinking. Maybe he craves hometown girls since he's been here. Maybe homemade mashed potatoes are what he craved all along." She pauses while I stare at her.

"I said I was okay with the 'cowgirl' and 'bumpkin,' but 'mashed potatoes'? Not so much."

"I didn't mean it that way. I meant Scott grew up with you. Maybe he craves hometown-clean beautiful. Not made up."

I brighten at her words. "You think I'm beautiful?"

"And wholesome. That's all I meant. My mouth gets ahead of me sometimes."

I like her. When I think about Mrs. Simmon's reaction to me, the venom in her eyes toward a little girl, and then Alexa's reaction when she thought I was sleeping with her fiancé, I have to give her props. She's too good for Scott.

I start to muse about my new life in Hollywood. "Isn't it funny we women all think it's about who's the prettiest? Has there ever been a supermodel that hung on to a man, ever? Yet we all think the prettiest girl wins."

"That eighties model is still married to Ric Ocasek from the Cars."

"Yeah." I wrinkle my nose. "Not a great example."

"Heidi Klum!"

"She kissed a few frogs first. Had a baby with at least one."

"Right." Alexa puts a finger to her chin in deep thought. "I'm sure there's someone who has been monogamous with Prince Charming."

"I'm sure there is, but maybe our odds aren't any worse.

'Our' meaning 'mine,' of course." I look at her. "You don't count, as you could be a supermodel."

"Ah, that is so sweet." Alexa's voice softens and sighs. "I suppose you can cook too."

"I make the best mashed potatoes ever," I tell her. "The secret is they have to be terrible for you. If they're healthy, they don't taste good."

"You'll have to teach me."

Alexa walks in her stilettos to get a few napkins. She does so with grace. Like a wild cat in the zoo, it's hypnotic and disconcerting, and everyone's eyes follow her, like at a tennis match.

"I can cook other things," I say, looking for something to feel good about as she walks back. "I learned early because my mother worked nights."

"You seem very sweet, Sarah, but very different than me, and if Scott is craving familiarity, I can't be that. My analyst says people want what they want and you have to accept that. Seeing you, I can accept that Scott was not looking for me as a life commitment. I'm in the process of accepting that." She tosses her chestnut hair and blinks those ice-blue eyes to wash away the sudden tears.

Her analyst. How Hollywood is that? She could have any man she wanted. The question remains why she wanted my cousin in the first place—this man who clearly has a little to learn in the chivalry department.

"Do you know what you want for dinner?" she asks me.

"Just order two of what you're getting."

She shouts the order at the guy behind the counter, and I shove money at her, which she pushes back at me. "My treat. I figure if I'm going to whine at you, it's the least I can do."

"Alexa, I don't know what happened between you and Scott, but I'm truly sorry. I don't want to be in the middle of it."

She waves the comment off. "But you are in the middle of it." It's not said with any malice, but I suppose there's plenty of truth in that statement. "You're living in our apartment. You know his new phone number. I just want an answer, Sarah. That's all I want. Can you tell him that much for me?"

"I'll do what I can. I promise. You seem pretty calm, and that's a good thing. I once saw my mother throw a guy's belongings out of a convertible along the highway when he broke up with her. His stuff was strewn there for ages until the snow came—and come summer, there were still remnants of the breakup. Not pretty."

Alexa laughs. "Really? I should have thought of that. But it's so white trash . . . no offense."

"In our small town, everyone knew the story after that. Someone put the guy's underwear over the signs along the highway, like those old Burma Shave signs."

She starts to giggle. "I do wish I'd thought of that, but I'd never have the guts to follow through, and this town's too big to have any lasting effect with something fun like that."

"Actually, it was more humiliating than fun. The whole town knew it was my mother."

I never liked any of the women Scott dated. They were always hard chicks who could throw back liquor to rival our parents and who dressed in low-cut t-shirts and pointy-toed boots. Alexa is about as far from that image as I can picture.

"Just tell Scott I'd like to see him to give the ring back. I'm not keeping it. It's not a gift; it symbolizes something that isn't. We both made our mistakes, but let's not make all our years together a sham."

I just nod. Her pain is palpable.

"Thanks for coming to dinner," she says. "This is good for closure. I wanted to hate you, but I don't. But you'll always be second to the work. Just be aware of that."

"Did you see me get tossed out on the street?" I ask with a laugh.

"I'm sure his excuse was some ditzy starlet who got kicked out of a restaurant, couldn't get into a restaurant, they didn't have the right colored M&Ms in her green room, blah, blah, blah. All stuff an agent does, not a stylist. But they call him instead. They love him. If he was smart, he would become an agent as well and double his fees."

"I don't think I could stand by for that. You're a stronger woman than me."

"You are standing by for that," Alexa reminds me. "Scott needs to be needed. Are you needy, Sarah?"

"I'm breaking free of a lot of baggage at home."

Her eyebrows lift. They are the perfect shape, and I can't help but wonder if she sees Anastasia, the eyebrow woman. "You're only trading the luggage if you're here with Scott." She hikes a Gucci bag over her shoulder as we walk toward the table. "I want Scott to be happy."

"Why?" Is she a walking doormat or what?

She laughs. "Because I love him. I don't think he wanted to get engaged to begin with. Maybe I forced the issue."

I shake my head. I can't stand it. "Women always blame themselves. What is it you love about him?"

I remember my cousin when he was as bright as the sky. Magic to be around. He was always selfish and a tad narcissistic. Ever the charmer, he was the fire that drew you closer. He made you feel special even when it was all about him. Now he's one giant ball of nerves, bundled tightly and ready to explode.

Alexa smiles, her scarlet lips parting slightly into a mysterious grin. "We both started out with nothing, Scott and me. Back then, he was dressing soap stars on salary at the studio, giving them big hair and greasy lip gloss." She shakes her head. "Hideous. He worked for this old lady who made him dress the women like a bad eighties nighttime soap opera. I was getting my real estate broker's license studying late. We had nothing but a goal. Even that was shaky at times." At this, tears fill her eyes, and I watch them melt into a paler shade.

"Memories are strong motivators, but they're not always filled with truth." Meaning that in all my phone conversations with Scott, I never heard Alexa's name spoken. Not once. Here, she's reliving all these warm memories, and I, his closing living relative, never knew about her. "Did you know Scott's family?"

"He said his father was dead from liver disease and there was no one else except one cousin."

I look down at the table rather than meet her eyes. May Alexa fare better than the Winowski women, anyway.

"Food's up. I'm starving." She clicks her heels toward the counter, where weird ingredients like artichokes, cranberries, chicken, and turkey are called out. If sausage was meant to be healthy . . . well, never mind. Californians do what they can to overcome the air.

I settle into the hard plastic chair across from Miss America and dig in. Alexa makes Cindy Simmons look small-time, and that in itself makes me smile. If I can befriend a striking auburn beauty who thought I was sleeping with her fiancé, maybe there's hope for me here after all.

As Alexa bites into her sandwich, all eyes in the restaurant watch her. She has all the power in the world; yet she's kryptonite to the one thing she wants. Well, we have that much in common.

As an unmarried woman,
I was thought to be a danger.
~ Grace Kelly

Yoshi didn't fire me. At least not yet. In fact, he hasn't mentioned the mishap and Alfalfa style from yesterday. Kreata walked out of the salon on lanky colt legs, her hair plastered down on top with an abundance of styling paste. She will wait ages for that to grow out, and I did that to her. I made her something to be mocked.

And I'm still orange.

I feel like death. Well, what I think it feels like to almost be lifeless, anyway. My legs are actually shaking, as if I'd spent the day hiking to the top of the Tetons just from walking on that stupid bamboo floor all day. *Get this, Sarah. Wash that, Sarah. Clean up that mess, Sarah. Extra foam, Sarah. Clean the scissors for the students, Sarah.*

Being a student of Yoshi seems to entitle you to treat Sarah Claire Winowski as your personal slave. That would never happen if I'd been born in Newport Beach! "Curse you, Sable, Wyoming."

I shake my head as I see someone look at me like I'm talking to myself and press fingers to my ear as if to readjust one of those Borg-like cell phones. Everyone else is talking to themselves, why shouldn't I? It's cultural, for crying out loud.

I should just call a cab and call it a day, but I want to walk Rodeo Drive. I'm orange, and if there's ever a night to walk, it's when I'm wearing my own headlight. If this all ends tomorrow, I'm not going home without a little sight-seeing. Nearly three weeks here and I haven't seen the ocean, and I haven't cut hair. With the exception of Kreata, who I unintentionally maimed.

Ann—long, lanky, blonde Ann—comes up beside me on the sidewalk. "Don't worry, we all looked like you in the beginning, Sarah. Just use extra concealer under your eyes with a little Preparation H for swelling until you're past this. The first month is the hardest. If you're not going to make it, Yoshi wants to know before he's invested too much."

"I've invested too much already. I can barely walk."

"Yoshi can teach anyone to cut hair. He can't give people a personality, so make sure he sees that!" A black Mercedes pulls up onto the street, and Ann waves at the driver, who remains cloaked in a mystery of darkly tinted windows. "You need a ride?" she asks.

I do, naturally, but I'm too proud to take one, and right now I want to be around my coworkers (read: slave drivers) about as much as I want to invite Isabella to dinner, and she made me orange. Even a limo doesn't look the least bit inviting if filled with Yoshi employees. "No, thanks. I thought I'd check out the Golden Triangle and get my bearings. Thanks, though."

"All right. Well, don't forget tomorrow night is mentor ing group. I left an open invitation on the employee board; we can always use more people. We're having a securities broker speak on investing. Maybe you can teach us something you learned growing up. Besides, we want you

to see our apartment. We could use another roommate; it's
to-die-for beautiful."

"Sure, it sounds great. I'll be there." I summon up the
strength for one more plastered smile.

Ann and Jaime, another stylist apparently joined at
the hip, hop into the waiting car and speed away. I exhale
deeply. It's over. I am finally alone.

As I walk toward Rodeo Drive, I realize cleanliness gives
a sense of false security. This may explain my mother's
penchant for bleach, but I notice it works in the middle of
a city as well. The brightly lit, clean streets of Beverly Hills
give me the sense of being in an adult amusement park.
I've read that a police officer will respond to any call here
in less than a minute, so I start up the street. Not taking
into account that I have no cell phone to actually *call* a
police officer, but I'm living dangerously.

"Sarah?"

I sigh. "What!" I'm expecting to see Yoshi barking another order at me. Instead, when I turn around I spy Dane
Weston approaching me. *The* Dane Weston. I blink several
times before looking behind me to see if there's another
Sarah standing about. *Nope.* I turn back, knowing I'm
probably gawking.

Dane is dressed impeccably. I hate to admit how the
sight of him makes me crumble. Like I said, my legs are
weak from working, so I'm sure it's just exhaustion. But
there's a quiet strength to him that makes me somehow
believe he holds the key to my future in his squared,
assured fingers. Of course, with the way I feel right now,
Orville Redenbacher could hold that key. I see him and an
old movie on DVD.

But then again . . . "Dane. You're home early!" I run
toward him and then realize he's looking scared. So I slow

and try to meet him casually. He reaches for me, drops his arms to his sides, puts out his hand to shake. I take it and pull him a little closer. I didn't mean to, it just happened.

"Got home this evening. Wide awake, thanks to a little jet lag. When you didn't come home for dinner, I worried your cousin abandoned you again."

How sweet is that? "I've been taking the bus home. Tonight I was tired, though, I was going to call a cab."

"Sarah Claire, have you seen a pay phone lately?"

I think about this for a moment and shake my head.

"Here." Dane hands me a cell phone.

"What's this? Well, I mean, I know what it is. Why are you handing it to me?"

"I had an extra line that an assistant used at the store, and I haven't turned it off. I charged it up today, so it's yours for as long as you need it. No woman should be alone in LA without a cell phone. This isn't Sable."

I look down at my feet, remembering my current Oompa Loompa look. Maybe the French women look worse; he hasn't noticed. "Why would you do this?"

"'Whatever you do for the least of these . . .' Which in LA I take to mean the person without a cell phone." He laughs at his own joke.

"Or a car? Or a thousand-dollar handbag."

"Can't help you with the bag, unless someone drops one off at the shop. I'll let you know." I feel like the world's been lifted from my shoulders as he takes my duffle.

"You don't look dressed to rescue a damsel in distress."

"I'm always dressed like this, and I never have anything better to do than rescue damsels in distress. I hopped on the plane straight from a meeting this morning."

My breath catches. "A girl could get lost in those eyes—I mean, words like that." I cover my mouth with the tips of my fingers.

"I thought we might get some dinner. No sense in both of us getting take-out and bringing it back to the house."

"Dinner," I say breathlessly, like a desert-crosser says water.

"You weren't planning on cooking, were you? I wouldn't want to miss that."

"I haven't been to the grocery store. Sorry."

"No worries. I wanted to check on my house. I was thinking we might pick something up and take it back to my place—if you feel comfortable with that, I mean. I just want to see how construction is moving along, and I'm interested in a woman's opinion."

"Your place?" Now I'm a girl of solid character—of staunch morals and a strict edict to live the opposite of my mother—but when he says *his place*, I don't think about any of those promises. And that's what scares me. "I'm really tired. I think I should just turn in. I haven't had the best day. Did you notice that I'm orange?"

"But you did get that awful haircut fixed. Not that it made any difference to your beauty. Having a bad one, I mean, not fixing it."

"I'm orange."

"You look stunning as usual. Sarah, I'm not going making a pass at you back at my place; it's just dinner."

"Trust me, I understand that. But why not?"

"Is that an invitation? I was trying to be polite, you being Scott's cousin, but if I had an arsenal, trust me, I'd make a pass. As it is, I grew up around old ladies and old furniture, so I'm not sure how I'd go about making a pass."

"Would you like directions?" I ask him with a boost of self-esteem. "I missed you, Dane. The house wasn't the same without you."

"I missed you too. If I were to get myself an education on making said pass, you would be open to the idea? In the Christian sense, I mean."

Dane, I am open till death do us part. I nod shyly, feeling heat in my moonshine face. I don't dare look at him, out of fear he'll know what I'm thinking and run for the hills, as the laws of commitment are known to make a man sprint.

"I think I might want to get an espresso if I'm going to be out like this."

He looks at his watch. It's a classic Seiko and it looks generations old. I think Cary Grant had one like it in his photos. "It's only eight o'clock."

"When there's nothing to do in town, eight is two hours past when they roll the streets up. Sable's so cold during the winter, we don't much venture out even for dinner. It's like two a.m. to me, and here you all are having a life."

"I know better than to mess with a woman who grew up in cowboy country. I've seen my share of spaghetti westerns."

"Did you go to college?"

"I did."

"Where?"

"Is this a quiz?"

"No, but I just wanted you to know I haven't been to college. In the interest of full disclosure before you make said pass."

"It's because of my car, isn't it?"

"Your car?"

"Yes, it's equipped with an emergency ejection button for all passengers who did not attend college. Like the air bag with kids in the car, I'll turn it off before you get in. Thanks for telling me."

"Very funny."

"I can't make a pass if you're going to act naïve about why I'm here. Why wouldn't I want the company of a beautiful woman to drive with me along the PCH and see my house and check on progress. And please note, it's after carpool hours on the 405, so this is from my heart, not out of the need for a passenger." He puts his hand to his chest.

"PCH?"

"Pacific Coast Highway."

"Ah. You mean the ocean?" I ask brightly.

He grins. "So that's what it takes. Yes, I mean the ocean. Is that enough to tempt you then?"

More than enough. He could lose the "ocean" and add "cesspool" and I'd be tempted. "Will my cousin wonder where we are?"

"Will he care?"

I shrug. "Good point."

Dane starts to walk and I come alongside him. "How did you find me?"

"I was parking behind the salon when I saw you walking, and I called Yoshi's to check when you'd be off, actually."

"I saw the edge of it from the plane."

His face expresses his puzzlement.

"The ocean. You asked if I saw it. I saw it from the plane."

"Seeing it from the sky is not the same as dipping your feet in the waves." He offers the crook of his elbow. "What do you say to a late dinner and the beach?"

"Just you and me?"

He looks around his feet. "I think so, unless you have someone else you want to invite."

It's only a ride to the beach, but all I can think about is *Would our baby have that great cleft in his little pudgy chin? Would he grow up smart like his daddy or overly cautious like me? Maybe both? Would we make the perfect child, and would science want to study it?*

On second thought, I think it would be a girl. Dane seems like the kind of man who has girls and who would teach them to get into MIT and take the world by storm. She would be a very bright girl, and I'd dress her well. She'd have it all. Parents who loved her, a brain for greatness, and really, really cute clothes. We'd take trips back to Wyoming for Christmas.

"Does my cousin need us out of the house? Is this a favor for him? Your coming here?"

"What kind of favor would I be doing your cousin?"

"I can't stand it when people answer a question with a question."

"Why?"

"Because—" I swat his arm. "You're infuriating me."

"I hear that a lot. I have an infuriating personality. It's why your cousin calls me Lurch. He claims I creep around. I'm quiet and tall; what am I supposed to do? Put bells on my feet like a toddler?"

"How on earth did you pick my cousin to live with during the renovation?"

"I could ask you the same question."

"But I have a normal answer: Scott's the only one I know in California. What's your excuse?"

He laughs heartily. "I like Scott, and he puts up with me. Let's get to the beach before it gets too late."

I stop walking and look up at him. "You seem awfully intent on getting me to the ocean. What's up with that?"

"Why are you unbelievably suspicious?"

"Cary Grant wore a hat just like yours in *Suspicion* to murder his wife."

"But he didn't do it. Because the studios wouldn't let Cary do it."

"How did you know that?"

"I live near the Chinese Grauman's theatre and the Hollywood Walk of Fame, and I furnished Cary Grant's old house at the beach when new residents moved in. I am nothing if not well versed in Hollywood history. How could I do my job otherwise?"

"Your job. Yes, about that. I noticed you were an antiquarium from your card."

Again he laughs.

Dane Weston is what I aspire to be—well, minus the guy part. He's elegant and professional in his pressed slacks or suit, and more important, he looks like he belongs in them. Not like he's inherited an older brother's clothes. He reads *U.S. News & World Report* and *BusinessWeek* for entertainment, and he understands what the Dow Jones Industrials are. By all appearances, you'd think he had a professional butler looking after him, but as his roommate, I can testify he does it all himself. He's regal, just like Cary. And though I find him the most attractive man I've met to date, I can't help but feel as though my flaws are highlighted neon yellow, cast underneath his long shadow. And that was before I was golden sunset in color.

"Your card *said* you were an antiquarium," I repeat.

He smiles. "You make it sound as though I collect fish. I'm an an-ti-quar-i-*an*." He says the word slowly. In separate syllables for the country girl.

I could die. Antiquarium, antiquarian. You say potato, I say po-tah-to. Neither word means a thing to me. It's been such a long day, and I feel the sudden sting of tears over my mistake. I'm sure it's more about Kreata's hair and my neon face than my own ignorance on antiquarians, but still. Although I blink wildly to hold them back, I held everything in all day in order to not stand out at work, and I let my guard down when I walked out the door. When all else fails, try honesty.

"I don't know what that is, Dane."

He stops dead, looks at me, and wipes an escaped tear from my cheek. His voice softens. "Sarah . . ." He comes in close so I can't avoid his eyes. *"No one* knows what it is; that's why I use it. The title makes me sound more exclusive. I'm an antiques dealer. I buy and sell European antiques in a small shop in Brentwood. It's only open to dealers, designers, and the more savvy collectors, not the public. My clientele prefer the title. It helps them charge their customers a higher premium."

I feel a strong headache coming on. "Antiques." The word rolls off my tongue. "I don't know a thing about them. Well, other than they're old."

"Not always. Sometimes collector's items for these homes are quite recent, but yes, the definition of antique is that something is old. I grew up around them. It was my parents' business. I'm not creative enough to strike out on my own like you. I wonder if I had a skill what I might have become."

"That's the nicest thing anyone's ever said to me."

"We need to fix that. If that's the nicest thing you've heard, you're not setting your standards high enough."

"So do you think Ben Affleck will have the same effect on people as Cary Grant some day? Will people buy his old house to relive an era?"

"I won't dignify that with an answer."

I giggle.

"Even the orneriest, snobbiest of people look good under a full moon at the beach. And I want you to see my kitchen, see if you like what I'm doing with it. Maybe you'll find me more to your liking. A man with a good kitchen definitely has potential, don't you think?"

If I found him more to my liking, I'd be doing the cavewoman bonk over his head and taking him home by the hair. And let's just say Mrs. Gentry would definitely not approve of that. It's not even what Dane says; it's that there's some kind of chemical combustion that goes on when we're together. Something impossible to explain but magic to encounter. I'm going to call it the X factor. In reality, he's probably the kind of man who saves worn stamps and metal lunchboxes in his closet, and I've created him to be nouveau Cary Grant.

Story of my life.

chapter 13

You must learn day by day, year by year, to broaden your horizon. The more things you love, the more you are interested in, the more you enjoy, the more you are indignant about, the more you have left when anything happens.

~ Ethel Barrymore

I feel the phone in my hands and gaze at Dane, thinking over his invitation. It's just dinner. I know that, and yet I know myself. I know how I feel about Dane.

"Dane, I have to make a phone call."

He shakes his head. "So make one."

I look down at the phone in my hand. "It's long distance."

"Believe it or not, Sarah, the cell phone will call long distance."

"But what will it cost?"

"It's free. It's an international line. Just make a phone call. Why don't you go over on that low wall and talk, and I'll window shop. I've been meaning to get down here to Rodeo Drive to think about Christmas anyway." He smiles broadly.

"I like platinum," I joke.

I walk over to the Louis Vuitton storefront and dial Kate. Of course, she's probably off fooling around, hiding from Ryan. Who's stalking me. As if I had something to do with it with any of the failing relationships around me. I have no idea why Scott dumped his fiancée, yet here I am, witness to the whole soap opera. Now I'm getting interrupted at work because Kate is having *thoughts*. What is this, the Dark Ages?

Kate answers on the first ring.

"Thank goodness you're home."

"Where else would I be, Sarah, it's ten o'clock."

I look at my watch. "Oh, right. Time difference."

"Is everything all right?"

I turn around and stare into the store window, whispering, "It's fabulous. I'm with Dane!"

"Dane. I thought he was in France or something."

"He's home early! And he came to pick me up, and he's lending me a cell phone!"

"Did you tell him you have a date with someone else?"

"Shut up. Listen, Dane invited me to his place, and I need you to tell me why that is such an incredibly bad idea. Go ahead and tell me about the girls who got pregnant in high school."

"You have serious issues if you can't go to dinner with a guy without your virtue suddenly being at stake. What's wrong with you?"

"So that's my support, huh? I'm feeling all warm and tingly. Really."

"Well, just be sure and close the door like they do in all your old movies. Like you wouldn't freak out that you're just like your mother. Please. You have issues, girl. Go to dinner and quit whining. No wonder you never had any dates."

"Ryan called today. He said you're talking strangely."

"I'm not talking strangely. I'm talking about what I really want in life. It wouldn't be strange if Ryan didn't want to tell me what I really wanted."

"Kate, Ryan loves you."

"I'm not willing to be who Ryan wants me to be just to have a man, all right? I'm not your mother."

"Kate!"

"I'm sorry. It's been a rotten day and I'm struggling. Pray for me, all right? I'm going to watch TV and forget this day ever happened. Oh, hey, call Mrs. Gentry if you have a chance. She's been dealing with your mom, and she told me not to tell you or worry you, but you know I can't do that, so call Mrs. Gentry."

"I will."

"Don't worry about Ryan and me. We're in the process of designing the way our life will look together; we're in negotiations, all right?"

"But you're not thinking of leaving Sable?"

"I don't know what I'm thinking. Look, Sarah Claire, I don't mean to be rude, but you're not one to speak to me on what kind of life I lead, all right?"

She hangs up on me.

My best friend hung up on me. *What the heck?*

In the past, I usually let Kate have her temper tantrum and we talked later like nothing happened, and that's what I'm opting for here. I look at Dane, who seems content looking at windows, though I know he's not interested in anything. "Dane, I'm going to make one more call! I'm sorry!"

"Take your time!"

I call Mrs. Gentry and breathe in relief at the sound of her voice. "Hello?" she answers raspily.

"Mrs. Gentry, it's Sarah Claire."

"Sarah Claire, is everything all right? It's nearly ten-thirty."

"It's only eight-thirty here, and yes, everything's okay. Did I wake you? I just forgot about the time change." And the fact that old people go to bed at eight-thirty. "I just wanted to check on my mother, and I thought you might know something. She's not returning my calls."

"Now, Sarah Claire, I hadn't wanted to worry you. How are you doing in Beverly Hills? You must be awfully busy, because the girls and I haven't received our promised letter."

Why is it that every time I talk with Mrs. Gentry I feel guilty? "I'm doing fine, Mrs. Gentry. How are you?"

"This Dane fellow, how is he?"

"He's fine. More than fine. We're going to have dinner tonight." I look toward him and he offers me a smile and a wave. *He's beautiful.*

"Kate's keeping us up to speed on your blooming romance."

"So the entire town of Sable knows."

"Yes, dear." She says this matter-of-factly.

"There's nothing to know, really. He's my cousin's roommate and he's my polar opposite, yet I can't help the way I feel about him."

"I heard all that. It's not like you to talk so glowingly of a young fellow, so I wondered why you were entertaining the idea of a date with another."

"The trainer, yes. I wondered that too. But he asked and I couldn't think of a good reason to turn him down. It doesn't change the way I feel about Dane." I smile at him.

"Nor should it, but there's nothing wrong with getting what you want either. You don't have to settle, Sarah Claire. You went to California to get what you want, so get it. You're nothing like your mother. You're loyal to a fault, and if your heart is telling you Dane is something special, why wouldn't you listen to that?"

"Mrs. Gentry, about my mother," I say, avoiding the topic. Romantic advice is not what I need.

"We'll get to her. What does your heart say about Dane? You're usually very good about knowing a person's heart. If you think he's a good man—"

"What if I'm wrong?"

"Was going to California wrong?"

"Well, I screwed up someone's hair today. Other than that I haven't cut anyone's hair. I lower toilet seats, empty garbage cans, and sweep up hair right now. Oh, and I make coffee, so you might say there were some consequences to my decision."

"That's just earning your keep, Sarah Claire. Nothing wrong with an honest day's work; we did much worse than you're being asked to do just to get our paltry paychecks back in the day. Because we were lucky to have a job, period. It wasn't about fulfillment, you know. It was about having enough money to put fruit in the cellar."

"Mrs. Gentry, my mother."

"I'll tell you when I'm ready to talk about your mother."

I shut up immediately. Mrs. Gentry is so amiable, so gentle, but she runs things like any good librarian would. She likes order and will not abide by the chaos of me jumping conversations.

"What I've seen is fear driving you, Sarah Claire. You don't want to end up like your mother, so you leave. But you're nothing like your mother—because of your mother. You were the caretaker; that makes you different because of your role in the relationship, don't you see? You can't run scared of romantic entanglements forever."

"Mrs. Gentry, I don't mean to change the subject, but my mother?" I plead. This time more forcefully. "There's nothing to talk about with my romantic ventures."

"She had another incident with the law. I think it's time she went into a program, Sarah Claire. She has no concern for anyone around her. She's blacked out a few times—once in Milly's when waiting for an order of coffee and once on the road the other morning before church."

I swallow hard. How do I get my mother to do anything she's supposed to do? For the good of humanity, herself, or anyone?

"I've looked up a few programs and—" I grimace in defeat. "How would I pay for them? I came here to make enough money, but I have to give it a little time—there are state programs, but I . . ."

Excuses. Just like my mother uses. She could kill someone, and I have to find a way to stop it I know that, and yet I feel powerless.

"She's going to kill someone if she isn't stopped." Mrs. Gentry voices my fears. "Al took her keys away, and the ladies have been taking turns driving her to work. But she's working at the bar, and the first thing they teach you in any addiction class is that you can't be near your addiction and what makes you crave it. You can't be sober and work as a bartender; it's not going to happen."

"She doesn't know how to do anything else." I wish right now I could just saw away the rope that keeps me tethered to my mother and her addictions. I know, it's selfish and completely unchristian, but I am so sick of the drama. I'm so sick of my life being halted by whatever stupid situation she's gotten herself into to make sure I can't escape.

"Sarah Claire, we'll pay for the program. You just need to get her into it."

"That's all?" I look up at Dane and wonder what it's like to have a life of normalcy. Did his mother make him sweets, pack sack lunches, and tell him bedtime stories?

"Give me a day. I'll figure something out."

"I love you, darling. Send us that letter and take some time to exhale, dear. You live your life too busy. You'll never feel at peace that way."

I look over at Dane. "Mrs. Gentry, how did you *know* with Mr. Gentry?"

"I knew when he looked at me. He made me feel like I was the only woman on earth, and for me he was the only man."

"Good-bye Mrs. Gentry. I love you."

"I love you too, dear. Let me know about your mom. We'll be set on our end. We need a little help getting her in, that's all."

A little help, she says. It will be like leading a lioness into a cage with, "Here, kitty, kitty."

chapter

*A kiss is a lovely trick designed by nature to
stop speech when words become superfluous.*
~ Ingrid Bergman

"Everything all right?"

"I'm sorry I took so long, I had to make another call."

"No problem. Just a little muscle atrophy from hunger."
His arms stretch over his head.

"You really want to go to dinner?"

"Wouldn't you show me the same hospitality if I came
to Wyoming, as a friend of Scott's?"

My insides warm at his words. "I would. But no one
would ever come there." We start to walk again, and I feel his
arm clasp mine a little tighter. "Isn't your car in the garage?"

"No, it's up here at the end of the block. Street parking.
Didn't Scott explain I'm a skinflint?"

"No, he did not." All I can think is how Scott said
Dane was off-limits. It breaks my heart he didn't think I
was good enough for him, but that's Scott. You can't expect
him to do anything out of the goodness of his heart; you're
just surprised when he does.

Dane's a *have*. We're *have-nots*. Scott is only trying to
protect me.

"I worry about you here on your own, Sarah. You
shouldn't be taking the bus."

"You don't have to worry about me. Trust me, I've been taking care of myself for a very long time, and I'm very grounded." *If you're going to worry, worry about my mother, whose been left without a chaperone.* "It's the whole 1940s way of thinking. Comes with the territory."

"My car's around the corner." He points ahead, and I try to match his long stride in my heels. When he looks down at me, I feel completely safe, like nothing could break into my peace.

I drop my head on his shoulder and gaze up into his eyes. Those sable eyes. We stop walking and face one another.

"Are you playing me, Dane?" I whisper.

His humor is apparent. "Sarah, I wouldn't know how to play you if you were an instrument. Let me tell you, a guy who's interested in ancient things is not a real turn-on to the Hollywood crowd."

"What does that mean?"

"I can spot a fake from twenty feet away. I think that eliminates three, quarters of my dating pool. And if you add in a Christian as a prerequisite, I'm done for. Help me, Sarah Claire, you're my only hope," he says mimicing Princess Leia.

I force back my smile. "Then why is your business here?" I ask with my fists on my hips.

"Because customers here buy what their designers tell them to. It's a profitable place for a man who knows the business of antiques. I've done whole houses for people who never see a stick of the furniture before they move in. Business, I'm good at. It's all the other aspects of life that trouble me."

Maybe I am too suspicious, but I let my eyes float from his head to his well-dressed feet. It's hard to buy the innocent act from Dane. Impossible, actually. Men who look like this do not have trouble in life, especially with the ladies. I may be from Wyoming, but the call of the wild is what it is. Gorgeous, well-off men are not lacking for comfort. Not in Wyoming or Beverly Hills. Either one of those attributes is enough, but together they're lethal.

"Is it really so hard to believe I'd like to get to know you better? That I felt something in my heart when you stole my hat?" he asks.

"Impossible, actually. In life there's something called a caste system. In India it's more formal. In America it's much less hard to define but equally rigid. Well-off men pay, and beautiful women jump."

"That's the most pessimistic thing I've ever heard in my life, Sarah. You can't possibly believe that as a Christian."

"Look at your church. How many rich men have ugly wives? When they looked for Queen Esther, did they look in the homely barrel?"

"Beauty is in the eye of the beholder, Sarah. I've got a client who collects Marilyn Monroe memorabilia. One of the most beautiful women in history and—"

"And she never married a poor man. So I rest my case."

"And no man ever married her either. Not who she really was. It's fascinating what you can learn about people's true selves when you start studying their belongings." He pauses. "Wait a minute, she married a poor man the first time."

"A politically correct answer; that was before she was blonde," I tell him.

"So you're jealous of blondes? Is that what this is about?"

"Of course not. Marilyn's color is easily duplicated. I'm an expert, remember? It's about commodities. The *haves* and the *have-nots*. Did you ever see *The Philadelphia Story*?"

"Is that a joke?"

"No, it's not. Cary Grant and Katherine Hepburn belonged together. Sure, she was tempted by the raw and charming Jimmy Stewart, but Cary's character knew her. He knew her world."

"And this has to do with commodities . . . how?"

"It's a business deal. Love is a business deal. I learned my place early on in Wyoming. You are Cary Grant and I'm the supporting actress, don't you see?"

Dane lifts his brows. "Not in the least bit. I keep trying to chalk this conversation up to jet lag, but you weren't on the plane."

"I'm just stating the facts as I see them. You are a *have*, I am a *have-not*, and whenever I've seen the two mix, the *have-not* gets the short end of the stick. So while I may dream of—"

"Are you talking to me?" Dane asks.

"What do you mean?"

"I mean, quite frankly, it sounds like you're arguing with yourself. Are you expecting a return answer?" He shrugs. "Because you know, I want to do the right thing here, and you agreed to help me out."

"I did?"

"This line of thinking is bigoted, you know. I'm a worker bee just like you, and even if you were competing on a beauty level, can you tell me the problem here? Because if you think there's a problem, I'm thinking eating-disorder material."

"In that suit you want me to believe you're a worker bee." I roll my eyes. "Listen, I've seen enough clothes here to know the good stuff. What did you pay for that suit? Just the word *antiques* makes you a *have*. We just call that stuff 'old.' My family can't afford Ikea; you want to up that, Mr. Worker Bee?"

"No, I don't. I want to know why you think that's a drawback. *I* can define an antique. I don't need to spend time with someone who has that talent, unless I'm looking for a business partner. Besides, what does any of this have to do with our getting to know one another?"

"I just don't want you to think I'm naïve and that I can be swept off my feet by someone with pretty words. Even if they do look like you."

"Tell me, how's my hair?" He pats his dark brown, grown-out curls.

I look into a storefront rather than answer.

"It's awful, right? You can tell me at dinner why I should spend more than ten dollars on a haircut because I associate that with the *haves*."

"Ten dollars! You pay that *here*? In California?"

He brushes his fingers through his brown locks, which curl at the ends. "I have to go into Hollywood, and my barber doesn't speak English, so I'm at his mercy, but it makes me look eccentric, I think." He uses the storefront window as a mirror. "An antiquarian should always have a bit of an Einstein look about him. It perpetuates the whole mad-genius thing, so people aren't questioning the prices."

"They only give the test in English and Spanish, so are you sure your barber has a real license?"

He pulls down a tendril. "Does it matter?"

I bite my lip to keep from smiling. "Listen, if I was going to find a *have*, you would be on the top of my list, Dane."

"Ah, see, you did notice my haircut and you weren't going to tell me. What's this about being honest with me? What if I'm a *have* with a bad haircut; don't you have any mercy? That's reverse discrimination."

"Dane, have you ever heard the term *baggage*? As in *emotional baggage*?"

"I have. When I have a designer with a difficult client, I always like to include a vintage Louis Vuitton trunk to add symbolism. It's an antiquarian's attempt at comedy."

"I'm an entire luggage department at Wal-Mart." I study my feet. "I have no idea why I'm telling you this. It's like my mouth won't stop moving, so let's go home."

As we stroll along Rodeo Drive, I wonder what it must be like to go into one of these shops and spend money. I'm not even tempted. I'd only be thinking about starving children or the East Side, which we drive through on the way into town. Living well to me isn't spending a lot of money.

"You're telling me because you're trying hard to resist my charms, but deep down you really don't want to."

"I need to make sure my head's on straight. That's all I'm saying."

"You're the girl next door. The real thing. Mary Ann and not Ginger. Genuine brunette. Authentic, stunning figure, with an aura of comfort surrounding your nature. We define the *haves* differently. You're exactly what every man in Hollywood is looking for."

"Ah . . . are they checking behind Jessica Simpson for me?"

"If beauty is a commodity, as you so eloquently are trying to tell me, then you are a *have*."

"Ah, see, that's not really true. If I am a beauty, as you're insinuating, that's where the myth comes in. I trade my beauty for your financial solvency and a deal is made, but that deal won't last."

"It won't?"

"Because my beauty will fade and then you'll start to

feel as though you were given a raw deal. A bait and switch, if you will. So you will look for a younger, prettier version of me."

"Or I may begin to see the inner beauty blossom and my investment pay off in spades. I may be the kind of man who believes a woman grows more beautiful as you get to know her deeply."

"Yeah, that could happen," I quip sarcastically, but as I say it I feel guilt bubble inside of me. Mrs. Gentry would burst into tears if she heard my attitude, and I have watched her grow in beauty while my mother withers. And I do know what the Bible says about beauty being fleeting. But still . . .

"So you want to be alone then? I was under the impression with the old Hollywood thing, you still had hope."

His question catches me off guard. "Of course I don't want to be alone."

"So where does God come into play in this commodity business? It seems to me He took a woman drawing water and gave her to Isaac. He took the mother of our Savior and placed her safely in the arms of a lowly carpenter. Seems to me you're limiting God on what He might have for you."

I am, and yet I'm hoping with my whole heart it's something more than I can fathom. I want to say, "I'm scared, Dane." But what I actually say is, "It's late, Dane. We should get home. I destroyed a reality-TV model's hopes today. That's enough of a day for me."

"I'm going on another buying trip soon to France. The piece I went after wasn't available yet. My house should be done by the time I'm home."

This stops me. The thought of him leaving again

makes me ache; yet the reality of continuing in this farce of a relationship looms. What if Mrs. Gentry's right about my feelings for Dane? What if it's time to risk something?

"I suppose I should say *bon voyage* then."

"Sarah, tonight is dinner. I'm not asking you for a lifetime commitment."

Of course he isn't. And he won't. Men don't marry Winowski women.

"You're hardly dressed for the beach."

"You're humiliated by my stuffy appearance? My anti-quated look?" He shakes his head. "You are a snob, aren't you? I thought maybe, just by knowing what a fedora was, you were different. What if I lose the jacket?" He puts my bag down and strips out of his navy blazer. My stomach churns again.

What if, for just one minute, I forgot all my fears?

What if I did what I wanted just this once and abandoned myself to emotions?

"Can I have that ride home?" I ask, though with all my heart I can't help but wish he'd take charge and kid-nap me to the Pacific. But I know his inner gentleman will rule out, and I'll spend the night with Cary Grant again.

"Perhaps it's me getting taken for the ride." He raises his eyebrows. *I love those eyebrows.*

We both stop walking and look at each other. No words are necessary. This dance we've been having in conversation has nothing to do with what we're thinking. It's avoidance. Pure and simple.

"Kiss me, Sarah."

That's what we're thinking.

He bends down and, unwittingly, I step back. He steps forward and suddenly something inside me breaks.

I will not back away from what my heart wants. Not this time.

Dane's lips brush across mine, and I relish the touch. He surrounds me with his arms and I kiss him like Ingrid kisses Cary in *Notorious*. There's no thought to the matter; I am lost in his touch, just as Ingrid was when she thought it might be her only moment to tell Cary how she felt. We fall into an embrace of all the emotion neither of us has stated in our conversational dance about beaches and antiques and commodities. The emotion we have fought every time we laid eyes on each other in my cousin's hallway. Every time I caught him peering at me over his business magazine. My chest radiates with the heat I've been avoiding through careless conversation. I'm lost in his kiss, tasting his lips on my own and kissing him back with a hunger I've never expressed before. Never felt before.

I close my eyes. I don't want to forget a thing. When I tilt my chin again, I feel his lips on mine, this time with more fervency.

"Get a room!" someone yells out their car window as they pass, and shocked, I step back, touching my fingers to my lips, hardly believing my complete lack of etiquette.

"The beach . . ." I pause, catching my breath. "Your house . . ." More breathing. "Not a good idea."

"No." He shakes his head. He exhales a ragged sigh that holds so much temptation for me, I shut my eyes against the emotion. "But do you see why your caste system doesn't hold water? Attraction is not moderated by logic, and I'm a very logical person, Sarah."

"Thank you, Spock." I hold my fingers up in *Star Trek* mode.

"I wish I could take you home." He shakes his head. I think he said that more for himself than me. "I'll drop you off at Scott's before I go."

With everything in me, I want to abandon logic for once and give in to this emotion that will take me straight to Dane's beach house. I want to get lost in his clutches from here to eternity in a scene that would make Burt Lancaster and Deborah Kerr blush. But thankfully, logic wins. If my mother taught me anything, it's that men—especially antiquarians—do not marry Winowski women. It's time for a cold shower and a Cary Grant fast.

chapter 15

*Mistakes are part of the dues
one pays for a full life.*
~ Sophia Loren

I'm just heading to my room for a shower when Scott, who definitely noticed that Dane and I arrived home together, bellows at me.

"What?" I call back to him.

"Sarah Claire!" Scott yells again from the kitchen. "Your mother's on the phone. Pick it up in your room."

Talk about waking up from a dream and finding yourself next to a dumpster. My mother. Brace for impact.

I shut the door to Dane's dangerous smile and enter the lion's den.

"Hi, Mom."

"Sarah Claire, you haven't called me. It's been weeks."

"Sorry, Mom, it's been busy. By the time I get home, you're working at the bar. The salon keeps me there until eight."

"Is it nice?"

"It's incredible, Mom, but more sterile than I thought it would be. I saw Trisha from your soap opera. She was getting highlights and all up in foils. I bet the *Enquirer* would pay for a picture like that. If she was a bigger star and all."

"Listen, I'm calling about something important."

"As if seeing Trisha getting her hair done isn't important?"

"I'm going on a road trip," she continues, ignoring my news of Trisha, when I was perfectly willing and able to tell her about the chunky blonde highlights and which brand they were and everything. I notice the important details. We could have duplicated it at home.

"A road trip, you said?" Now what this means in city speak is that you pack up the car, the family, and head to another town, preferably stopping at a roadside motel along the way to some national landmark. To my mother, it means she's met a man and he has a big enough hog for two, and they'll be tearing up the streets in leather. A month later, she'll be home in tears.

"Mom, you can't go anywhere. You're awaiting trial. Mrs. Gentry said—"

"I told you not to talk to those old biddies about me. They need to mind their own business. Al knows I'll be back in time for the trial."

Al is our bail bondsman. And yes, we're on a first-name basis.

"Is that such a good idea? I mean, you can't really afford to take off from your job right now, can you?"

"Clyde's driving. He's got a beautiful Harley, Sarah Claire. It looks right off a showroom floor."

Wyoming isn't so backwoods that I think motorcyclists are tattooed hoodlums without a place to call home. We have our share of wealthy Harley riders who own cattle ranches bigger than some states. However, all that being said, that is not who my mother has found for her planned escape from town. She has found some dreg of society who either got drunk at the Hideaway or knew some friend who got drunk at the Hideaway. Magic was made, and my mother found someone to keep her codependent self company now that I'm gone. It didn't even take a month. If I wasn't so disgusted, I'd be impressed.

"I'm entitled to a vacation, Sarah Claire," she barks.

Suddenly, leaving her behind isn't feeling like the best way to the top. "Mom, I don't know how to say this, but you need to focus on your future right now."

"That's exactly what I'm doing."

"You met a man, Mom?"

"Who said anything about meeting a man?"

"Are you trying to tell me you didn't meet a man? Who's Clyde?"

"I meet a lot of men, Sarah Claire. I work in a bar and more than half the clientele is men." Clientele. Now that's stretching things a bit. It's akin to the title "gentleman's club." No one's falling for it.

"So translate 'road trip' for me," I say.

"I'm taking my bike up to Glacier National Park."

"With Clyde?"

"Don't smart-mouth me, young lady. If I cared what this town thought and ran like you did every time they called me a name, I wouldn't have my self-respect."

Ah, when the going gets tough, act like a mom.

"Mom, you don't have a bike."

"I'm borrowing one."

"So you're just leaving the house?"

"You didn't worry about the house when you left, did you? But in fact, I'm not just leaving the house. A friend is staying here while I'm gone. He'll take care of everything. Your cat, watering the plants."

"We don't have any plants."

"He'll just be taking care of things, all right?"

A friend. There isn't a soul in Sable that everyone doesn't know, so why she feels the need to hide who it is can only mean one thing. She's handing the keys over to some stranger who ambled into her bar last night. I wonder if her alcohol will still be alphabetized when she gets home.

"So will you be checking in with me? How will I get ahold of you?" *Translation: if they find you in a ditch somewhere, how will they notify me?*

Here's the thing about being raised by an alcoholic. You learn not to expect anything and that pointing out the practical is pointless. Just go with the flow; it makes life bearable.

"I'll call you, Sarah Claire. I'm not going to Mongolia, and I'll be back before the trial."

I can't help myself. "Mom, do you know this guy well enough to be going off with him? What if he's wanted by the police or something?"

"You have such an imagination. You just worry about your studies and doing everyone's hair pretty, all right? I'm a big girl. Your scandal has blown over, and now everyone will be back pointing fingers at me. It's time to go."

My scandal. I roll my eyes.

"Mom, can't you just sit still until things straighten out?"

"And do what, twiddle my thumbs waiting for you to return?"

"No, I was hoping you'd further your education or maybe move to a different town."

"I'm not leaving here, Sarah Claire. I have ties in this town. Clyde is not dangerous, sweetie."

"Is there anyone named Clyde who's not dangerous, Mom? How long have you known him?"

"That's none of your business. You make it sound like your mother's easy."

"Well, call me, Mom. All right?" I try to keep the desperation out of my voice. "You remember what you promised me—that you'd make the most of my absence. If I don't get to stay at Yoshi's, does this person at our house know that I might be coming home?"

"You won't be coming home, Sarah Claire. I've rented out the house. How do you think I can afford a road trip? Don't worry about me. I'll call you from Canada."

"You can't leave the country—"

I hear her giggle and then a man's voice.

"It's against your parole."

"Gotta run, baby. Give Scotty a kiss from his aunt."

Click.

Scott bangs on my door as I hang up. "What?" I say too sharply.

"Here's some more clothes." He tosses them at me. "I have tons right now because everyone's looking for an Emmy dress. I don't need this casual stuff. They're given to me for advertising. I'm sure you're not exactly the kind of press they're looking for, but right now it's what I've got. Work them into conversation, understand?"

"These labels are like hieroglyphics. 'Hi, I'm Sarah Winston. I'll be your shampoo girl today.'" I turn my derrière toward Scott. "'Today I'm wearing wide-legged trousers by Dolce & Gabbana with a fitted shirt, courtesy of Chloe.'"

"Perfect," Scott says. "The tags are still on most everything; look for a label if you can't find one. Study them like they were your next pop quiz. Do an Internet search if you need to."

I look at him, at the tired eyes. He's tense, and I don't think it's entirely because of the Emmys. With my own romantic experience still tingling my lips, I decide to play

Cupid. "Have you talked to Alexa lately?"

His eyes flash in warning. "It's over."

"Scott—"

"Give me the benefit of the doubt, will you?"

He shuts the door and I slide down the wall, cupping my arms around my knees, still dreaming of Dane's kiss. I begin to rock and pray. I know God is here, somewhere. I know He comforted me all those dark nights when my mother left me alone. But Dane is here also. Dane, the light sleeper.

chapter 16

*Hollywood is a place where they'll pay
you a thousand dollars for a kiss and
fifty cents for your soul.*
~ Marilyn Monroe

Obsessive. That's exactly how I would describe Southern California. Celebrity is a drug here, and everyone seems to drink deep from the same shot glass. I didn't sleep well last night because my cousin was in his room talking to himself about "cutlets"—little rubber things women put in their bras to enhance themselves. I think I could have gone my entire life without having some of the Hollywood secrets exposed. A little mystery is good for the soul.

Of course, regardless of what Hollywood does to perfect themselves, they still look better than me without the help.

My thoughts haven't left that kiss. So much fire. *"It is better to marry than to burn with passion."* Now I know exactly what that verse means, and it leaves me with quite the dilemma: no one's asking me to marry, and I don't think I could be around Dane long without putting my faith on the shelf. It's not like we have the luxury of time behind us. I barely know the man. Which makes me wonder how real my faith is if I can just forget it and get lost in a simple kiss on Rodeo Drive like a common prostitute. What would Sable say to that?

Never mind. I do not want to know.

At least I'm not orange any longer.

Obsession runs in the family, so I come by it honestly. Scott spends his entire life shopping for other people's clothes and will throw hissy fits over a necklace being wrong. That's a strange occupation for anyone. Speaking of which . . .

"I am never going to find anything! The Emmys are two days away!" Scott is pacing frantically.

"Should she have her dress by now?"

"She should have had her dress and three fittings by now. Look at this girl, Sarah." He pulls out an eight-by-ten glossy, and let's just say, you know how Dane can spot a fake? Mr. Magoo could spot these fakes from the next town. This girl's so fake that her shirt is a testimony to the engineering of Lycra.

"That is *not* attractive. And look how pretty her eyes are. Not that you'd ever notice."

"I don't know what I was thinking taking her on as a client. This girl couldn't look good in anything. She has virtually destroyed any hope of wearing couture."

"I think that's the point, isn't it? I don't think that figure is meant for clothes."

"I took her on as a favor to a producer who's got her in a new series, but she is impossible to dress. Couture? Are you kidding me? Couture is meant for women with the figure of Kate Moss, not a human Viking ship." He drops his head to the counter. "What am I going to do? I'm going to be a laughingstock backstage. The stylists will all mumble as I walk by."

I watch his face fall. Understanding all the garments used to stretch, pull, flatten, and lift has clearly ruined my cousin on the mysteries of women. He probably just looks at them and sees what size cutlet they need and where they need a little more elastic.

"What about a shawl?" I ask, knowing he probably doesn't need my advice.

"Cover her completely, you mean?" My cousin looks at me over his glasses.

"If she wants to be legitimate, wouldn't that be best? You should go shopping at Bed, Bath & Beyond and get a bed sheet and fashion it into a shawl. She'll have the only outfit that's 600 Egyptian thread count." I grab a water out of the fridge. "I'd tell her she either covers up or you'll give her back to the stylist at Frederick's of Hollywood."

Scotty laughs at me, but he begins to nod. "You know, you're right. I'm stressing for nothing. It's her producer that she needs to impress, and he called me. I'll just threaten her with quitting, and she'll wear a curtain if I demand it."

He's goes back to sketching ideas for shopping, planning the day out and obsessing himself silly over this poor mutant girl.

"I'm off to work."

"Yeah, have fun." He doesn't look up from his sketch pad. I am invisible. But I guess next to his client everything is invisible. She's like a human car accident—you don't want to look, but you have to.

I pack my cell phone, smiling at the thought that I have a cell phone. I'm so calling Kate again today, who I am sure is safely back in the reality she's created for herself in Sable. She and Ryan have had these tiffs before.

❧

I've spent the entire morning learning the proper way to wash hair. *As if.*

"Massage the fingers deeply . . . deeply. Feel the skull

base at the back of the ears. Press deeply . . . massage deeply."
Magnus—which sounds like a dog's name but really belongs to a slight, white man of about thirty—makes the
instruction sound lewd. I mean, there's only so much pleasure you want a client to get out of a shampoo, am I right?

"Pressure points are key." Magnus lifts up a soapy
finger. "You will study the diagram of the head tonight,
and I want the name of the central acupressure points on
the head. Tomorrow, each of you will give me a shampoo,
and you will be graded according to proper pressure,
finding the right acupressure points, and finally, an overall
relaxation score. Any questions?"

In Wyoming, they told us shampooing was just like
milking a cow. I never had any complaints. But I wash the
fake head at least twenty times. Which is ludicrous; you
can't practice washing on a fake skull. Still, I obsess like
everyone else in this town, feeling for the bony parts of the
plastic skull. It's as good of a diversion as anything. I think
this is just a town of human ants, and there's something
about being here—one has to keep moving or die.

"And now!" Magnus lifts the other soapy finger as
though the crème de la crème of shampoo facts are forth-
coming. "We will use *real* Yoshi shampoo, and you will
work on the texture of your head and select the right
products for your personal head using the information you
were given in your manuals last night."

We all look at our identical plastic heads and wonder if
it's a trick question. A hand goes up, and my fellow student
Angie has guts enough to ask the obvious. "How is my
head different from hers?"

Magnus ignores the question and accompanies this
slight with a taut jerk of his head. "If you'll all *feel* your
hair and write down the products you would suggest for

that client, I'll take your answers before we work with real product. Once we bring out the Yoshi organics, we will not use more than necessary. Are we clear?"

My fingers are raw—the *real* shampoo doesn't come out until the end, so we got the "texture" and "feel" of how much is needed by using bulk dishwashing detergent, purchased at "Hollar for a Dollar" by *moi*. (Don't even get me started on how many bus rides it is to the local dollar store from Beverly Hills.) My fingers are stripped of their outer layer of skin—it's a blue peel for the hands—and this is probably the time to commit a crime if I have need, since I'm sure it took my fingerprint with it. One good note: if I need to remove wallpaper, I now know a really cheap alternative, and it's all mine for a dollar.

When Magnus brings out the gentle stuff, I can almost hear the angels singing over the shampoo's halo. He puts a small bottle at the head of each shampoo bowl and one large one in front of me. "You'll fill the little ones for everyone and we'll begin washing together. Put your heads away; we'll be practicing on each other."

I hold the bottle. My first inclination is to clutch it under my arm and run away with the booty, but I take a deep breath and reset—pirate fantasies notwithstanding. Washing plastic heads all day is doing nothing for my brain cells.

Opening the bottle, I head to the first shampoo bowl. Fellow trainee Gretchen has made no bones about wanting my spot as the paid position, and she's done her level best to talk to the entire room about why I shouldn't be there.

"Gretchen, can you open your bottle?"

"You can open it," she says without moving. Did I mention she looks and sounds just like Cindy Simmons? I move on to the next student and fill until all five bottles are filled, including my own. Gretchen's sits there closed and empty. Childish? Absolutely. But I am not playing. I made that mistake as a child.

"Magnus," Gretchen says with her hand lifted. "Sarah skipped me."

Magnus thins his eyes at her. "Well, what do you want me to do about it, take away her crayons? Is this kindergarten? Ask her to fill it and open your cap. Did you ever think she can't fill a closed bottle?"

Gretchen looks at me with a pout as I approach her bowl. "You did that on purpose," she says through clenched teeth.

"Did what?" I hate conflict, but this girl is getting on my nerves. As if washing plastic heads with battery acid all day isn't enough to do that.

Suddenly Gretchen bats the bottle out of my hand, and thick bubbles of Yoshi gold pour out onto the floor. My mouth just drops open. *Cindy Simmons has followed me.* My new demon is named Gretchen.

Terrified, I bend over and try to channel the shampoo back into the bottle, but it's not working, and there's a giant puddle of lavender-scented liquid oozing along the floor. I try to cup the spill with my hands, and it pushes the wetness onto my knees and soaks through my jeans. Well, someone's jeans anyway; they're Scott's.

Something makes me look up to see Yoshi standing in the doorframe. Magnus is horrified at the scene, and the entire group stares at me, then back at Yoshi. He looks relatively calm. For a looming tsunami, that is.

"Sarah."

"Yes, sir."

"Do you know how much product that is lying there on the floor?"

"Four hundred and eighteen dollars' worth?" I ask, giving my best shot at a *Rain Man* answer.

"Yes, well." Yoshi claps his hands together. "Someone get the mop!" Everyone scurries into motion. Except me; for the moment, I am the human mop. "Sarah, stand up please."

I do and feel the shampoo ooze from my knees to my feet. I pray this is as organic as he claims, because if it doesn't come out, these jeans are most likely my first paycheck. If not more.

"Sarah and Gretchen, you'll be washing each other's hair today. You've had more than enough practice on the heads." He goes on to pair the rest of the class, but I don't hear any of it.

"Yoshi, I'm so sorry. It was—"

"Come with me, please."

I follow him into his office, thankful that my shoes are not trekking shampoo with me. Thank goodness I'd filled the other bottles up before getting to Gretchen. *What was with that psycho?*

I'm trying to keep my breathing quiet, but it's strained and desperate. I can't go home yet. Not without one paycheck at least. For one thing, I can't actually get there financially, and I haven't even paid off the debt to get out here to my cousin. No, this is definitely not going to work.

"Yoshi, I—"

"Sarah, you need to learn when to speak." He slams the door behind him and settles himself at his desk chair with a good view of himself to the mirror.

"I'm sorry—"

"You're speaking again." He motions toward the extra chair and I sit down, bracing myself for my own failure. This has nothing to do with my mother. This is mine alone.

"I can pay for the shampoo—"

"Sarah—talking again. And no, you can't. I know what I pay you."

"Right. Sorry."

"Gretchen wants your position, no?"

"No. I mean yes."

"This is a cutthroat business. I can't protect you from every scheming stylist, do you understand?"

"I do."

"But you've got to learn to play a bit dirty. You never had a catfight in Wyoming?"

My jaw drops, not because I'm surprised, but because I don't know if I have it in me to play dirty. It's hard enough putting energy into a shampoo that's more choreographed than an automatic car wash.

"Maybe one."

"Gretchen will never make it, do you understand? I can teach anyone to cut hair, but I cannot teach them humility—that styling is not about them but the client. She will never understand that; therefore she will never work in my salon."

"So why's she here?"

"Because there are a thousand like her right behind her, and they pay good money to be here and learn. But you need to deal with them. Let yourself out." He says this into the mirror, but I assume he's talking to me, so I shut the door behind me.

What I wouldn't give for a good pin curl and hair tease about now.

❧

I spend the rest of this never-ending day making advanced espresso. If you want a half-caf soy latte with extra foam, baby, I'm now your girl. Not a bad accomplishment after being virtually espresso illiterate less than a month ago.

I'm a little buzzed after all the taste tests, though. I should be thoroughly on fire for Ann's mentoring group, since sleeping is probably not in my immediate future. And since I think a mentoring group is the secular world's answer to Bible study, I'm anxious to hear what intellectual stimuli I might get from Hollywood employees in the know.

chapter 17

You can only sleep your way to the middle.
You have to claw your way to the top.
~ Sharon Stone

I last ate at seven a.m. when I had an energy bar. No wonder everyone's skinny here; there's no time to eat. What I wouldn't give for a hot dog or a chicken sausage from Jody Maroni's. If you're only going to eat once a day, why not make it something in the sausage family?

"I'm starving," I say aloud, thinking too hard about Jody's. I place my hand on my stomach, hoping to soothe its empty cry.

"We'll eat at mentoring group." Ann is spritzing her long, luxurious blonde hair, though I never did see one strand out of place. She has the kind of beauty where it's like her hair wouldn't dare misbehave. "Someone's in charge of bringing dinner; it's usually Rock because she pinches it from the leftover catering trays for whatever movie she's on."

I think about questioning this, but I decide it's just better not to know. I'll eat whatever's put in front of me, provided by Rock, Tree, or whomever.

"Are you ready?" Ann is perched at the door, waiting for Yoshi to extricate himself from the premises. She still looks as fresh as a daisy, as though these hours have no effect on her beauty. She spent most of her day doing color. There has to be a serious lack of hydrogen peroxide in this town because everyone's blonde! You think that's a myth about LA, but nope, everyone's a blonde, unless they're Asian or African-American. Weirdest thing ever because, quite frankly, not everyone has the coloring for blonde.

Oh, wait, there are a few bad redheads too. Ann said there were more now that the *Desperate Housewives* redhead and McDreamy's ex-wife on *Grey's Anatomy* came to the forefront. This phenomenon has brought out the control freak in me. I just want to pick them up off the street and bring them into Yoshi's for a real dye job. Even worse than an olive-skinned blonde is an olive-toned redhead.

Of course, I wanted to kidnap people in Sable, too, and rid the world of blue and pink hair dye, which is actually difficult to purchase in this day and age. Sable seems to have a lifetime supply in someone's warehouse. There are only so many things in life you have control over.

"I heard you spilled shampoo all over the floor today." Jamie walks up with a giggle. "Did Yoshi totally spaz or what?"

"He was really nice about it, actually."

Jaime's smile straightens. "He was? I hope you don't get fired tomorrow. I think I'd rather have him spaz." She looks at Ann and they nod, convinced of my imminent departure.

I spend all day with these women, and they're like two cardboard cutouts. In our salon back in Wyoming, the whole day was social, a virtual gabfest, but there's a serious nature to this environment—as if we're performing surgery and solving global warming, all at the same time. The fate of the universe rests in our organic hands.

I miss relationship. I miss Kate and Mrs. Gentry and Mrs. Rampas telling me what to do. I miss someone caring about me.

"So what's our topic at mentoring group?" I ask, changing the subject.

"Securities," Jaime answers. "But we don't need a topic; our topic is mentoring. Whatever we have to share with others." She rolls her eyes with a, "Duh."

Not having biblical thoughts at the moment.

Jaime has a mass of natural curls that blossom from her head and dangle in spectacular ringlets like clinging vines. Jenna says Jaime's father is black and her mother is Puerto Rican, so she has this exotic look with creamy dark skin and blue-green eyes. Needless to say, she makes the blondes envious, but it makes me wonder if those curls aren't pulling on some vital brain cells.

"The girls will be at the house at nine," Ann says. "So we have to run."

A group that starts at nine. I just can't get over how weird that sounds. I've got my Bible tucked into my bag; I've decided to act like this is a Bible study. Maybe I can mentor someone in the Word while I'm there. Or maybe meet another believer. Being here, I've found my life compass is way off. I don't know which way to turn. Admittedly, I haven't had any trouble meeting men for the first time in my existence, but discerning exactly what they're up to is proving difficult.

A gym trainer with a serious ego problem and an antiquarian who could eat me intellectually for lunch. In the real world, these men wouldn't look twice at me, and I'm hoping the mentoring group will provide some answers as to the why before I let myself get carried away into a sad Hollywood ending I've seen too many times on the pages of *People*.

The mysterious Mercedes is out front when we come out of the salon, and Ann ushers me in. "Good evening, ladies." The driver turns around and he's a dead ringer for a younger George Clooney. This entire town seems to be magazine-worthy. My self-esteem is taking a huge hit. Does anyone really want to be Mary Ann in a town full of Gingers?

There's a cab behind him, and I wonder if that isn't my ride, but the taxi simply follows.

"Sarah, this is my boyfriend, Kyle," Ann says with no mention of the car behind us.

He reaches over the seats and shakes my hand. "Pleasure to meet you. How's being the fresh meat at Yoshi's?"

I smile. "It's not as bad as all that. I've learned there's an art to everything, even making coffee and washing hair."

"Kyle's the chauffeur for the Wilshire. When he's not busy, he picks us up and drops us off at the complex. It's right across the street from his hotel." She turns back to Kyle. "We think Sarah should move in with us."

Kyle stares at me and back at the road. "Yeah, that'd be good."

The girls, who have barely said hello to me each morning, are looking for a new roommate. Apparently, my predecessor Yoshi apprentice was fired without warning, leaving them with an extra $1,000 a month. I can't likely pay that when I'm going to go into debt if the church ladies pay for my mother's rehab, now can I?

Upon arriving—an easy walk, I might add—I see Ann and Jaime don't really live in an apartment complex at all. I believe it should be more appropriately stated as a *suite-cluster*. Yes, that's my own word.

"The apartments are available furnished or un-furnished. We have a furnished model." Ann lowers her voice. "A lot of people come here to recuperate after plastic surgery. They go to a place that takes care of them, then move on to here when the deep healing is done. The recovery centers are only for the early days. This just gives them a chance to regroup while their bruises and scars heal. There're a few stars that stay while filming a movie, though the really big ones rent a secluded house or stay at the Chateau Marmont."

"Hmm." This is an obvious sales pitch for the third place in the apartment, and I'm broke, ladies!

"We have a maid service every week. It's forty-five dollars a person, but it would only be about thirty if you wanted in," Ann offers. "We clean all day at Yoshi's. I don't want to smell any cleaning products when I get here." She opens up the fridge while I pick up various photos about the room. "That's Abby. She'll be coming tonight."

"She's beautiful."

"She's a model."

I'm intrigued by a photo of someone who is pretty by all standards but much less so by Yoshi standards. "Who's this?"

"That's Rock. She's a stuntwoman. She's broken her nose five times, and I think she's about to get it fixed finally. Want something to drink?"

"I'd love a water."

She tosses me an Evian. I have to say, this stuff smells like dirt. Imagine my surprise when it tastes like dirt too. Maybe I'm spoiled in Wyoming, but I will never get the fascination with Evian. I chug it down anyway. *When in Rome . . .* My stomach grumbles mercilessly as I do so.

The doorbell rings again and I sit down on the sofa, anxious to see what new gorgeous starlet will enter the room next. But there's a commotion at the door, and somehow I just know it relates to me. I close my eyes instinctively.

"I know she's here. I followed her here in a cab. Let me in."

No way . . .

The door swings open and behind it is my mother. My jaw drops, and my first thought is that I hope they're not paying too much for their security guard. My second thought is that my mom looks worn and I want to help her. But selfishly, I'm thinking of my job too.

I look around the room, shamed by the fact that I don't want to acknowledge her, but all eyes bore through me with the intensity of an automatic drill.

Yes, she belongs to me!

"Excuse me, won't you?" I walk toward my mother, who smells like the back alley behind the Hideway, and pull her out the front door into the hallway, shutting the door behind me.

"Mom, are you all right? How'd you get here?"

She nods, and I notice a tear falling down her cheek.

"What are you doing here?" I whisper, praying no one else arrives for mentoring. I'm ashamed to admit it, but I can't help but feel what her presence does to me. It changes me into the caretaker, and right now I need to take care of keeping my job.

"What do you mean, what am I doing here? I came to see my daughter. My only family."

"Right."

"Did you think I'd stay there in Wyoming, waiting for Al to put me away once and for all? To just wait for you when you felt like coming back?"

"I didn't leave you there, Mom. I just decided to do what I wanted for a change. I'm an adult. It was time to start making my own decisions."

"It's all about you, isn't it, Sarah Claire? You want to hang out with these shallow, beautiful people? That's what I raised you for? To ignore your mother in a room full of strangers?"

"I want to make something of myself, and I'm a great hairdresser, Mom. If you'd ever let me cut your hair, you'd see I have a gift. And I didn't ignore you."

She scoffs at this. "In the end, family is all that matters, don't you know that? Men, they come and go, but we're here for each other."

Here for me? I bite my lip rather than say what I'm thinking. "I'm following my dream, so maybe it's your turn to be here for me. It was one of two coasts, and I picked the closest one. I did that for you, Mom."

"I lost my job," she says plainly. "Al says your thousand dollars is his since I skipped the state. Sorry about that. I'll pay you back when I find a new job."

No, she won't. If I had a dollar for every time she said that, I wouldn't need to be in California. "Sorry about the job, don't worry about the money. I'm just glad you're safe and not with this Clyde character."

"He didn't want me. We only got an hour or so up the road and he said his wife had just left him and he'd made a mistake."

"Mom, there's this great rehab center not far from here that Scott told me about and—"

"Sarah Claire, I do not have a drinking problem just because I have a relaxing drink at the end of the day. Why must you make everything of crisis proportion with me? Have I ever let you go hungry? Who hasn't passed out after working all day?"

Okay, I know this argument would be obvious to normal people. I hate that we're not normal people.

"I've been looking into it. They have programs, and I think I could find a place that's affordable for us. Now that I have a job, I could get credit. This is our chance to make things different. Mrs. Gentry says—"

"Don't you dare bring up that woman's name to me." She looks around the hallway. "I would think if you're bandying about with these types of folks, a thousand dollars feels like a lot of nothing to lose."

"I've been here for less than a month, Mom. Do you think I found my fortune at the end of the rainbow?"

"Don't take up an attitude with me, little girl. I think you've been stockpiling it all along is what I think."

"Mom, just go back to Wyoming and face the music. Al has always been on your side. Get this legal garbage over with so you can move on."

My mom pats her chest. "Al has a soft heart, honey. He couldn't stand to see me go to jail. He wants me to start fresh, not waste time on a poser like Clyde." She holds up a wad of hundred-dollar bills.

A poser. Now there's a word I haven't heard since high school. I'm feeling the sudden desire to call the IRS and turn them loose on Al's Bail Bonds. He lets my mom out of jail and gives her my money; how very generous of him. But then I remember he took her keys away, and I am truly grateful for that.

"Mom, I have no place for you to stay, and after tonight, I might not have a place to work. Do you know what Yoshi would do to me if he found out I was harboring a criminal? Image is everything in his salon."

"Don't be such a drama queen. Your mother's visiting. I'm sure those girls' mothers come to visit all the time."

Chances are they're sober when they do it. Maybe bring them some homemade cookies, that kind of thing.

"Mom, I can't support you here. It's too expensive."

"Did I ask you to support me?"

"Where are you planning to stay? Scott has a full house, and you're not exactly his favorite auntie."

"The weather's nice here, or I can probably find a friend at a local drinking establishment."

"Sarah Claire Winowski?" Two police officers enter the hallway.

My mother points at me. "That's her."

"Mom!"

My mother starts to run down the hallway, and the two burly men in black follow her and bring her back to the doorway as she bicycles her legs like an upturned cockroach.

"Just a few questions, ma'am."

Feeling sick, I look into my mother's eyes. She refuses to look at me. She would have let the police take me. My own mother . . .

Somehow that changes things for me. Once and for all, I realize she has totally abused and neglected me my whole life. Perhaps I'm slow that it's taken me this long, but at this moment, I feel every shred of anger I've held on to all these years rise in my throat to the point where I let out a carnal scream that is anything but human in nature.

The front door of Ann's apartment opens slowly, and Jaime peeks her head out. "You all right, Sarah?"

"I'm fine."

At the sound of my name, the police officers come toward me. "You're Sarah Claire Winowski?" He holds out a passport with my name on it and my mother's picture.

She didn't.

"Yes, but I have a feeling you're not really looking for me. I don't actually have a passport. Never did."

"I didn't do anything!" She points at the cop. "You can't prove anything."

I'm thinking they can prove a fake passport pretty quickly.

Jaime shuts the door gently, an act that brings me to a full boil when I look at my mom. "You just had to do this, didn't you? You just had to ruin anything I did on my own. It wasn't enough that you had an entire town disgusted with me; you had to follow me here and ruin it all. Whoever my father is, he was right to get away from you."

I regret it as soon as it's out. But it's out. She mumbles under her breath but doesn't look at me when she says it. "You ungrateful little minx."

"Ungrateful? I'm ungrateful? Were you grateful when I had food waiting for you when you came home from work? When I schlepped down to the food kitchen to make sure there was food in the cupboards at ten years old? When I alphabetized the cans because I knew what you'd say if the beans weren't in front of the corn? Were you, Mom?"

"Ladies, I need to see some identification," one of the officers says.

I'm shaking, not in fear but in distinct anger. These cops can't do anything to me that my mother hasn't already done. I stare at her antiquated beauty buried beneath the years of alcohol abuse, and I realize I've reached my limit. Enough is enough. One day at a time is one day too much at the moment. I've been an idiot, playing into all her manipulations. There's no excuse for what I've let happen! No wonder Mrs. Gentry thinks I don't speak up for myself.

"I have to get my ID in the apartment."

I creep into the apartment as quietly as possible, but all the girls are huddled together in a circle, and their whispers stop abruptly when I enter the room. "I just need to get my purse. Thanks for the invitation, Ann and Jaime. I'll see you tomorrow." Maybe.

No one answers me, and I pad back to the front door

like a repentant child and watch as my mother is hauled off in handcuffs.

"We have our suspect, ma'am. Thank you for your cooperation."

*Dramatic art in her opinion is
knowing how to fill a sweater.*
~ Bette Davis

I wish I had a door to slam rather than this stupid, sliding elevator door into my cousin's condo. Sometimes a girl needs to make a statement! If I looked at the sunny side of life, I'd see that at least I know the door's combination now, and where I live, and I possess a working cell phone. Since I can spell my middle name, I can officially graduate from Kindergarten of LA and maybe even own a library card. Oh, wait a minute, still need to learn my phone number by heart for that.

"What happened to you?" Scott looks me over.

"You don't want to know." I toss down my bag and flop on the couch next to Dane, who's reading a giant biography of a dead president. "You're not actually reading that, right? It's just hiding a copy of *MAD* magazine?"

"*MAD*? How old are you?"

"I'm telling you, she's from another era, Dane. It's like someone dropped her in a time machine of her own making. She's Doc Brown gone awry."

"You know, Scott—" I slam my purse down. "—just one small moment of peace. Please?"

"I take it by your mood your mother found you," Scott

says. "She called here looking for you. I tried to confuse her by telling her the salon was called Ishi—you know, California's last Indian—but she had it written down."

"How does she do it, Scott? How does she not have money to pay the water bill but manage to get out of parole, get on a plane across three states, and stumble into my mentoring group in less than twenty-four hours? Did she get me one of those dog microchips while I slept? Is this all some dire plan and I'm really the daughter of a KGB agent who poses as the town drunk? If so, maybe I can go into a witness protection program and hide from her."

"She's a professional. That's what cons do. They spend more time looking for how to make the scam work than just doing things the honest way."

Dane is avoiding eye contact. I'm sure a lifeless president is far more interesting, but due to our kiss he owes me more attention. "Ahem."

Still nothing.

"It's all right, Dane, I'm aware that you can't relate to my *have-not* family issues."

He looks up with that "Wha—? Huh?" look men have perfected. "Sorry?" He puts his book on the sofa. "I wasn't listening."

He was, however, listening when I said I'd come to the beach house with kisses, wasn't he?

"I said can I cut your hair? I haven't cut hair in a month, and I'm getting itchy fingers. I need to style someone. And if you aren't screaming for a new 'do, I don't know who is. Come to the kitchen."

"I—uh—you didn't say that. I don't think—"

"You're eccentric. I know." I grab a kitchen chair and my kit from beside the door. "Don't worry, I'll keep you slightly off-key, but you need a haircut. It's driving me nuts. You're like Hugh Jackman as Wolverine. David Beckham with a ponytail. I can't take it anymore; it's not natural. Good-looking men lacking proper hygiene is not right."

"Hygiene? I'm clean. Are you insinuating I'm not clean?"

"Don't you watch *Grey's Anatomy*? Dr. McDreamy is all about the hair. Do you know how many men are coming into the salon asking to look like him? Well, here, I mean. In Sable, no one ever heard of him, and they certainly wouldn't want to look like a neurosurgeon. It's all about the cowboy there."

He pats his head nervously. "I don't think I really need a cut. I was just asking you yesterday as a topic of conversation, but it's really not bothering me."

"Are you kidding me?" Scott asks him.

"Let me rephrase my answer," Dane says, with his palms up as he backs away. "Sarah, darling, you're angry, and it's a strict policy of mine never to let an angry woman near my hair—or anything else, for that matter—with sharp instruments. I may not be a rocket scientist, but this much I know."

"Sit down." I have my hands on the back of the chair and I pick it up and drop it slightly. "I'm not playing. I need to get back in to it. Do you know how many garbage cans I've emptied? How many times I've lowered the toilet seat?"

He shakes his head.

"That man uses a small can for garbage on purpose. Do you know how much hair I swept today? Without cutting any of it? Do you know how many soy lattes I made?"

"Yeah . . ." Dane shakes his head. "I'm not letting you near my head."

"Dane," I growl.

"No." He laughs. "Did you ever see *The Barber of Seville?*"

I step toward him, and he steps back. "Only the Bugs Bunny version. Don't try to impress me."

"The opera is not as bad as all that. The Count and Rosina are married at the end. It's romantic."

"Are you proposing?"

He gets that caged-animal look.

"So a haircut isn't sounding all that bad." Scott laughs.

"Can I trust her?" Dane asks Scott.

"She's the best Sable, Wyoming, has to offer."

"I'm better than that. Really."

Dane fingers his hair. "I'll relent on one condition."

All I can think about is cutting someone's hair and having an actual "after" following several weeks of not working. "Whatever you want."

"We watch a movie first or we play a board game. When you calm down, I'll trust you with scissors." His eyes narrow, and it makes me smile. "Or you can watch that worn-out DVD of *Notorious.*"

I can't wait to get my hands on his hair. "I'm not *that* angry," I whine. "Well, maybe I am, but it won't affect my work."

"I'd like to see the results of haircuts following that statement. I imagine they're something like, 'I haven't had that much to drink, officer.' Or perhaps the visual equivalent of a Rorschach inkblot image."

"Monopoly's not my thing. I'll wash your hair first. How's that? That's relaxing, and there are no shears involved. I've learned to do that the Yoshi way. You'll love it. I think it's illegal in other countries."

My cousin is in the kitchen, his shoulders shaking with

laughter. "Go ahead, Lurch. I'm here to chaperone if you're scared."

Dane finally relents. I mean, *accepts* my offer of a haircut. We head to the kitchen sink and I pull out my first bottles of Yoshi shampoo, which he charged me a small fortune for—at cost. Give me a break. It contains seaweed amino acids, tea tree oil, and a host of other reasons to charge three times what it's worth. It smells divine, though, even with the tea tree oil, which usually smells nasty. It's hypnotic in some ways, but maybe that's just Dane's distrusting gaze, eyeing me as if he's my lamb to the slaughter.

"I'm not going to hurt you. Come here and bend over the sink. I'll rinse your hair and give you a wash."

Dane's glare is unnerving me. I keep reliving the kiss every time I look at his lips. They're all I can see. Rodeo Drive and the lap of luxury and I will forever think of it as my first foray into PDA.

He bends over the sink, taking one look back at me. "You're going to be gentle, right?"

"It's the Yoshi way." I shrug and push his head down. "If you came into the shop after hours, I could do this at a rinse sink and it would be much more comfortable."

He lifts his head up, looking back at me again. "I don't think I want to feel much more comfortable with you, Sarah."

I watch my cousin's brows lift and shake my head at him. *Nothing's going on*, I mouth.

That's not good. It's getting easier to lie without guilt.

A wave of warmth shoots through my system, and my hand releases from the sprayer, halting the water's flow. Scott is staring at me as if he knows the entire story and my little flirtation is no longer secret. Granted, the mauling on

Rodeo Drive told anyone driving by the same thing, but this is different. We *know* Scott.

"What's the matter?" Dane asks. "You stopped the water."

"Nothing," I answer. "Nothing at all." I look at Scott and shake my head slightly. Scott gives me a look, and I turn the water back on so Dane can't hear, then lean over to whisper, "Don't say a word. I'll get over it. I got over Steve Harris."

But I'm not going to get over it that easily. Dane will always represent what I wanted in life: an intelligent *have* with a hint of charity for simple country girls. Cary Grant for the cerebral set.

I'm rubbing my temple when I hear a hollow clunk against the stainless-steel sink.

"Oh, Dane, I'm sorry. Are you all right?" I surround his damp head with a towel and help him stand up right.

He rubs his own temple. "This is what Yoshi teaches, huh? You say he's a rich man?"

"I'm so sorry, I was thinking about something else and Scott looked at me . . . It was Scott's fault!" I point toward my cousin.

"I knew you were a little too angry to be touching sharp instruments. Even the kitchen sink is a weapon."

When he looks at me I forget all about Scott being near us. "I—I was thinking about Rodeo Drive."

The corner of his lip curves. "I'll never feel the same way about overpriced merchandise again."

"Am I missing something?" Scott asks.

Dane and I look at each other, but Dane speaks first. "I picked your cousin up from work last night and offered to take her to the ocean, but we walked Rodeo Drive instead."

"Did you get some clothes there?"

"Oh, sure, I picked up some Michael Kors after my trip to Tiffany's for a new tennis bracelet. The old one was getting *so* five minutes ago."

With a *Whatever* look, my cousin stalks off. I gently unwrap the towel, place Dane's head back down, and rub where I slammed him into the sink. Okay, I didn't slam him, but I feel as though I did.

The worst part is that I mentioned Rodeo Drive, and now that's all I'm thinking of—while I'm massaging his head. *Not good.* I start to repeat Scripture silently to get my mind off where it shouldn't be. *"Marriage should be honored by all, and the marriage bed kept pure, for God will judge the adulterer and all the sexually immoral."* There's a reason I memorized that one.

Dane lifts his head slowly and tilts his chin toward me with his brown eyes ablaze. "Let's just cut this part short, shall we? I already washed it this morning."

"I didn't use conditioner on you," I ramble. "It's definitely not the Yoshi way. The head massage is generally five minutes or more." He looks at me and we both nod. "Right. We'll cut it short."

Dane takes my hand at the wrist. "Sometimes . . . too much of a good thing is—" He looks down at me and I'd swear he was going to kiss me again. I forget the Scripture I was thinking about, which makes me feel like a complete and utter failure.

With Dane settled into the chair, I comb gently through his hair and position my scissors. All thoughts of my mother and my angst have disappeared. *Who's in jail again?* Dane's hair is thick and soft, with subtle curls at the end. "You'll never go bald."

He nods. "My dad never did." His eyes meet mine.

"So I'm going to put some layers in. It'll be much more

manageable in the mornings."

"I'm not really a *product* sort of guy, Sarah. I pride myself on being the one man in LA who can say that."

"Fine, it will still be perfectly acceptable even if it is a little frizzy on foggy days. Your choice."

"You make it sound like I have one. It's humid here; you're supposed to have a little frizz. It's how you know something's going on in my head. Lot of static-electricity action."

"Oh no, that's where you're wrong. Frizz is never good."

Scott has disappeared, and I feel our solitude intensely.

"Do you have any idea how beautiful you are?" he asks very quietly.

"I'm trying to cut your hair evenly."

"Why don't you come to France with me on my buying trip? I would love to take you to the Louvre and to see where Dumas wrote *The Three Musketeers.* You know they say he embarked on his career as a romantic by fighting his first duel and having his pants fall down. He's my romantic muse, you know."

"Dane, is there a normal fact you can share with me?"

"*Casablanca* was filmed in France."

"Dane."

"*To Catch a Thief* also."

"Dane."

"I'm serious. Separate rooms. No monkey business."

"Do you think that's possible?" I ask him, our chemistry sizzling like a live wire. "You won't even let me wash your hair."

"No." He slaps his knees. "No, I don't, but I had to ask."

"Besides, I'm poor, Dane. Rich people don't understand that real people have no money. By that, I mean *no* money. Not 'I have to wait for a CD to mature,' not 'I'll pay a penalty to pull it out of my 401K or get a second mortgage to finance the cash I need,' just simply 'I have no money.' I'm at my cousin's house out of need, not because my kitchen is getting remodeled in my fabulous beach house. I don't have a trust fund to fall back on or a travel write-off or any of those other tricks you people with money have."

"*You people.* Again with the bigotry! I wasn't asking you to pay for the trip, Sarah."

I nod slowly. "I wouldn't want to feel as if I owed you anything, Dane. I might be tempted to pay."

He stands up resolutely. "That wasn't what I was asking at all. I wanted to show you the Louvre. Where Cary Grant played a notorious jewel thief. Okay, that was in Nice, mostly, so maybe not there, but where he was chased by Audrey Hepburn in *Charade,* where Dumas wrote *Camille,* where it played in the theatre. It was a spontaneous thought. Nothing more."

"Of course it was. I wasn't accusing you of anything. I was protecting my own very tentative virtue." *I have spontaneous thoughts too, like let's forget that you're a* have *and I'm a* have-not. *And let's run to the nearest church, profess our faith and say we can't burn with desire any longer, and get married as quick as they'll let us.* But of course, those are the kind of thoughts that get you a one-way trip to the closest mental institution, so I don't share them.

"Hollywood moves at a pace I'm not used to, Dane. A cattle roundup is fast for me. I don't want to make any mistakes."

"This has nothing to do with Hollywood. Or California, for that matter. I was asking for your company because I can't stand to be away from you already, Sarah. You're under my skin, and I hate it that you're there."

"That's romantic."

He walks away from me toward his room, his hair half cut, half layered. Then he pauses, comes back for his dead-president biography, and takes one last look at me. "I'm sorry. Values are not something you share because of how much money you have, or even that you have the same religion. Values are how you live. I like the way you live, Sarah. Who you are. So sue me."

He slams the door to his bedroom and my cousin reappears, mocking me with a deliberate clapping.

"Well done."

"Let it go, Scott. I don't see you with anyone either. You can't even break up with a fiancée properly." Gathering my tools, I start to put them in the bag, then drop my scissors and rub my forehead again, in that migraine motion that seems to be a new habit. "It's not every day I get invited to France."

"What are you going to do, run off with Dane to the Louvre?" He sneers. "I thought you Christians didn't act like that. You're above the carnal nature, right?"

"Apparently, we're not. Would that make you happy, to watch me screw up like my mother? It would prove so much to you about my faith, wouldn't it?"

"Listen, if your religion helped you through your childhood, I have nothing against it. But look at what it's doing to you and Dane. You're both tormenting yourselves. For what?"

"Maybe because we want to do things right. Giving into temptation did so much for you and Alexa."

"Sarah!"

I feel horribly as soon as I say it. "I didn't mean it that way. I meant that we're both screw-ups and so what? I believe God is going to rescue me from my debauchery, because I've asked him to take it upon Himself. You're just hoping He's not noticing. But it's all right; I know you think I'm the stupid one."

"I don't think you're stupid, Sarah. But I do think some people find religion but it has no bearing on their life."

"So you think Dane and I are that way? You think we're hypocrites?"

"You've known each other for less than a month. What are you doing, Sarah Claire? He's not going to rescue you. Not going to take you away from the responsibility of your mother. That's yours to own."

I look up at Scott, my eyes wide. "I've known Dane for less than a month. It seems unimaginable. I feel like I've known him my whole life. I feel like I know what he'd do in an emergency, what he would read before bed, and what kind of future he wants. B—but really, I don't know any of that, do I? All I know is what's in my gut, and there's no logic involved in that.

"Dane means well, Sarah, but he's misguided in his ways. He thinks everyone wants to be like him, live like him. Alexa and I paid the price for that."

"What's that supposed to mean?"

"Nothing. I don't mean anything."

"You seem to be blaming Dane for you and Alexa."

"Why don't you just go to France? What's it going to hurt? Dane has the money, and I imagine with his stimulating personality, paying for companionship is not all that odd of a thing for him. Factoid about eighteenth-century operettas, anyone?"

"How can you be so cruel?"

"Is *my* mother sitting in a local jail while you have an *Out of Africa* experience with Dane in my kitchen? I told you he was off-limits; you completely ignored that. So fine—do what you think is best."

"Don't make fun of me. I got caught up in something."
The realization stuns me. "Ann and Jaime have probably
already called Yoshi. Maybe I *should* pack my bags and go
to France. It beats Sable, and if I have a ticket out of here,
France is by far the better option."

"See, Sarah, you can't trust someone because they say
they're a Christian. I've heard Ann say how her faith has
changed her life. Please. I've never heard a truly sincere
word out of that girl's mouth. And the only reason she
invited you over tonight was to get some rent out of you
for her overpriced box of an apartment. Self-serving people
ready with a sermon and their hand out."

"I never heard Ann say she was a Christian, and I don't
care why she invited me. At least she invited me. Besides,
that's not why I trust Dane. Because he's a Christian, I mean."

"Nor should it be."

The intercom buzzes frantically. I may not know Morse
code, but I know that buzz is code for *frantic*. Scott pushes
the button. "Yes?"

"Scott, it's me. Flora Fawn. Can I come up?"

"Do all your clients' names sound like porn stars?"

"Shh! She'll hear you." He pushes the button again.
"Come on up." Then he looks back at me. "Don't you
know who she is?"

"Let's just say the visual I'm getting helps me. I imagine
she knows Dr. Rey intimately?"

"She's starring in the new Spielberg movie opposite
Tom Hanks. She's a legitimate actor, and she's been on one
of the hottest TV shows with a huge following."

"Right. I'm going to bed."

"Don't you want to meet her? In six months you're not
going to have to make an appointment be able to get a
glimpse of her."

"They said that when Sable's *Rambles* became the most popular bull in the PBR too. I think I've had enough of today. It's time for it to end."

"You're really not going downtown to bail your mother out?"

"I'm really not. I'm going in my room to pray."

I walk toward my room and shut my door before the elevator opens. As I lean against it, I wonder if Dane is imagining Paris as I am. Can he see us walking the *Champs-Élysées* like Rick and Ilsa? Or is it all, once again, just a figment of my overactive imagination? Which I have to admit is better than the facts: my mom's here in jail, my would-be soul mate is locked away in his room with his hair half cut, and my best friend has gone crazy on me and can't decide whether to marry her own soul mate. Oh yeah, I need reality like I need a hole in the head. Curse my Cary Grant fast!

Failure and its accompanying misery is for the artist his most vital source of creative energy.
~ Montgomery Clift

The phone rings, but I'm deep into the Book of Romans, wondering what it must have been like for Paul the apostle to travel his whole life. He never really nested. I don't think I could do that. I'm a nester by nature; is it my fault my mom just built it in the wrong place?

Scott breaks into my musings and bellows like I'm in the apartment a few blocks over. It's nearly eleven! This house is Grand Central Station.

I pick up the line and am relieved to hear Kate's voice. "Sarah Claire?"

I sigh my relief obnoxiously loud, just so she'll know how much she's annoyed me. *What are friends for?* "Kate, you hung up on me. What's going on?"

"Sarah Claire, I'm not your mother. I'm fine. It's me. I've made a decision. I talked to Marge. Prayed over it and everything. Speaking of which, have you gotten to church yet?"

"You don't want to know. What's this about Marge?" Marge was our boss and she's pretty much what you'd think of as a Marge. Big hair, styled once back in 1979, and she liked it so much she never bothered to change it. Being the only salon in Sable for years, she unfortunately tainted the whole town with her version of styling. Big. Bigger. Perfect.

". . . and Marge can handle the entire town of Sable's thinning gray hair." Kate's been rambling for a moment now.

"What did you say?" I must be hearing things.

"I'm in a hotel in Hollywood."

"Wait a minute, you can't be here. You didn't say you were here, here."

"I did say that."

"I just talked to you on the phone last night."

"On my cell phone. I was at LAX when you called. Wow, what a fiasco that was."

I feel betrayed. I feel betrayed for Ryan and for myself. "How could you not tell me you were coming? I would have met you at the airport. What is wrong with you? Does Ryan know about this?"

"I tried to tell him, but he wouldn't listen."

My heart clenches at the thought of Ryan waking up, bringing Kate some coffee, only to find she's left town without warning. The night is gray and overcast with ocean fog, and I can't help but think there are other things awry.

"Does your mother know?"

"Sarah Claire, I just needed to get away for a little while, okay? I haven't abandoned my whole life like you have."

"Where are you?"

"I'm in Hollywood at a hotel."

"Actual Hollywood or just LA?"

"It says Hollywood on the keychain."

"Is it a dump?"

"Hmm." I can picture assessing the place. "Oh, yes, it's an incredible dump. I can see the outline of the person who was in the bed before me, and I'm just hoping they left here alive. And there's dog hair on the sheets, which I actually prefer to human hair. But there is no chalk outline of anyone, and for that I'm thankful."

I slam my Bible shut. The world has gone crazy. "Are you nuts, Kate? I can't afford for you to go nuts. You are my stability—now you're going to start acting like my mother and just taking off when you feel like it? If you were planning to come, why didn't you take a flight with me instead of scaring everyone half to death?"

"I've left Ryan, the Hideaway . . . my life, really. But I haven't made any decisions about it being permanent. I needed to get away to breathe. I can't breathe there. With all the wedding plans and the ladies at church coordinating every detail of my future, I thought I'd burst."

The world's gone mad, I say.

"Who's washing and setting Mrs. Gentry tomorrow?"

"Is that all you worry about? The salon? People's hair? My life was being written for me, Sarah Claire. Did you like that when people did it to you? When they told you what kind of person you were, whether it was true or not?"

"Of course not, but I'm worried about your fine specimen of a fiancé who is right now at home, worried sick. Or he will be when he finds out what you did. What do you mean you've left Ryan? If you're going to leave someone you have to actually tell them. It's the rule."

"He wouldn't listen."

I try to hold back my *Duh* here. "Yeah, any sane person would have told you this was a hare-brained stunt. What are you doing here? And why am I suddenly so popular that the town of Sable is immigrating to California?"

"I was coloring Mrs. Rampas's hair and she told me how lucky I was to be marrying Ryan, what a kind and gentle soul he was, and that someday he'd own the town and give your daddy a run for his money."

"And this is bad because . . . ?" I mean, should I mention that the man I have a pending date with is only around because I'm too big of a wimp to say no—both to espresso and his pushy, buff self? And that the man I *do* want to date is in the next room with really bad hair and a lingering invitation to France. That I, who had a desperate need to coif Hollywood, am suddenly wanting to learn more about antiques so I might appear brighter to his suit-clad, hot self?

Kate is still talking. ". . . I realized even the best life in Sable isn't what I want, Sarah Claire. It took you leaving to realize that without you, I've got nothing there."

"I'm asking how you found all this out now. You couldn't have figured this out when I was planning my trip?"

"When you were planning your trip, I was planning to take over your clients at the salon. I was too busy to realize I didn't want to stay either. I just took my grandmother's money, kissed my mother good-bye, and took off."

I crash back on the bed. "Explain this to Ryan, Kate. He'd go wherever you want to go. I know he would. He said so."

"No," she squeals. "You of all people should understand. Do you want to be what everyone in Sable expects you to be?"

"Well, everyone in town expects me to be the town whore, so I'm thinking no. But you're supposed to be the town's matriarch; somehow that seems better. Call me crazy. Ryan's collecting cows for you. You know that old story about the wife being worthy of ten cattle and how the guy pays more for the ugly bride because he wants her to feel worthy of ten cows? You know that story? That's totally you."

"Sarah Claire, quit it with the cows, will you?"

I shrug. "It's a good story. I want to be worth ten cows."

"Ryan is still old school. Once he even said he wouldn't have asked me to marry him if he'd known I had desires like you." She pauses before continuing, I suppose so I can grasp that Ryan thinks I'm scum too. "That you were going to end up like your mother, chasing a rainbow."

"Ryan said that about me?" *Okay, I might want to pull back my support until I know more.* "Ryan said that?"

"He didn't mean it rudely. He said he didn't want an ambitious wife; he wanted one who would stay home and be satisfied in raising a family."

"Well, that's fair. There's nothing wrong with that."

"It is fair, Sarah Claire. Only when you left, I realized it wasn't what I wanted at all. I mean, it is what I want, but I don't want it with Ryan."

I shake my head, even though she can't see me. "Kate, I have nothing else. I'm here fantasizing about my roommate and covering it up with thoughts on the Apostle Paul's travels. I'm pathetic, so I have to ask, are you certain about this?"

"I'm in a seedy motel on Franklin in Hollywood. I'm sure."

"I don't want it to be too late for you."

"The idea of ending up like Mrs. Rampas, Mrs. Piper, and even Mrs. Gentry scared the daylights out of me. What if my highlight for the week was getting my hair washed at the Hideaway? He wouldn't want me to work, Sarah Claire. He'd want me to have kids. Right away. The right man makes those things desirable. They're not desirable to me, and I had to stop and ask why while people were telling me about wedding menus and flower choices. I got more and more frightened."

"How do you know for sure? How do you know you're not just chasing a dream like Ryan says I am? You have a choice to be a Mrs. Rampas. I don't. What if you left your soul mate?"

"You're a lot of help. I had a huge compulsion to run and I ran. Would I have a compulsion if he was my soul mate?"

"You might. You can be impulsive."

"I supported you, right? When everyone laughed at your idea of coming out here, I said no, she'll be fabulous! She'll make it because she's Sarah Claire."

My chest heaves with a sigh. "You did support me. But I left my mother. You left Ryan!"

"So I have better taste than you. I always did."

"Kate . . ." I rake my hand though my hair. "My mother's in jail here because she did something at the airport. I have no idea what yet. Scott is feeling crowded, and my job at Yoshi's is anything but secure—how can you choose right now to become unstable?"

"Did I ask you for anything?"

This feels like a slap across the cheek. "Well, no, but I can hardly let you stay in that dump."

"Sarah Claire, my grandmother's money is now well over twenty-five thousand dollars. I can stay anywhere I want. If I wanted to head to the Wilshire, I could. But you know, I passed the Chinese theatre, the Galleria, the Roosevelt, and I didn't want to leave Hollywood. I wanted to experience it, so here I am. There was no one to tell me it was a stupid idea, and I did what I wanted to do. It's powerful, you know?"

"Couldn't you have experienced it *at* the Roosevelt?"

"They were full."

"Can you use some of that money to take classes at Yoshi's?"

"No, Sarah Claire. That's your shot. I'm going to use my money and play at the beach for a time, figure out what I want to do with my life. Maybe I'll go to college. Who knows? Do you think I'd be a good coed?"

I feel myself start to tear up because Kate was who I always wanted to be, and here she is mimicking my train wreck of a life. "Kate, can you come here at least? Scott won't mind."

"If you're going to do that weird thing where you look in my eyes to see if I'm telling the truth, I am. I'm young, Sarah Claire. I don't want my life laid out for me at twenty-six. I think I might go to college, major in something people would never expect of me. Maybe engineering."

"Engineering? Gosh, I want my life laid out for me." I look at the door and imagine my roommate. "In fact, if Dane came in here right now and said the elevator could take us to another era . . . if he whisked me away to a new life, I'd totally go."

"You would not."

"He wears a fedora. I totally would. He makes me believe it could work with a *have*, know what I'm saying?"

"What's a *have*? He wears a hat and you're going to bet your life on him? Maybe you should just call Al now and get a deposit in on your first bail bond."

This makes me laugh out loud. "Dang, I missed you. Get over here. Who do you think you are coming into the town where I'm living and not seeing me, you little snot."

She laughs too.

"I just don't want you ending up like your mother 'cuz a guy wears a hat, know what I'm saying?"

"My mother ended up the way she did because she had an amazing ability to throw back a vodka tonic, not a hat fetish."

"Sarah Claire, you're here to be the next Vidal Sassoon . . . Focus!"

"Exactly what Scott said. Go back home, Kate. Not before you see me, but go back home. It's not what you think here. It's like sitting outside one big popular table in high school. Everyone who was homecoming queen or head cheerleader is here trying to make a living out of being beautiful. Go back home where the people are real. Where the traffic reports are not six minutes long but consist of 'Joey Billing's truck broke down again on Rocky Road. Stop and give him a jump if you can.'"

Kate's still giggling. "I need to try it, all right?" She pauses. "Wait a minute, back up. In the midst of you and your elevator fantasies, did you say your mom was here? Here in California?"

"Yeah, we know she got arrested for using false ID at LAX, but we're not sure why or where she is just yet. They arrested her in my coworker's hallway. She'd left the false ID with them. At least that's as much of the story as they'll tell me on the phone." *Granted, I haven't exactly scoured the town for her yet.* "Their police department called the sheriff when he found out there was an arrest warrant, so I got most of the story from back home."

I look at the clock.

"I've got to go get her." But in my heart I don't want to. Not one bit. I don't want to rescue her anymore if she's just going to keep living this life. I can't help her if she chooses this life.

"Ryan will follow me here," Kate says. "You know he will."

"You said he wasn't interested if you wanted a career."

"That doesn't mean he won't try to convince me of the error of my ways. I need you to do me a favor."

"Noooo," I whine. "Kate, I don't want to hurt Ryan, even if he does think I'm a loser."

"Please, Sarah Claire. You know he won't listen to me."

"I'll do it on one condition."

"You don't even know what the favor is yet."

"Like heck I don't. Kate, I' have known you since kindergarten. I know exactly what it is. Since I was five I've been doing your dirty business so that the whole town sees you as the sweet girl. Your reputation is intact."

"All right, what is it then, smartie?"

"You want me to break it off with Ryan."

She's silent.

"And give back the ring, because I know you're still wearing it," I continue. More silence. "Is there more?"

"No, that's it. I just hate you for getting it right."

"He's going to blame me anyway, but I still think it's weird you're not doing it yourself. You'll never be able to show yourself in Sable again. *I'll* never be able to show my face in Sable again. You do realize they'll say I corrupted you and that they warned your mother not to let me hang out with you."

"What's the condition? You said there was a condition."

"You have to check out of the seedy motel and get over here to Scott's. There's someone I want you to meet. I need the opinion of a trusted friend, because my logic isn't working so well at the moment."

"I hate men in hats."

"You won't hate this one."

"I'll come in the morning. I want to watch Letterman and sleep."

"I should go look for my mother anyhow." But for the first time in my life, I am truly not tempted to seek her out and fix her problem. For the first time in my life, I have something I want, and I see that my continual quest to fix Mom's issues hasn't fixed a thing. I don't want to rescue her anymore if she's just going to keep living like this. I can't help her if she chooses this life. "On second thought, maybe I'll catch Letterman too."

"It's not selfish to avoid enabling, Sarah Claire."

"It's so much easier to know what the right thing to do is when it isn't a real person. I mean, anyone else and I'd be telling them to let her go, she's never going to get out of trouble. But she's my mother, and I want to have hope. God forgive me, somehow I still have hope for her. I keep seeing her having this dramatic conversion and becoming the mom I always wanted."

"What do they put in the water out here?"

"I'll see you in the morning. Come by Yoshi's when you wake up. But you have to meet Dane. I'm not doing your dirty work until you meet Dane."

See, this is how life is: you change your life so there won't be any problems, and then all new ones crop up that you can't possibly anticipate happening. My issue is the same old issue that keeps popping up. And her name is Janey Winowski.

chapter 20

If I had my career over again?
Maybe I'd say to myself, speed it up a little.
~ James Stewart

Hoping to find solace and escape in someone's world that sucks more than mine, I reach for my ragged copy of *Camille*. The book, which I bought for a quarter at a library sale, always brings me peace. It's not exactly a happy story—it's about a courtesan (a nice French word for a kept woman or your basic high-end prostitute, but I digress) who falls in love with a young man of means, and his father asks her to leave him for the son's sake. Basically, your typical *have/have-not* love affair, and once again, the *have-not* ends up in the gutter while the *have* goes merrily along. Maybe merrily is a little harsh, but she's dead at the end, and that's definitely worse off than the young man. He is still alive and rich.

When Sable would call my mother names, I'd think of Camille, the woman who loved Armand so deeply she sacrificed everything for him only to die alone. I guess I hoped my mother would come to this place and give it all up for me. I hoped that deep in her soul it wasn't about her, and she'd dramatically tell the men it was over. She needed to be a mother!

Considering she's in jail and I'm out my latest thousand

bucks, I'd say that dream has gone up in smoke once again. Unrequited love is mine once again. The gift that keeps on giving.

Camille loved Armand with a purity of soul and his best interest in mind. (Though he never appreciated the gift until she was gone. Typical.) She proved her love in the end. That's my goal. It's so biblical, really. Didn't Rahab prove her worth? My mom is clearly not going to do it, so I'm going to try to die to self and make it up for her. I will change the direction of the Winowski family single-handedly.

I'm trying, God. I pray that counts for something.

There's a knock at my door and I throw my tattered copy of the book at the wall. I should have watched Letterman.

"Sarah Claire, come out here. I need your help." I open the door and see my cousin looking pale. "I have a hair emergency."

"Your hair looks fine."

"Not mine! Come out here."

I walk out to the living room to find a woman crying. Her hair is a pale, sickly, pond-scum shade of green. I've seen this before. It's the kind of color mishap that isn't going away with a bottle of anything, but I know better than to say that to a grieving woman. These are the moments that great hairstylists are made from.

"Did you use henna?"

She sniffles and nods. "Can you fix it? I had to wear a hat to get over here. I snuck out the back."

I walk over and finger a few strands. It's like straw. Fresh spring straw. *It's bad,* I think to myself, worse than when Carrie-Lynn went ballistic with the *Sun-In* and lemon juice. But one never wants to let someone hear their greatest fear out loud. Hair emergencies in Hollywood make a hair emergency in Wyoming look downright comical. This girl is stressed.

"Please say something," she sobs.

I give the prognosis as gently as possible. "There's no way you're ever going to get it back the way it was, and it's not strong enough to hold extensions, but that doesn't mean we don't have options. Your cheekbones give us a ton of options."

Full-blown blubbering ensues. "I have a screening for the studio tomorrow night! I've got my dress borrowed from Badgley Mischka!"

"*I've* got her dress borrowed from Badgley Mischka," Scott corrects.

"Scott, we have a hair emergency. Little easy on the ego, all right?" I mean, *really*.

"Do you have a great wig?" She sniffles. "Maybe I can just sweep it on top of my head or wear a bathing c—aa—p!" More sobbing.

"Just calm down for a minute." My voice is soothing, like a country creek. "We're going to talk options." I'm all business; it's going to do her no good if she doesn't trust me or think I'm not in complete control. "It's not going to retain any form of blonde like this." I finger a few strands to let her hear that crisp, crunchy sound. "The green is going to peek through."

"So a wig?"

"A wig is too dangerous at a premiere because there will be so many photos, and you don't know which angles you'll be taken from. It's impossible to ensure."

"She's right, Flora, we can't do a wig," Scott adds, as if he has any idea what I'm talking about. I purse my lips at him.

"If we could do extensions or a hairpiece, that might work, but I don't think your hair is strong enough for that."

More whimpering ensues.

"I think you should go shorn and dark," I say resolutely. "Cover up the problem until new hair grows out and it's strong enough to take a lighter pigment again." I shake my head slowly. It's the hairstylist's equivalent to, *I'm sorry, ma'am, there's nothing more we can do.* "I know that's not what you want to hear, but with these cheekbones and the right makeup, it's going to look like you planned this for your premiere."

She's weeping, cradling her face in her hands. "What am I going to do, Scott? I'm the *new* blonde!"

"They're calling her the next Marilyn Monroe," Scott explains.

Please. They call everyone that. And in my lifetime, there has never been another Marilyn. Nor another Elvis. Nor . . . the list goes on and on: Cary Grant, Clark Gable, William Holden . . . Hollywood needs a new line promoting their wannabes.

I try to console her by patting her shoulder and fingering her hair to see if there's some way. *Any* way. But it's not going to happen. It's toast.

"All the more reason to go dark," I reason. "You can show them you won't be boxed in to any corner. Like Madonna, you can be anyone you want to be. Blonde, brunette, redhead—you are Fawn Flora." I have to spit out the last part. *That name!*

"It's *Flora Fawn*, actually," she says quietly.

Scott rolls his eyes.

I just shrug. Is there a difference? What can I say, really? It's a stupid name. I mean, Winowski at least sounds real, am I right? "If you let me go ahead, we'll have to lift this product out of your hair. It will look worse for a while tonight. Are you willing to see it through?"

She fingers her hair. "I'm going to lose my hair!" Her face crumples into a wail.

"You already did lose your hair, Fawn—I mean Flora. We're just going to remove the dead body."

She's reduced to a loud squeal.

"Flora," Scott says with authority. "My cousin is the best. She'll make you look like a superstar. You just have to trust me. Have I ever let you down? When you said you wanted Mischka, did I not get you Mischka?"

She sniffles, nodding her head with each pout of the lip as she looks up at my cousin, the biggest liar I know and love. "Do you promise?"

This is how women end up pregnant.

"I promise you," Scott purrs.

"I'm a color-correction expert, and I've done this before. I'm going to cut your hair because I think you have such beautiful facial structure you can handle it short. Not many women can, so be grateful for that. Tomorrow night, you'll make a statement no one is expecting."

Flora has massive green-blue eyes, and even though her face is puffy and swollen from hours of crying and fretting, when she blinks, it's still heart-stoppingly beautiful. Her cheekbones look as though Michelangelo formed them from marble to commemorate God's handiwork. She has a pert, straight nose and full, round lips. This girl's hair won't make a bit of difference, but I'm only too happy to fix it for her.

"Generally, this would take a few visits. I'd pull the product out, have you come back and put something in. I don't know if your hair is going to hold any color, so I want to treat that as well. We're going to have a long night. Are you ready for it?"

"Do I have a choice?"

"Actually, no."

I take the mirror away from her, but this being my cousin's house, there is no shortage of them. Dane comes walking out of his room, and Flora puts her elbows around her head. "Who's that?"

"It's just Lurch, my roommate. Don't worry; he has no idea who you are. He's only interested in people and things that have been dead for a few centuries."

Not quite, I think to myself with a smile.

Dane gives him a dirty look and takes his sideways haircut into the kitchen, grasping a glass. "You didn't cut his hair, did you?" Flora cries.

"No, she didn't," Scott interjects.

"I'll get what product I have." Luckily, I bought some, and it's not organic. Organic is what caused this disaster. In situations like these, a girl needs chemicals! Better living though toxicity.

"I have a ton in the master bathroom."

"Of course you do." I shake my head at Scott. "I have what I need. I brought it for the color codes to compare to Yoshi's products."

"Oh, you cut for Yoshi." Flora exhales loudly. "I thought you were just some chop-shop girl."

I'll ignore that. "You're going to have to devote your week to this, I'm afraid. I'll get you set up for tomorrow, but it's going to take a few visits to get it right. I'm going to spray you tomorrow night with something to make sure you don't lose color, but you'll want to be careful the rest of that evening. Stay away from water, and don't put any product in your hair after I finish."

"I promise. Whatever you say. Just fix it."

"First, like I said, I'm going to lift the color and see what we have, just to make sure we need to cut it. If we can keep it, we will."

I head into my bedroom and pull out all the product.

"You'll need to be at the showing?" my cousin asks me when I reenter.

My first thought is of clothes. As in I have none, and going to a Hollywood anything is not in my wardrobe vocabulary. But taking a look at Flora's hair and then my cousin's concern over his own career, I have my answer. "I just need to be outside of it. She'll be fine for a few hours." It's not brain surgery, but this girl's hair obviously means way too much to both my cousin and, consequently, me. And Yoshi, if word gets out.

"I'm going to get you a ticket, just in case. This gal is my cash cow, Sarah Claire. You can't screw this up. She's got a percentage in this movie, unheard of at her level. If the buzz is good, I am set for a long time."

"Thanks for keeping the pressure off." I gather up the bottles and cradle them in my arms. "I'll keep your client gorgeous, but . . . I need to find my mother before I get started."

Scott whips his head back and forth. "No."

"What do you mean, *no?*"

"I'm putting my foot down here. She's sat in jail many a night, Sarah Claire; she's not going to mess this up for us. Not this time. It's not going to kill her to be there, and at least you know she's safe."

What he says sounds completely reasonable. But I told myself I was going to do this. "It's just a phone call."

"It's not, Sarah Claire, because after she's manipulated you on the phone, you'll want to go downtown and take my checkbook, and I'm saying 'enough.' She's sat in jail before."

"With the Sable sheriff and Al, her personal bail bondsman. It's not like she's in her element at the LA county jail. They'll eat her alive."

He taps his foot. "They'll eat your mother alive?"

"All right, maybe they won't, but she'll still want out."

"Then she should have thought of that before she snuck past LAX security."

"How do you know what she did?"

"She already called here, looking for bail."

"And you hung up on her? She gets one phone call, Scott!"

Dane comes up, holding a glass of water in his hand. I clamp my mouth shut about my mother. It's one thing that he's a *have*, it's another altogether to reiterate my *have-not* status complete with police action.

"I'm sorry I was rude earlier, Sarah," he says without preamble.

"No, that's okay. It's me that owes you the apology. I was agitated. I'll finish your hair when I'm done with Fawn."

"Flora!"

"Whatever."

Dane looks over at the once-blonde bombshell, and his eyes linger a bit too long for my liking. "I'm not in a hurry." He takes a long, slow drink from his water and wanders off.

"Do you have any mineral oil, Scott?"

"Mineral oil?"

"Like baby oil. Do you have any?"

"I think so." He runs toward his *Sephora* bedroom.

"And sterile cotton balls!" I yell after him.

Dane is standing in the kitchen, and I'm ready to usher him right back into his bedroom. "So you'll let me finish that?" I look at his head.

"I like it this way," he says dryly and goes into his room, slamming the door.

Men.

My cousin returns, and I fan my hair cape around the crying beauty. I coat Flora's hair with rubbing alcohol. "This is just the first step. I'm sorry it smells, but beauty is hard work. Why did you do this, anyway?"

"Scott told me I could benefit from brighter highlights. When I couldn't get into my salon, I thought I'd try henna at home."

I purse my lips at Scott, and he just shrugs and mouths the words, *"I wanted her to come to you."* Then he turns toward Flora. "Homemade highlights the night before an opening? You had to know I wasn't suggesting that!"

Three hair disasters in two days and I'm to blame for all of them. Hairstylist to the stars, my foot.

I coat her hair with mineral oil and follow with a lifting product, hoping her hair will feel soft and shine again, but no luck. She still looks like a bleach-bottle blonde with stringy, lifeless locks. "I'm going to have to cut it."

I let Flora go into the bathroom and have a good cry. When she comes out, she nods as if being led down the gangplank in the middle of the Pacific. "Let's just do it."

"I have some hair vitamins from Yoshi. They won't help instantly, but they will provide you with the right nutrients to help your hair grow back healthier than ever."

"Thanks . . . I just realized—" She bats her big eyes at me. "—I don't even know your name."

"Sarah Winston. I'm Scott's cousin." I finger her fried hair and change my opinion. "I think I could color it blonde again, but I still recommend you go darker because it has the oddest green tint to it that I don't think the blonde will cover. I've never seen this color green with henna. It's not a good sign for how your hair might react."

"Just do what you need to." She clasps her eyes shut as if I'm going to inflict bodily harm. Being in Hollywood and "cutting her crown," I imagine I am.

It pains me to do it. Pains me even more to know I can't use these long, formerly gorgeous locks for Locks of Love. But the hair is gone, and there's no sense crying over spilled milk. I take my first cut and Flora wails at seeing it land on Scott's kitchen floor.

"You're going to be gorgeous. Your cheekbones were made for short hair."

Another snip. Another wail. Another compliment. 'Tis the cycle of these things.

Dane has returned to get himself a new glass of water and meets my gaze. Must he walk around like this? Does Flora really need an audience at the moment? She doesn't need to know he's walking around with his haphazard haircut courtesy of me. Of course, he's the one who walked off in a huff like a big baby.

"I like it better short," Dane tells Flora, looking directly at her with his dimples. *My dimples!*

Flora looks up at him and smiles coyly. A surge of jealously rushes through my system, and I steady my hand to keep from chopping off the rest of it and giving the two of them matching haircuts.

"Thanks, even if it isn't the truth." She runs her hand through her cropped hair. I hate that she looks darling without hair. Granted, that's my job, but at the moment, I'm not feeling it. "Do you really like it?"

Oh shut up. Really now. Why don't you ask her about your

dead president, Dane? See if she knows he was our president, or if she just knows him from a five-dollar bill. I can hear her giggling now: "Oooh, it's Abe Lincoln. I just love that he didn't cut down the cherry tree."

And Dane with his dry laughter: "Now, honey, that was George Washington and there's no proof he ever did that."

Gag.

I keep snipping away, using my razor scissors to cut some jagged edges and give Flora a harder, more contemporary look.

"You're known for being the 'girl next door' in your movies?" I ask, and sure, I don't exactly feel Christian asking it because she doesn't exactly exude girl-next-door qualities. Although at the moment, I could say my life doesn't look much different from someone who professes to be an atheist, so who I am I to talk?

But why Dane? Why does she have to flirt with Dane? Why do I have to watch it? *Ask me how generous I feel at the moment.*

There are, after all, two men in the room. So my cousin's done his idle best to perpetuate the gay myth; he can't act macho for a minute? But I suppose you *want* a man to be gay when he's stuffing rubber cutlets in your bra.

I'm sure when he and Alexa broke up, the Hollywood who knew Scott confirmed their suspicions. But I thought women liked the challenge of a gay man anyway. Didn't Elizabeth Taylor pine after Montgomery Clift for years?

"Would you like something to drink?" Dane asks her, lifting his glass of water.

I smack my tongue a bit to show I myself am parched, but Dane doesn't offer *me* anything.

"I'd love a water. Do you have any Evian?"

French water. They tell me the entire city of Paris smells like urine, and people want to import their water. *Come to Wyoming, people! I'll give you water.*

"I import French antiques. I spend a lot of time there, so no, we don't have any Evian." He laughs. "We have some Pellingrino."

We have some Pellingrino, I mimic soundlessly.

"Did you say something, Sarah?" Dane asks me.

"Just humming." This razor is feeling itchy. What was that about the *Barber of Seville*?

Why I feel any ownership of a man I've known for a few short weeks is beyond me, but if I could brand him with a big "S" I probably would. It probably has something to do with the wild PDA on Rodeo Drive, but I'm thinking it was that first moment he came out of the elevator. I need an hour of confession just for the last five minutes alone. Out of fellowship. Out of resources.

It takes me a long time to get the razor though all the strands and shape Flora's hair. It's thick and the straw consistency is not making the razor cut any easier. I've made scarecrows easier than this. After I clip my last piece and watch it flutter to the floor, I look at Flora to ensure the cut is even. This is the part Dane walked out on, and if he doesn't let me get back to it, I doubt anyone is going to buy antiques from his crooked-headed self.

Next up is the dye for Flora's hair, and I paint it on generously and wrap her head up in plastic and foils. Not because she needs them, but it makes me feel better to see her looking not quite as perfect. She's looking anything but the Hollywood starlet, and still Dane hasn't noticed. He's milling about, bringing sparkling water and ignoring that dead president altogether.

"Don't you have a little history to bone up on, Dane?"

"Me?" he asks. "No, why?"

I shrug. "Just thought you had some reading to do."

"I can read it on the plane."

Yes, I'm sure you can, but I really wasn't concerned about you finishing your biography.

He's leaning over the counter, with Flora carrying on a conversation as though I'm merely the hired help, not anyone to include in the discussion. I try to avoid eye contact with either of them and just focus on the work, but I'm afraid he's going to ask her out right in front of me, and I just don't think I can take that. I've withstood a lot in my day, but my prayer is God won't make me endure that. Not today.

Twenty minutes later it's time to rinse Flora and see how this all turned out, but I don't want Dane to witness the "after"—not that the "before" wasn't pretty good to start with—so I keep waiting for him to leave.

"What time do you have to be to the office, Dane?" My voice is perky and yet uninterested. "Early tomorrow with your trip coming up and all?"

"I can go in anytime. That's the beauty of owning your own shop."

"Oh, you have your own shop?" Flora coos.

"It was his parents'," I interrupt.

Dane gives me the hint of a smile. He knows exactly what I'm up to, and I hate being so transparent and small.

"Well, I'll leave you girls to your beauty. I've got a biography to get to."

"I read a biography once," Flora claims.

Dane stammers at this. *Yes, Dane, she did say "once."*

"Really?" I ask. "Who was it about?"

"I can't remember. It was for a script, but it was clear I wasn't going to get the part, so I didn't finish it."

As she says this, I suddenly feel bad for her. This poor girl has had her beauty all her life, so her wits were hardly an issue. Who am I to judge? I'm Cindy Simmons for the cerebral set.

"Did the movie get made?" Scott asks.

"Yeah, it was *Capote*. He was a writer, I guess. I read for a small part, but it was clear I wasn't right for it. She was a country girl who walked in on murder victims. Anyhoo, the piece has to go and get nominated for an Academy Award. I would have tried harder had I known it would be famous, but it was about a writer. Writers are boring, so I never thought . . . no one's going to take me seriously until after this movie comes out."

"I think your new hairstyle is going to help that along. It's hard to take a confident woman with short hair for granted," Scott says.

Dane is not leaving, so I rinse Flora's hair out, grateful that the nonporous strands are accepting the color—even if it's just for a time. I condition it well and wrap her head in a towel. Back in the chair, I blow-dry her hair with a cool dryer and diffuser. And I finish with a curl-enhancing serum.

"I'm going to dry cut the rest. You need a little more texture in the cut, and I can't see how it's going to lay until it's dry."

She sniffles her answer, though it seems more for Dane's attention than her own emotion. She's still acting, as long as someone's in the audience. I pull out my texturing scissors. They have six shears and this wakes up our princess. "What are you doing with those?" She reaches for the back of her head.

"You need to thin it out a little to have it set right. These just thin the hair lengthwise instead of across. Your hair won't poof out this way. You have to trust me."

"I don't have enough hair to poof," she wails.

I finish the cut while she moans and then add some shine products. Dane watches the entire event as if he's at the premiere. Normally, at this time Yoshi would add finishing makeup to make sure the client was at her best. *Like that's going to happen.*

I smile at her and nod my head. She looks great. Oh sure, she looked great before, but now she's going to make a statement, and it won't be *Step away from the henna.*

She pats her head again. "It looks great."

"You sound surprised."

"I just have to go home and act like I planned this."

"That's where those acting skills come in. You're going to be great," Scott says.

Flora stands up and wraps me up in a bone-crushing hug. "Thank you so much, Sarah. I won't ever forget this." She releases me and looks at Dane. "Would you date a woman with hair this short?"

"Short hair is hot," he says uncomfortably. I don't think Dane is the type of person to use the word *hot.* He must have picked it up from Scott. "But everything Sarah does is hot." He winks at me from across the room.

"You'll be there tomorrow, when Scott comes to dress me?" She grabs her handbag and pushes the elevator button, looking at me over her shoulder.

"My best friend is in town—"

"And she'll be there. No problem," Scott finishes.

She rakes her hair with her free hand and nods her head. "This is going to be good, Sarah. It's going to be good." When she looks at me, I can see there are tears spilling over her long lashes, the liquid only making her blue eyes bigger and more brilliant. She actually glistens under the halogen lights in the entry hall.

She reaches out and pulls me aside to the elevator. "Listen, I've never had anything like this. It might all end tomorrow. But Sarah, I won't forget you doing this—even if it was only a favor to your cousin."

"You're going to be wonderful tomorrow night." As I say it, I realize Flora is really a sweet, young woman. She wants to be told she's beautiful and worthy, just like every one of us. I could just do without her being beautiful and worthy in my house. In front of Dane.

Before the elevator doors envelop her, Flora pushes the button to hold them open. "Are you interested in coming tomorrow night, Dane? To the screening, I mean. It's not a premiere, just a casual screening for the studio execs and the cast."

It's worse than him asking her out. See, I shouldn't have ever prayed for something negative. God's only going to show me my wicked heart and make me watch her ask *him* out.

Dane shakes his head and grabs his book again. "Thanks for the offer, Flora, but it's your night, and I haven't seen a movie since I saw *Return of the Jedi* in my jammies at the drive-in for Stephen Sweat's birthday party."

"You did not just say 'jammies.'" I'm stunned.

"Yes, Sarah, I did wear jammies back in the day and always at sleepovers. They had Darth Vadar on them, and I carried a very big flashlight in the shape of a light saber. It was the proper thing to do, you know."

"You haven't been to the movies since 1983? What planet do you live on?" Flora is incredulous. "This is Hollywood."

Dane just laughs. "Oddly enough, I don't feel I've missed a thing. No offense, of course."

"You missed *Kate & Leopold.*" I look at Flora for support. "Isn't there something so romantic about a guy traveling outside of time for you? Oh, sure, it's impossibly ridiculous, but still overwhelmingly romantic."

"I'm still getting over the fact that Dane hasn't been to the movies," Flora says. "So I take it that's a no for tomorrow night? I can get your date a ticket if you're worried about that."

Ouch. I don't care what era you're from, that's gotta hurt.

The world just drifts away when I look at Dane's brown eyes. I can hear Flora and Scott conversing, but I have no idea what they're saying. Nor do I care.

Flora looks incredible, as though her mistake was a gift from above. She is more mesmerizing than ever, and at the moment, I wish I was her.

"Sarah, you have to come tomorrow night. I want you to handle any questions about how this was planned."

Meaning: lie.

"Flora, it's your night and as I said, my best friend—" I don't want to mention I have a date. I don't want to have a date, but I have a date with a man who has trouble putting his arms down by his side. Meanwhile, I turned down an offer of Paris from Dane. Something is not right with me. This can't all be bad luck; at some point, my stupidity and blatant disregard for what I'm thinking has to come into play.

Scott practically falls over himself getting to the elevator to push the button again. "She'll be there."

I exhale as I watch Dane make his way to his room without saying good night. An hour ago I had the opportunity for France with a man I desperately want to believe can save me from a life of unrequited love. Now I have little more than I had in Sable a few weeks ago. So close and yet so very far away.

*I wish I were supernaturally strong so I
could put right everything that is wrong.*
~ Greta Garbo

As soon as Flora's gone, the realization of what I've done to my mother comes back to haunt me, and it feels like the blood at Carrie's prom. (One of my mother's boyfriends was fascinated with this cult classic—I can't ever get that image from my mind!)

My throat is tight; my stomach clenches imagining her in a dank cell somewhere in the bowels of Los Angeles. There are moments that I want to strangle her for her self-importance and blatant belief that she is above the rules. The law. But then the memories of her crying on the sofa when she'd get home from work flood my brain. I remember the messages on the answering machine every time some guy announced his abrupt departure from our lives . . . and I can't do it. I can't leave her there all alone or I'm just like them.

I grab my tattered copy of *Camille* off the floor and my woefully expensive bag from a collection of years gone by that Scott gave me. Maybe Scott is right. Maybe I should leave this book behind and start reading something with more power in it. I'm a wimp. I push the button to the elevator.

"Where are you going at this hour?" Dane comes out of his room at the sound of the elevator bell. "It's nearly one a.m."

"The day that never ends, yes, I know. I have to take care of something. If Kate, my best friend, comes by, tell her to make herself at home in my room, or I'll see her at Yoshi's."

He looks at his watch. "Sarah."

I drop my bag on the couch. "You want me to finish your haircut."

"No, I don't care about that. You're not going out in the middle of the night by yourself."

"Kate will probably just come to the salon; she's trying to make a dramatic entrance." I swallow hard as I admit the truth, which he probably knows in full anyway. "I'm going to get my mother because—" I pause. "Well, because that's what children of alkies do." I look at his big brown eyes across the room. "I left her there." I let the tears fall. Why bother hiding what I am? "I left her there in jail so I could do a starlet's hair."

"I'll take you down there. Let me get my keys."

"No, Dane, it's mine to do, and I should have done it hours ago."

He walks toward me and places his hand on the small of my back. "Let's go."

"Don't." I hate to see his sympathy, his pity. "This is my cross to bear, what God gave me in life, and I'm failing. I wanted to do what I wanted to do for a change, but you never really leave who you are anywhere."

"Who do you *think* you are exactly?" Dane looks at me with tender eyes. It's hard to believe we've only known each other a short time with all I see in his eyes. He has a way of getting right to the heart of the matter when I don't want to let him in there.

His five o'clock shadow roughs my lips when I kiss his cheek. "Thank you. I'll finish your hair in the morning. I want to do this myself."

"I'm sure you do. You have some sort of death wish, it seems."

"I beg your pardon?"

"I know you're from Wyoming, and I don't mean to scare you, but you don't walk in LA at night by yourself, and the only way you're getting a cab is if you call one. This isn't New York. If you don't want me to come, at least take my car."

I stand at the elevator, my face flushed. I want to be a woman who can take control, who marches down to the jail and bails her mother out with what's left on her measly Visa, but I can't even get down the elevator without a myriad of obstacles. The latest being I do not want to drive these streets, where cars slingshot their way toward their destinations, pausing only momentarily at red lights before rocketing onward. It's cosmic, I tell you.

Dane's still staring.

"I don't want to take your car. I'll call a cab. Is there a phone book?"

Dane grabs my wrist as the elevator opens. "We'll go in the morning, Sarah. She's probably sleeping now anyway. She needs to sleep it off, I'm assuming. You need some rest, and we'll do it in the morning. You're not thinking clearly."

I'm still sniffling. The elevator door closes again.

"You know, not all men are pigs in a blanket, and you're not the only one with a messed-up mother, all right? Some of them might hide behind a higher label of alcohol, but when they're face down in their sheets, drool lapping over the mattress, they all look the same." He shakes his head like someone who's familiar with the scenario but doesn't offer up more information. And since I've been asked too many similar questions, I don't ask any.

We drop onto the black leather sofa and he looks down at my book while I focus on his half-done hair and my unpleasant memories of him and Flora.

"Are you're going to let me fix your hair?"

"It's depressing, isn't it?"

"Your hair? I don't know if I'd call it depressing, but—"

"No, the book. *Camille* is depressing."

"Not really. It depends on your point of view. Unrequited love isn't always depressing, not when it remains in your heart. You know the adage: 'It is better to have loved and lost than never to have loved at all.'"

"She dies," he says, tapping the book. "Without her great love. Maybe I'm too practical, but even for a romantic, that's hard to take."

"Thanks for ruining it for me."

He laughs. "Your choice might make some downright suicidal, though it is refreshing to discuss *Camille* with someone who's actually read the book versus just seeing *Moulin Rouge*. That's what LA is missing: great readers."

"LA is missing more than that. You can't tell the homeless people from the business people because everyone wears those Borg cell phones in their ear. You don't know if they're talking to themselves or putting together the next big deal. It's missing normal conversation in favor of imbedded cell phones, Treos, and iPods. It's like you won't work here unless you're attached to something electronic. Everyone's chest arrives in the room before they do, and there is not one person in this town who remembers what their original hair color was."

"It takes some getting used to. Everyone's a multitasker, trying to fit in as much life as possible."

"But how do you do it? How do you actually reach people here?"

"You act as though you want to." He grins. "People are starving for attention."

"Unrequited love is not always depressing," I say, reverting to our previous conversation. *Though if it were me, it would always be depressing, albeit the Winowski way.*

"Armand wasn't worthy of her." He sits back on the couch, draping his arm over the back of it. I am calmed by his peace. Everyone else around here is too frenetic; they don't sit still unless they're getting a beauty treatment or making a deal over a meal.

"You don't think so? I mean, I don't think so either, but I'm a girl." I get up to thumb through the phone book, looking for bail bondsman and a cab.

"Are you now?" He smiles. "I hadn't noticed. If they'd married, he always would have thought himself above her and treated her as a courtesan."

"See, exactly what I was talking about earlier with the *haves* and *have-nots*. Humphrey Bogart—Rick—loved Ilsa enough to let her go and be who she was meant to be."

He stands up again and walks closer to me, "I'm more selfish than that. I don't find anything romantic about being without the woman I love."

The way he says it indicates there's something between us—the thing I've hoped for—but something stops me from daring to believe. I'm Sarah Claire Winowski. Things like love at first sight do not happen to me.

"Armand was young and impetuous in *Camille*." Inside I'm thinking, *Also stupid and completely selfish*, but I continue to stand up for Armand. After all, I spent many an evening with the man. "*Camille* died alone." I look down at the book. "That part's sad."

"Not in the movie. He comes to see her in the movie." Dane moves a little closer. "See? Hollywood isn't all bad. Of course it was Garbo. She wanted to be alone."

"I thought you didn't see movies."

"I don't see movies made after 1985. Flora's hair looked great by the way. I imagine your days of being an unknown are coming to an end."

I don't hear anything he's said about me. "Flora looks good regardless. She could be a hairless Chihuahua and she'd still have that bone structure."

"I hadn't noticed. I was too busy noticing the beautician."

I laugh at the word. "You do live in the fifties, don't you? You didn't seem like you were noticing."

"If I hadn't noticed her, she wouldn't think you were doing a good job. Am I right?"

He grins at my glare. "That sounds like a good excuse. For someone who didn't notice Flora, you sure looked close enough."

"Jealous?"

I fidget. "No." I fidget a little more. "Maybe."

"You're the one who has a date on Friday—a perfectly good day for us to go to the beach and you're eating out with someone else. Will you kiss him on Rodeo?"

"How do you know I had a date?" I want to burst into tears because I don't want a date, but I have one, and it's with the wrong man, and the right man knows. See, this kind of garbage cannot be coincidence. Somehow I am Murphy's Law come to life.

"Your cousin told me you had a date. He's trying to make sure I know you're off-limits."

"I didn't tell my cousin about my date!"

"But Jenna in your salon did."

"I didn't tell Jenna."

Dane shrugs his wide shoulders. "That I can't help you with, only to say that the world is wired here. If it happens, it's only a matter of minutes before it's broadcast. Who's your date with?"

"Aren't you going to tell me?" I ask him. "You seem to know as much as I do."

"Brad Pitt?"

"That's Saturday night. We're going to watch *Somewhere in Time* together." I wink at him.

His eyebrow cocks. "To a man, that movie is so long it's painful. It's what they should show in POW camp; men would be surrendering in droves."

"I beg your pardon."

"I'll never get those hours back, you know."

"So if I stay in Friday, I take it we're not taking the movie to the beach?"

"It's one of those movies that makes me thankful for my Christianity. I have eternity to make up for those lost hours."

"I have to go."

"So, are you going to tell me about your date? Who I need to send my guys to check out?"

"Your guys? I wasn't aware the antique business was so unseemly. Is there a Louis XVI mob?"

"You'd be surprised," he growls.

"Are you going to let me fix your hair?"

"What's wrong with it?"

"It's crooked. Didn't you look at it?"

"I'll wear a fedora tomorrow. You've done enough to-night."

"You look like a homeless person."

"In a good suit, though." He smoothes his slacks. "It's amazing what one can pull off in a good suit."

He moves closer still to me, and I look down at my shoes. "Don't, Dane."

"I'm not letting you go out in the middle of the night by yourself. I'm just not. Maybe I don't want you to fix my hair because I know who did cut it. I want to keep it this way for posterity. Tomorrow, you'll probably be famous."

"Don't tease me, Dane. You are not keeping it that way. You look ridiculous."

At his proximity, my breath quickens. I can't take my eyes off his lips, praying they'll take that last step toward mine, but he stays just far enough out of reach to where I'd have to make the first move. And I am not that kind of girl. I pull away.

"And that, Sarah—," referring to my distance "—is why I can wait. It's late. You're beautiful and vulnerable at the moment, if I may say so. I'm only human."

"You think I'm vulnerable?" I ask, wondering what kind of woman wouldn't be vulnerable to a man who looked like him in a suit, inviting her to Paris with all the right words. Not to mention the added benefit of sleeping down the hall from me. I don't call that vulnerable. That's just lucky in my book.

"Your mother coming to town," he reminds me. "Your best friend?"

"Oh, right."

"Having to cut off all the hair of one of Hollywood's beautiful starlets? That didn't make you vulnerable?"

"She's not *that* beautiful." I'm not above fishing for a compliment, and Dane had better take the bait.

"I meant according to Hollywood, not my own assessment. I just used her presence to make mine known to you."

He shoots. He scores!

"I can't stand it. Sit over there." I point, and I'm not taking no for an answer. He ambles over to the stool, and I start fixing his hair—trying not to touch him. It's like he has rabies.

"I can't talk much about cattle drives, so we have to stick to my strong suit. My parents traveled all over when I was young. Books were all I had while they did business."

"Me too. Well, that and the old movies. They were all I could get at the library." Of course, I leave out the fact that it was because my mother was drunk half my childhood. *We'll save the happy memories for later.*

"I think being rich is overrated. You put too much stock in money solving your problems."

I let out a labored sigh as I check the cut for evenness. "People with money always say that."

"Someday you'll see. I knew your cousin before he made money. He was happier then. He just wasn't as busy."

"He likes to be busy. Everyone here does. It's a way of avoiding actual relational contact." Setting down the scissors and refraining from running my fingers through his hair yet again, I step back. "You're done."

He stands up without even acknowledging I've fixed the avalanche that was his lopsided haircut. "I've delivered furniture to a lot of very wealthy, unhappy homes."

"Not all of them are unhappy. You know, I'd like to try a little of that unhappiness. They say youth is wasted on the young? I say money is wasted on the rich. Those people are pathetic. The world isat their fingertips, and they whine that things aren't perfect." I pick up the phone book again.

"Not all poor people are unhappy either." He takes the book from me and opens the cover, fanning through the pages. "In fact, I've known more happy poor people than happy rich people. Happy is a state of mind."

"Maybe you're just hanging out with the wrong rich people."

He smiles that devastating grin. "So tell me, are *you* happy, Sarah?"

"I'm happy and poor; does that bode well for your research? Well, except for my mother's issues still outstanding. And my best friend skipping out on her fiancé and she wanting me to give his ring back. And the fact that I have a quarter for a father. Okay, so I'm not entirely happy; you've proven your point, I guess."

"If I paid to fix your mother's problems, would you be happy?"

"No, because then I'd be in debt."

"Exactly!" He points at me. "It's always going to be something."

"No, that's not it at all." I cross my arms, angry he tricked me. "You're going to be happy with your mother sitting in a LA jail? I don't think so."

"She's safe. Right?"

"I still can't leave her there. She's my mother. At least in Sable I know the sheriff is going to take care of her. She's probably just another number here and—" I pause, looking into his dark eyes. "I don't want to talk about this."

"Why not?"

"It's personal."

"It's actually a matter of public record. So technically, not all that personal."

"Stop it! It's personal to me. Stop twisting my words around like a television lawyer. I have guilt, okay? I'm entitled to a little guilt today. I'm here in a penthouse suite and my mother's in jail."

"Your mother did something illegal and she's paying

for it. Hasn't she watched the news? You don't evade LAX security and expect to get away with it. She's lucky she wasn't shot. Why should you have guilt?"

I'm about to argue the point, but instead I say, "Well, duh?"

Dane starts to laugh. "'Duh'? That's your debate?"

"You're telling me if you had everything right now, and your daddy did something—let's say he stole some antiquity from Europe and now he's in jail awaiting extradition to France—"

"France's justice system is liberal. He'd be all right."

"Change it to China—he's imported an internationally famous statue of Buddha out of perfect jade, and he's in jail. You're going to just go to the beach like nothing happened?"

"I'm not going to sit and feel personally guilty about it. I either can do something about it, or I can't. And you can't, Sarah. But if you feel more comfortable with a shawl of guilt, you go right ahead. I won't stop you."

"I'm going to call the jail." I head toward my bedroom.

Before I can do anything, though, I hear Scott coming back in, having delivered Flora. I open my door a tad and look down the hallway, eavesdropping.

"Dude, I see the way you're looking at my cousin. Get over it, you hear me. You're better off with Flora."

Dane shakes his head. "Whatever."

"I told you she wouldn't go to the beach with you. She's not that kind of girl, and like I said, she's off-limits. What part of that did you miss?"

"The part where you run my life just because you're letting me live here," Dane fires back.

The briefest blip of guilt fires through my brain, and I think to myself that I should close the door, but the thought is quickly extinguished by the desire to know what they're talking about. Is Scott going to tell Dane who we are in Sable? What would Dane's family think of me if they knew?

"I told you my cousin was off-limits. I told you that plain and simple. You two are wrong for each other—wrong, do you understand?"

I don't know why my heart's pounding. This is all information I know, but to hear it so blatantly laid out for Dane. That I'm no good—and coming from Scott, it's excruciating. He changed his course; why would he stop me from changing mine?

In *Camille,* Marguerite ran away from her abusive, dysfunctional family. Clearly, I didn't run far enough. The gutters of Paris are calling . . .

I'm tossing that book. It always did depress me. When I'm tempted to reread it, I'm going to grab *Pillow Talk* instead and cheer myself up.

chapter

I'll cry tomorrow.
~ Susan Hayward

Kate walks into Yoshi's as though she owns the place. She ambles right past Jenna without even stopping to explain herself. I see her from the shampoo room and laugh out loud.

"You have no respect," I say when she meets me.

"It's a hair salon, not lockdown."

"It's Beverly Hills. People want it to feel exclusive."

"Yeah, well, whatever. Show me around. The receptionist looked at me funny."

"She's an office manager."

Kate rolls her eyes. "I assume she puts her pants on like me." She looks back at the reception desk. "Albeit a little lower on the hips."

"It's the style here, and Jenna has been very good to me, right from the start."

Kate looks back again. "All right, do you want me to invite her to be in my wedding, or what?"

"I thought there wasn't going to be a wedding."

"Oh, right. Before I forget." She hands me a grey velvet box.

"You're really not going to give this back appropriately?"

"He'll just try to tell me I'm making a mistake."

"And what if you are?" I ask her.

"I need more time. You don't have to give it back to him yet. He doesn't even need to know you have it. Let me stall a little, that's all." Kate makes herself right at home in Yoshi's, opening cabinets and even the door to Yoshi's office.

"May I help you?" I hear him bellow.

"Sorry, thought this was the bathroom." She smiles and closes the door behind him. "That him?"

"That's him."

"How did he know I wasn't a client?"

"You don't have Barbie skin."

"Yeah, what's up with that? Why does everyone look like that? Are pores illegal here?"

"It's the chemical peels and Retin-A in massive doses slopped onto their skin. They run down to Mexico if their doctors won't give them enough of it. The skin cancer rate here has got to be phenomenal. They say it's the sun, but it's totally that they peel off their top layer of skin."

"Well, the salon is gorgeous. I've gotta run. I'm going to Newport Beach today, and I want to make sure I have the whole day."

Kate is like a stranger to me right now. She's never done anything on her own, and now it seems as though she's allergic to anyone who tries to get near her. "You know, getting cold feet about the wedding is perfectly normal. But you don't have to escape *me*, do you?"

"Sarah, you know how everyone in Sable knows exactly how everyone is going to react to something. If your mother is in jail, for example. Al bails her out, he puts her in the holding tank until she's sober, and then the next day starts again. The sheriff usually lets it slide, acts like she hasn't been in there a million times, like she's not driving a bullet with someone's name on it."

"Is there a point about you in this?"

"I don't want to be the kind of person who just fits into life, the kind of person who is going to wear the blue sweater on Tuesday. The person who will bring the potato salad to the church picnic—not the snickerdoodles, not the pecan pie, but always the potato salad."

"You make good potato salad."

"I do make good potato salad, but I don't want to have to make potato salad."

"So this is about salad? Make a noodle salad."

"Yeah, that will change my life. A noodle salad. Why didn't I think of that and save myself some hassle?"

"People are ridiculous."

"What's that supposed to mean?" Kate's arms cross in rebellion.

"It means if we don't have real problems, we have to make some up. That's not a real problem, Kate."

"You're trying to tell me the need for organic shampoo is real? The need for Yoshi in there to have a spotless garbage can—that's real?"

"Shh. He'll hear you." I look to Jenna to see if she's heard, and I notice Dane talking to her. "What's Dane doing here?"

"Dane!" Kate exclaims loudly enough for him to hear. His head turns in our direction. "Dang, girl!"

"I know. Can you blame me?"

"Ingrid Bergman wouldn't blame you."

We look at each other and giggle like we're in fifth grade as Dane approaches us. I pull them both into a shampoo room before Yoshi comes out and accuses me of having a social gathering on his time. "What are you doing here?"

He holds up a paper bag. "You forgot your lunch. I thought you might get hungry."

"Oh my gosh, that is so cute," Kate says. "He brought you your little lunch. Is it peanut butter and jelly?"

"Shut up, Kate. Dane, this is my best friend, Kate Halligan."

"From Wyoming?" Dane asks.

She nods and they shake hands. "It's a pleasure to meet you. I've heard so much about you and your hat." She clears her throat as I slap her gently. "Don't hit me, Sarah Claire. It's rude."

Dane laughs.

"You have to ignore her."

"So how did you two cuties meet?" Kate asks, knowing full well how we met.

"I'm living temporarily with Scott," Dane says, his lips curving.

"Because you're unemployed?"

"I am gainfully employed, but I'm getting my house renovated. I graduated summa cum laude from Missouri State in classical studies with a major in antiquities. I have a clean credit report. I'm up to date on all my vaccinations, and I plan to take Sarah Claire to church with me at Mosaic in downtown Los Angeles. I don't have a dog because I travel too much, but I have excellent dental hygiene and I floss daily. Anything else I can clear up for you, Kate?"

She shakes her head. It's the most hilarious stunned silence I've ever witnessed.

"Thank you for bringing my lunch." I take the bag from him and he pauses for a moment before kissing me on the cheek.

"See you later. Bye, Kate, it was a pleasure."

"No one flosses daily," Kate says as Dane walks out.

"He kissed you. That was not the look of a man playing around."

"You sound disappointed. Did you think he would be?"

"Just be careful." Kate's eyes thin as she watches him exit the door. "You haven't known him very long, and he looks at you like he knows who you are inside. I don't like it. It's too much, too fast. No one knows you that well except me."

"You better get on the road to Newport Beach. I have to locate my mother this morning, and there are toilet seats to be managed." I start to line up the shampoo shelves then realize what's made me angry about Kate coming here and noticing what she perceives as a character flaw in Dane. "You know, Kate, you're not the only one who doesn't want to be pigeonholed. Maybe Dane sees who I really am, not Jane Winowski's daughter."

Kate rolls her eyes. "I gotta go. See you tonight after work . . . maybe."

She brushes out as casually as she walked in here while I stand there with teeth clenched. But then it occurs to me: Kate Halligan is jealous of me. As ridiculous as it seems, I'd know that emotion anywhere. I've lived with it my entire life.

Almost every girl falls in love with the
wrong man, I suppose it's part of growing up.
~ Natalie Wood

The screening is a pre-premiere, without most of the glitz and glamour. The purpose being to quietly screen the film for investors and pray they're happy with the outcome. It's about starting film buzz, and it's when Hollywood tends to get religious (because there are a lot of prayers said before a screening). I say this as though I'm thoroughly unimpressed with the event. Blasé even. But I've never witnessed such a sparkling event where the people all seem beautiful and confident. They walk like everyone is watching them, and the fact is everyone can't be watching everyone, so it's interesting to see who they do watch. I'm watching Flora. Her hairstyle will be the talk of the town tomorrow, and what they say will have a distinct effect on my career. No pressure or anything.

"Oh, my gosh. Rob Thomas!" I squeal.

"He wrote the soundtrack. Sarah, you have to maintain," Scott says calmly.

"I love Rob Thomas!" I scream this a little too loud because he turns around and waves. "That." I point to Rob. "That right there was the highlight of my life."

"Which is beyond sad."

"And yet so realistic," I say. "This would have been so much more fun with Kate." I harrumph. "She would have stargazed with me and acted appropriately. You act like they don't love it. They're here, aren't they? They're posing for the cameras. Look at Rob Thomas's wife—you're going to tell me he's not proud as heck to have her on his arm? They look like a wedding-cake couple."

"You're here for Flora's hair; would you pay attention to her? Isn't it bad enough you had to bring your date along?"

"Yes, yes it is," I say, looking at Nick Harper handing out business cards. *At least he's wearing a shirt.*

"Where did you find that loser?"

"He sort of found me, crying on Cary Grant's star."

"I don't even want to know."

"No, you don't, but if you hadn't said Dane was off-limits, I'd have a decent date for tonight, and he's really very nice."

"Dane is off-limits for your own good. I can't imagine why you don't trust me on things."

"Because your room is a torture chamber of under-garments, perhaps?"

"I know you both well. Don't you think if I thought you'd be right for each other, I would have said something. I'd like you to break the family curse, Sarah. I think you're the perfect candidate to do so, but not with Dane."

"I'm just appalled that you think your opinion matters that much, that's all."

"You both can do better."

I smirk at Scott and turn my attention back to the stars milling for attention. Man, it's like a high school prom gone awry. There are familiar faces and some unfamiliar, walking up a red carpet, all dressed to the nines, and they pause, in obviously well-practiced poses, when they reach the white tack paper with sponsors' names written on them.

A collective gasp is heard through the crowd, and I see Flora approach. As I look around the crowd, I see she has everyone's attention, but I'm still unsure if it's good attention or if the hair is a complete flop. I hear the words *blonde* and *brunette* shouted with surprise, and I wait to hear their assessment as I stand behind the press. *Please let them love it. Please let them love it.*

"Flora! Flora!" A blonde nestled snugly into a creamy mermaid-shaped gown waddles toward Flora. "Sydney Carlson, *Hollywood Tonight.* The hair! We love the hair!"

Flora runs her fingers through her short crop, and all I can think is *Please, color, stay on. Please, what's left, stay there.* Isn't that how we are? One prayer is answered and we immediately go to the next.

"Isn't it great?" She throws a hand like she's talking to her best girlfriend. "I'm telling you, Sarah Winston at Yoshi's is, like, a total genius." She points to the camera. "And don't you all be calling at once. She's so mine. Get in line!" She runs her hands through her hair again.

I could kiss her.

Immediately, there is press by my side, and I turn and see why. Scott is pointing at me. "Yes, yes, this is her. The creator of the new look."

Whatever happens in my lifetime from here on out, Flora Fawn made me a success today. (Well, her and Rob Thomas.) I will always be able to say my hair was recognized on *Hollywood Tonight.* It's the Oscars for me right now, and I'm ready to thank everyone who made it possible, but then I look over and see my date unbuttoning his shirt and flexing his pecs and all joy drains from my face. He's not doing that! He's not. He seemed so normal.

Flora walks toward me and the reporters get their pens ready. "You did more for me than my hair, Sarah. You gave me my confidence back. This is your moment, and I will not shrink from saying your name at every possible opportunity tonight." She winks at me and heads into the awards ceremony. I turn away from my date, who is preening in front of the one journalist who will listen. Probably community television.

"Miss Winston," all the reporters say in unison. I feel the tears falling down my cheeks, and I try to take a hint from Flora and pull it together and field their questions like I'm Mike McCurry.

"We understand from Flora's stylist, Scott Baker, that this is the creator of Flora's hair. How many people will be heading into their salons tomorrow for this cut, Scott?" Sydney thrusts a microphone in front of me.

"I—uh—" I panic. It's my moment in the sun and I blow it.

Once again Scott rescues me. "As Hollywood's leading stylist, I should warn the women of America not everyone has the confidence to pull this style off. Flora is confidence personified. She's like Rambo in an evening gown." He laughs and Sydney joins him.

Sydney pulls me closer toward her, and I see the red light on the camera. It feels like all the blood in my body has drained away, and I know Sydney is talking to me. Again. She's giving me another chance to make an idiot out of myself. She's asking me something, but my heartbeat drowns out any sound.

Scott nods. "She is a genius with shears. Yoshi brought her to Beverly Hills because he knows how to find talent."

"Well, Sarah, a pleasure to meet you, and I'll have to get your number when my hairstylist isn't listening," she jokes.

I said nothing.

I did nothing.

I dreamed of that moment for a lifetime, and when it came, I did nothing.

I am a Winowski forever.

At this point I'm thrust in front of the paparazzi and my picture is snapped about a bajillion times. At least there are no microphones. As a deer in the headlights, this works for me. It's all surreal, so it feels like a dream when I suddenly see Nick, my date on the red carpet, coming toward me. His shirt is buttoned, thank heavens. Isn't it my luck to have a date who makes me want to flee? I want to run, but there's nowhere to go; Spielberg is coming, and as the throng of photographers rapidly loses interest in us, we're pushed toward the back. A screening is supposed to be a quiet affair. I think this is what buzz looks like. My hairstyle is going to be seen everywhere!

Nick comes up beside me and puts his arm around me while the photographers take pictures. I could die. *Go away. What is Dane going to say tomorrow?*

This can't be happening. But somehow it is. At least it can't get any worse.

I look over and see Alexa. She's standing at the edge of the crowd with a hot young model-type on her arm. *It's worse.* "Scott."

"Just a minute, Sarah."

"Scott, I think you should look at something."

"Busy, Sarah," he says through his clenched smile.

"Alexa's here." Somehow she managed to finagle an invitation tonight.

Scott's eyes narrow as he sees Alexa, and his eyes flash at the sight of her date. "Stay here, Sarah. Go and check Flora's hair."

"Nick Harper, trainer to the stars. That's H-A-R-P-E-R. Smile pretty, darling." Nick leans his cheek in next to mine and flashes his toothy grin.

"Excuse me, Nick."

The press somehow takes this as me wanting to talk. "Miss Winston, can you tell us the styling products used on Miss Fawn's hair?"

"The color?" Another reporter asks.

"What were you trying to accomplish with this look?"

I see Alexa tug at her ring and my cousin pulling her away from her date. They're definitely having words and I'm hopeful. I pray he might see what he stands to lose. Or at least that she'll get her answer.

I watch my cousin beleaguer Alexa and her date walks away. Scott is very aware of the press around him and is trying to make it look like the friendliest of exchanges, but I can feel the tension from here. And in that instant I vow I won't let that happen to me. I won't let misunderstanding and pride come between me and my true love. Right or wrong, appropriate timing or no, I'm in love with Dane Weston. He was meant to be my husband, and I don't care if he's a *have* or if he has nothing. He's the one God meant for me. I know it. As surely as Flora is not the next Marilyn Monroe, I am the next—the only—Mrs. Dane Weston.

"Flora's hair is fabulous. She wanted to try something different, not be pigeonholed. She's an adventuress, willing to take risks. That's why Spielberg believed in her for this role. All Flora's products will be Yoshi of Beverly Hills." Of course, I used cheap, chemical product on Flora, but all upkeep will be Yoshi, and I'll be a person of my word.

I have no idea where that little surge of publicist came, but all I can think of is getting home to Dane before my cousin ruins everything and I lose my nerve.

Scott's face is now red, and I watch as Alexa sashays away with her gorgeous date on her arm. The ring is still on her finger as she moves toward the theater, and Scott looks as though he might explode. But he catches himself and breaks into a huge smile for a nearby camera. At the same moment I feel an arm slip around me. Nick Harper is looking for his moment. My wretched date talks to Sydney as the *Hollywood Tonight* camera's red light comes on.

"Funniest story. She was sobbing on Cary Grant's star. How could I have known she was a hair genius? She has no shoes on because her heels were bothering her, and she'd just passed by my gym! 'Of all the gin joints in all the world—'"

"No," I stammer, shaking my head, but I see from Nick's expression he's been in the background long enough. He wants his opportunity to shine.

I look straight at Sydney. "Nick is too humble. He was running near Hollywood and Vine, and he works his clients hard. He didn't get this body sitting still."

Sydney reaches out and clutches Nick's bicep and I see a moment to escape to Alexa, but as I move she turns her attention back to me. "Well, I certainly see that your girlfriend is camera shy. She's definitely content to be in the background. Back to you in the studio, Kim." With a shake of her head, she and the cameraman move on.

"I have to go, Nick. I have to make sure the hair is okay. I'm sorry to abandon you tonight."

"No, no. I'm thankful for it, actually. If it brings me even one client, maybe I can be on my way."

"I'm in love with someone."

He laughs. "Since last week?"

I nod. "It's a long story, but—"

"It can't be that long if it happened in the last week."

"I'm allowing myself to admit what I want even if I don't get it, but please, pray I'll get it." Without a backward glance, I extricate myself from the crowds. Scott runs toward me.

"Sarah, you've got to go into the ladies' room. Flora's losing color. Did you bring some temporary?"

"I did, but—" I point back toward where Alexa was. "Did you talk to her?"

"I can't talk to her, Sarah."

"Why not? She just wants an answer."

"Because the answer hurts, all right? I want to be able to say I can forgive her." He pushes me toward the wall to make sure no one sees our emotions high. "I want to forgive her. I love her, but I'm slime, all right? And every time I see her, she only reminds me of that. Now go find Flora! It's why you're here." He shows his backstage pass, and I'm ushered into the ladies' room, where Flora is conversing with the bathroom attendant and signing an autograph.

"Sarah, thank goodness you're here. My hair is losing color at the root. There's that green tint back again."

I just nod. "Sit down." She sits at the vanity stool, and I wrap her in a towel used for show in the bathroom and spray her hair until all the spots are covered. "You'll have to come in as soon as the movie's over. We'll need to make sure the mineral oil doesn't make you lose more color, but you need the moisture right now or it will show like straw in photographs."

"Sarah, are you all right?" Flora looks at me in the mirror, and I see my nose is red.

"I'm fine."

I paint the color on and spray it with setting spray.

"How do you know if you're in love, Flora?"

Flora's eyebrows raise. "You're asking me? I can't even get a date to my own screening." She laughs. "You might want to look into that roommate of yours. He seemed interested enough in you last night." She looks into the mirror and breathes in deep. "I'm ready." She kisses my cheek and dashes out of the restroom. I hear the hush of excitement as she walks through the crowd.

I have to reach Dane. I have to tell him, even if he turns me out flat on my ear. Whatever Scott told him, I need to tell him my truth.

I call Dane on his cell phone. No answer, so I rush out of the restroom and meet Scott. "I've got to go home before intermission."

"You're not leaving here. You'll never get back. Do you know how many limousines are back there? This is as busy as any screening I've been to. I guess that's what Spielberg will do for a movie. Besides, Dane's packing for France."

"Dane's going to France again already?"

"He'll be there when you get home. Chill."

But I can't shake the feeling I have. The feeling that this night of success—the one night I've dreamed about my whole life, to make someone so beautiful that the world noticed—is like a blip in time compared to life without Dane. Sometimes you just know. There's no proper time involved, and there's no reason. There's just this man I know was made for me.

My cell phone trills for the first time. "Dane? Oh my gosh, I'm so glad you called. I was worried."

"Sarah Claire, it's not Dane. It's Mrs. Gentry, dear."

"Mrs. Gentry, I'm sorry, it's just not a good time."

"Well, dear, what I'm calling about is very important. It needs to be said."

Exhaling deeply, I try to refocus, "What is it, Mrs. Gentry?"

"I'm in the hospital, dear."

"What? Are you all right?"

"Oh, I'm fine, but I needed to tell you something because I don't want you to hear it from anyone else, should something happen to me."

"Just a minute, Mrs. Gentry. I need to get to a quiet place. Are you going to be all right? What's happened to you? How can I pray?"

"Relax, Sarah, it's just my bad arteries; you know how they give me trouble sometimes. All that butter so many years ago."

"Should I come home? Do you need me home?"

"No, no, dear. I'm just going to have a stent put into my heart, and I needed you to hear the truth before I go into surgery, that's all."

"The truth? Mrs. Gentry, you never lied to anyone in your life." I laugh.

"Sometimes, there's the sin of omission, dear."

She has my attention now, and I slowly lower myself onto a padded bench in the theater's lobby. "Go ahead."

"This is your mother's tale to tell, and I always hoped that she would be honest with you. But since she hasn't, I feel I must."

"My mother?"

"Sarah Claire, Bud Simmons is not your father."

And just like that, I can't breathe. I struggle for each gasp of air, looking to find more oxygen. "Not my father?" I reach for the quarter I take with me everywhere as a reminder to pray for him.

"Sarah Claire, your father was my husband."

My head shakes from side to side. "No. No, Mrs. Gentry,

it was Bud Simmons. No one wanted to say because he was the head of the town, but it was Bud Simmons."

"I'm sorry, darling. I wish that were true, but my husband—well, he was an elder at the church when he got involved with your mother. She was doing some secretarial work after school, and one thing led to another . . ."

"No, Mrs. Gentry, why are you telling me this? This isn't true. Your husband was a man of God."

"A very flawed man of God, Sarah. He tried to make things right, but he knew going public would only hurt your mother more. She begged him to keep it to himself and he did, until the day he died. He told me that day."

I can't help it. I start to weep. Ugly, blubbery cries of anguish come out and I could care less who sees me. "That's why you spent so much time with me at the library?"

"I couldn't have my own children. When Albert died, Sarah, you were a part of him. All I had left. He gave me a good life, left me well cared for, but he was a weak man in many ways."

My father's name is Albert. Albert Gentry.

"How did you bear it?"

"See, that's the thing when you really love someone. You're called to love them despite their flaws."

"The Bible says you can be released from marriage for infidelity."

I hear her laugh. "Don't think I didn't consider it, but I loved Albert, and in his heart he loved me and knew he'd made a terrible mistake. Your mother wouldn't take his money. She wanted to punish him, and I can't blame her. She was barely a woman when she fell victim to her passions."

"How can you stand it? How can you think about it?"

"When you face your deepest fears . . . ? Sometimes that's how you receive your greatest blessings."

"What does that mean?"

"It means I thought my greatest fear was having a husband not be true to me. But that wasn't really true. My greatest fear was being alone. There was a time I let bitterness take root, and I threw your father out. Out of the house and out of my heart. But I didn't like who I'd become. I forgave him because it made me a better person. And out of my greatest trial I received one of my greatest triumphs—you in my life and a man who I knew would spend his life trying to prove his love."

"I'm praying for your surgery, Mrs. Gentry. I've got to go."

"I'll call you when I'm out, dear. Don't do anything rash. This is a lot to digest, and I'm so sorry I had to tell you over the phone. But I couldn't go into surgery without a clear conscience, and this heart just acts up too much. Tell Dane thank you for this number, and find yourself a decent living situation, young lady."

❧

The movie goes on forever, and I pace the Kodak Theatre until I'm sure I've worn down the carpet. My cell phone trills again, and I pray that it's Dane, but it's Yoshi. Dane is home taking messages for me and passing on my cell number.

"Sarah, excellent work on Miss Fawn. I knew you had what it took," Yoshi says, but I'm shell-shocked. I can't even appreciate his cold words of praise.

"Tell that to the poor model with an alfalfa sprout," I say. After news of my father, I hardly have time to care what Yoshi thinks.

"That was my fault, and she'll learn to overcome her flaws for the camera. It was a positive thing for her."

Yeah, sure it was. "Yoshi, I'm sort of busy. Can I help you with something?" *Did I forget and leave the toilet seat up after one of your rude male clients?*

"Sarah, I just wanted you to know I'm promoting you to master stylist; we'll sneak in private classes after hours. As far as anyone is concerned, you're a Yoshi master stylist. I'll be sure you're licensed by the end of the month."

"Thank you, sir." I let out the sob I've been holding inside. I know this is totally about Yoshi and someone else stealing me before he can get to me, but I'm still grateful. Yoshi brought me here and I feel loyalty to him, even if I did get on a first-name basis with the toilet.

"We'll see you in the morning."

The phone clicks as I emerge from the restroom. I see Scott across the room.

"Scott, please, can you finish Flora's hair for the night? I have to get home to Dane. I think he's mad at me."

"No. This is your night; this is what it's all about. You have to be seen with Flora for the rest of the night. Sarah, this is what you came here for."

"Oh, yeah." I look down at the carpet. "It is, isn't it?"

My cousin suddenly dashes into the men's room. Startled, I look up and see Alexa coming toward me. At this point in the evening, I'm too exhausted to show more than mild surprise as the leggy blonde stops in front of me, clad in a stunning shimmery gown. *This is just too surreal.*

"He did not really just do that," she says as the door shuts behind Scott.

"What are you doing here? I saw you with Scott earlier."

She grimaces. "Believe it or not, I accepted a date with someone connected to the movie just so I could try to talk to Scott. Pathetic, I know, and a lot of good it did me. It took me forever to find someone coming here."

I refrain from agreeing and we stand a minute looking at the bathroom door Scott escaped behind. Finally, a sigh ruffles out of Alexa. With a nod, she pulls off her engagement ring.

"I give up. He's obviously not going to see me. Give the ring back for me, will you, Sarah? You know him—I trust you to do it right."

"Are you going to tell me what happened?" I say, clasping the giant diamond.

She laughs. "It's funny, if you think about it. Ironic. Scott told me that he didn't want to be a father, that he came from a long line of terrible parents and he didn't want to bring a child into this world."

"He's wrong. Scott and I are excellent parents. We've already done it once for our own parents."

She smiles, her fantastic blue eyes shimmering. "I got pregnant."

Oh, no . . . now I understand. My heart aches. "What did Scott do?"

"I wasn't going to tell him, but Dane did."

"Dane?"

"He thought he was doing me a favor, that Scott would do the right thing and we'd be led out of our sinful lives."

I nod.

"I'd gotten drunk, saying I had to get rid of the baby."

I feel sick. "I don't want to hear anymore." Sin's consequences seem to go on forever. No one wants to look at that aspect of living exactly how you want.

"Dane was convinced if Scott knew about the baby, he'd ask me to marry him. So Dane told him. He said Scott was a better person than I gave him credit for."

"I don't understand."

"I thought Scott asked me to marry him because it was time, so I got . . . I took care of . . . the baby because I knew he didn't really want to be a father."

My heart is breaking. I bury my head in my hands. "Alexa."

"I've cried all the tears I can cry. What I did was a simple conversation away from being a different life, but I can't cry the same tears. I made a mistake. I will pay for it in my heart for the rest of my life, and your cousin will never be able to look me in the eye knowing what I did to his child."

Alexa straightens up as a man walks toward her. She squeezes the diamond in my hands and whispers, "Take care of him for me, Sarah. I love him, but there's too much water under the bridge."

"There isn't. There's forgiveness."

"Scott never will forgive me. I'm finally coming to understand that."

I clutch the enormous engagement ring in my hand. Who would I be in the same situation? Mrs. Gentry or Alexa? Sadly, I can't even say, and that doesn't speak well of my faith. My mother had me. For all her other flaws, she gave me life. And while I shouldn't judge her or Alexa, I certainly have. I've spent my life judging.

As I said, I began losing confidence in my instincts, which is tough and very bad for an instinctive person.
~ Kim Novak

When I'm finally allowed out of the parties and countless ridiculous conversations about someone's life being newly defined by a hairstyle, I run home to the apartment. I rush down the hallway to Dane's room. He's not there.

"Sarah, he's gone." Scott drops his bag of tricks in the kitchen. "Come have some of this piroshki. It's to die for."

"Scott." I grab him by the tie. "What do you mean he's gone?"

"He went to France."

"Without saying good-bye?"

"He does that sometimes. You haven't noticed he's a bit odd? He told me before the premiere he might have to leave early if he caught another flight. Oh, and don't forget to call Kate, Mrs. Gentry, and your mother. And he left you something in your room and said good-bye."

I run to my room, sliding along the hardwood floor and banging into the wall at the end of the hallway. There's a bag with gold embossing from Dane's shop on my bed. I run my hands along the shiny lettering. "Dane," I whisper. I should have acted like my mother. For once in my life, I should have taken a risk and done what my heart wanted to do.

All the secrets people have lived. For what? What did it accomplish for any of them? My mother is alone. Scott and Alexa are alone. Kate's alone. Mrs. Gentry's alone. "I don't want to be alone!" I yell to the ceiling. "I want to be in France with the man who sets my heart on fire!"

I know the reality of the situation, and right now I just don't care. I don't care at all. I only know he's gone, and I blew it. I'm left alone here with a fancy job, a client list Scott created that would make the average producer fall prostrate on the ground, and no Dane. I thought success would make me happy. Complete. It's made me just like the rest of them. Alone.

I'm alone again. Just like my nights in Sable, only now I'm surrounded by more people and a better financial future. *I don't want Dane to complete me, Lord. I want him because he makes me a better person. He makes me want to get up in the morning.*

I pull Alexa's ring out of my pocket and set it beside Kate's, then go to the kitchen, where I rummage through the leftovers Scott took from the party and open a can of Pepsi. Back in my room, I prop the two rings up. I could open my very own jewelry store at the moment. Naturally, no one would want what either bauble represents.

If I had known what success would cost me, I would have paid my fees for failure and called it a day. I thought my quest for financial solvency was a higher calling, a way to prove to my hometown that my mother and I had value and worth. In the end, I stand here with my feet in two separate worlds, belonging fully to neither.

There are two engagement rings before mc on the expansive, stainless steel countertop. One is from Tiffany's, a classic platinum band and solitaire that I'm sure comes with all the proper GIA ratings. The other is from a mall jewelry store, miniscule and flawed, but sparkling with promise. This might give the impression that there's a choice to make, but there isn't. Neither man would have made an offer had they known the truth.

"And the truth shall set you free."

I shut the boxes on the engagement rings. They should represent hope; yet all I see is brokenness in them. Ryan's heart is broken as Kate flies solo for the first time in her life. My cousin's life is broken, but he doesn't know it. Essentially, he made the same choice my mother did; he made a choice for bitterness and being right over a life of love.

I want to be like Mrs. Gentry. I want to choose love.

I call Dane's cell phone and get voice mail again. Part of me wants to rush to LAX and have my Hollywood moment where I tell him everything. Where I tell him that I'm a romantic victim of Cary Grant movies and men in fedoras. And I tell him I've fallen in love with him, and I don't care how ridiculous it seems. He is everything I want.

Finally, I open the bag he's left me. It's a very worn copy of *La dame aux camélias* dated 1868 and published by Maison Quantin. Inside the cover is a very old copy of *Camille* in French. Its cut-edge pages are yellowed and crisp, but its condition is nearly perfect for its age. Inside the book is an envelope with Dane's handwriting, reading, "Sarah." I run my hand along those letters, thinking how ironic it is that my own unrequited love is written in ballpoint pen along with the gift of an antique book.

I stare at the envelope for a long time, not wanting to know what it says but needing to know. Then, with a breath, I rip open the letter and look at Dane's beautiful script.

Dear Sarah,

By the time you read this, I should be on my way to Paris. I found this book through a friend in England and—humor me—here are some facts about it. It has a color frontispiece, with engraved plates and tinted vignettes. Albert Lynch, the artist who did the renderings, was born in Peru in 1851 and made his name as an artist and illustrator in Paris. You'll notice they spared no expense with books in those days. They were a luxury item. The dark brown morocco with raised bands, gilt-decorated compartments, and the spray of flowers was most contemporary for its time. Aren't the marbled endpapers with their gilt edges the height of beauty?

I have to stop the letter and laugh at Dane's love of all things fact-oriented. He's a walking encyclopedia. While Scott finds him highly annoying, I find him completely charming and entertaining in his love of history. This should prove once and for all that I am in love.

I do realize, of course, that you can't actually read it in French, but its value is so much higher in the original French, and I wanted you to have the best. This story and its effects on you are misguided, but if I've learned anything in my years, it's to give the customer what they want.

You are not Camille and you never were. Camille made ill-informed choices, and while I do question your not coming to France with me, I know you chose not to come for intelligent reasons—not because you were ruled by your heart, but because you had the wisdom to see that we are not in full control of our emotions around one another. I don't wish to be loved to the point that you would die to "save" me. What man would?

Unrequited love is not romantic. It's a waste of the life God gave you. The beach house with its new kitchen, trips to France with a man who loves you—that is romantic.

When you're ready, I'll find a new owner for this book. I'll sell it and give you the profit. Give up the myth for me, Sarah. Time travel with me into the future. Our future.

With love in Him,
Dane
P.S. I enclose a rendering of Alexandre Dumas and his son for your realistic analysis of them as heroes. Cary Grant they are not.

It's too easy, God. Men do not write letters like this. Men do not offer themselves up for the price of a book. I don't believe it. I can't believe it. But without the hope of this book I hold in my hands, I have only the illusion of success. Why have I been so fearful to state what I really want? Why is it so dangerous?

The answer is as clear as Wyoming air: I want to be loved. Not just by God but by a man God has ordained for that purpose. I want a man to get old and saggy with, someone to laugh with about the latest article in *U.S. News & World Report.* Together. Old. Saggy. We would be the types of people you don't want at your party because we will laugh at our own jokes, and Dane would have a new fact to share with everyone about the latest nonfiction title on the Gettysburg Address.

I am a *have.*

Scott slams open the door. "Enough of this."

"What are you talking about?"

He takes the book from me. Looks at it. Frowns. "Dane is the wrong man for you."

"I don't understand."

"I've tried to be honest. I've tried to be a good friend to Dane. But Sarah, he didn't grow up a good Christian boy like you're thinking. He's not the preacher's son with the ideal background and stunning education that will rescue you. He would be toxic for you."

"Scott, I'll be the judge of Dane's character for myself."

"Dane's an alcoholic, Sarah Claire. He found Jesus in AA. Everyday he walks a tightrope of sobriety. Now, tell me, can you really deal with that?"

All of my hope drains from me. Anything but that. *Anything.*

chapter  25

Cars, furs, and gems were not my weaknesses.
~ Gene Tierney

Yoshi finally bagged Johnny, who went out with a law-
suit and a laundry list of Yoshi-inflicted torture for a
jury, but I can't complain. As my first cover is readied for
InStyle on the very hot/haute Flora Fawn, my career is
currently sizzling. So much so that Scott and I found
my mother in a homeless shelter after her brief jail stint
(too brief, as far as I'm concerned) in Anaheim and sent
her for treatment at the Betty Ford Clinic in Rancho
Mirage. She brags that she now has more in common with
Elizabeth Taylor than just married men. Although Liz
says she's one woman who only slept with men she was
married to (though there was that whole Eddie Fisher/
Debbie Reynolds scandal), and that sort of deflates the
commonality. My mom's husbands usually belonged to
someone else.

Someday, I hope she (my mother, not Liz Taylor,
though I wish her well too!) will be well enough to tell
me about my father and how she let one man ruin her
future. Or maybe she'll find the solid truth and tell me
how her own choices certainly contributed. She's working
on it; one of her steps was apologizing, and I have to say,

she was sincere. Mrs. Gentry said so too. I have hope. Guarded hope.

It's been a month since Dane left for France. I kept myself busy by styling hair and consulting on new looks for starlets. It's funny how my duties of sweeping up hair and flipping toilet seats were abandoned as soon as I appeared on *Hollywood Tonight*. But even with my superstar status at Yoshi's, Dane's never far from my mind or my heart. I know I can't be with him and risk the nightmare of a continuation of life with my mother. But I check my e-mail daily, and not a word from him. It seems so long ago that I read his words of warmth in the original letter with the book, and I can only assume if he felt something for me, it's burned away in the skies of Paris. Love is fragile. I wish I'd known how fragile.

"Okay, so you have everything you need," Kate says to me now as she stands in line at LAX. "You'll be home at Christmas?"

"I wouldn't miss it."

"Mrs. Gentry says you can stay with her, you know."

"Yes, Kate, I do."

My BFF enrolled in UCLA, but in the end she was overcome with loneliness for good beef and the man she loved. I thought of telling her who my father was, but I couldn't bring myself to do it. I just told her Bud was not my father and Cindy Simmons was not my sister. My mother will eventually tell everyone. She promised me. Of course, she's been lying for twenty-six years, so we'll see.

"Aren't you forgetting something?" I ask her. I pull out her engagement ring. "I think Ryan will want to see this on your finger."

She gives me a warm hug. "Thank you, Sarah Claire, for giving me the time and space I needed."

I nod. "Sure. Thanks for giving me a choice. *Not.*"

She laughs. "You really don't want to come back home for the wedding, do you?"

"I'll take the Fifth on that."

"You were right to leave there, Sarah Claire. I never realized how bad things were until I saw you here."

"I'll see you at Christmas."

"Sarah Claire . . ." Kate clears her throat. "Try to see beyond Dane's problem, all right? I've seen the way he looks at you. It's something I don't think you can see yourself. I believe he'll do whatever he can."

My heart skips a beat and I just shake my head. "I imagined the whole thing. Who always told me I had an active imagination? And now you're trying to back out of it? I don't think so."

"I'm not always right," Kate admits.

"No!" My hands cup my cheeks. "You're kidding me, right?"

"I know it's hard to believe," Kate says. "But I was wrong. I was wrong about you leaving Sable, and I was wrong about love at first sight. It happened with me way back in high school, and I saw you and Dane with my own eyes."

I shake my head. "I can't do it anymore, Kate. My mother was enough. I have everything I could want. I'm ready to move out on my own, I have a fabulous job, and I've made something of myself. My mother's in rehab. Life is good."

"If you think cutting hair for a lifetime is going to fulfill your purpose here . . ."

"Alcohol, Kate. *An alcoholic.* The only thing I cannot take on." I let out a laugh. "Ironic, but it's the plan God seems to have for me. Let me dream a little and then crush it like an ant at a picnic."

"Sarah Claire, it's different with your mom. Dane hasn't touched a drop in a long, long time. Even Scott vouches for that much, and you know he's not going to say anything for the sake of someone's reputation."

"Where's all this compassion for alcoholics coming from? You were the first one to defend me when my mother would go schizoid. Do I want a life of alphabetizing the booze? I'm thinking not."

Kate shakes her head. "It's not like that with Dane! He had a problem. He got help. He loves Jesus. He's the real deal, Sarah Claire. For another, he'd have to be OCD and an alcoholic to alphabetize booze, and really, what are the chances?"

I manage a smile. "With me? The odds are pretty good, thank you. Don't worry about me. I've got Cary Grant to keep me company, and maybe I'll try another date with Gym Boy. Maybe I didn't give him enough of a chance."

She exhales deeply. "Gym Boy has bigger boobs than you. You're going to have enough to worry about in the intimacy department; you don't need that pressure."

"You are not making me feel better. Are you trying to make me feel more like dirt?"

"Just think about Dane and give him some time to prove himself," she lectures and pats my head. "At least I know you have employment." She picks up her suitcase. "Thanks for dropping me off."

"No problem." I can't bear to send her off without at least a little bit of hope. "I'm going to Dane's house in Santa Monica. He needs the house readied for his return, and don't think I'm not going to check every nook and cranny for a bottle. If he has cough syrup in his medicine cabinet, I'm out for good."

Her face brightens. "In other words, you stole the key from Scott?"

"Never mind. For someone who's not a romantic, Kate, you're going awfully Saturday-morning black-and-white movie on me. I have no intention of being there when Dane gets home, but he asked me before he left, and I intend to keep my promise."

Kate tilts her head. "If you're over him, why are you afraid to face him?"

I hate best friends.

"Afraid to face him?" I echo back, annoyed. "When times get tough, what's to say he's not going to fall back? That he's not going to order a Coke and ask the bartender to slip in some vodka to take the sting out of the day."

Kate tilts her chin. "Well, I believe in him."

I manage a smile and hand Kate her carry-on. "See you at Christmas."

She nods, hugs me tight, and turns away.

I watch Kate walk toward the security guard as tears spring to my eyes and run down my face. Like Mrs. Gentry, Kate means well. I get the message: no relationship is perfect. Marriage is hard. It's excruciating sometimes, and whatever you worry about happening usually won't happen. It will be something different. That's what Mrs. Gentry tells me. But you better make sure who you walk the path with is right. I can't imagine anyone beside me on the journey but Dane, yet I know I can never survive life with another alcoholic. Of all the gin joints, he had to walk into one too many.

∾

As I unlock the door to Dane's beachside bungalow, I'm mystified at how it's better than I imagined it. I purposely have not gone to the beach since I've been here. Dane's promise of the waves lapping at my feet with him beside me is exactly the way I wanted to experience it the first time. Though of course, I did see the blue-green ocean driving his car to the house.

The interior of Dane's house is warm with rustic travertine on the floors covered by antique rugs. The entry hall leads straight to the kitchen, which Dane has redone in his carefully manicured style brightened with a love of history. It's not modern like I would have thought based on his ease in Scott's home. Everything has a rustic feel to it. The stove is refurbished, something from the 1940s era. He's even painted it that seafoam green that was so popular after World War I.

Soon the house is spotless, smelling fresh and clean. I back away toward the door, car key in hand, smiling. I resist the urge to leave a note that would elicit a response from Dane. To what end? The vicious cycle that was my mother's life? *Love me . . . No don't . . . Yes, love me . . . No, wait a minute . . .*

Shoot! I hear voices at the front walk, pivot, and peer out the peephole on the door.

It's Scott.

With Dane!

Instant panic. Like a deer in headlights, I have no idea where I should go or what I should do. The door starts to jiggle, and I know if I don't get out, I'll be running straight into Dane's sable eyes. So I do the only sensible thing: I run for the back door and rush through it—only to have the door start blaring an alarm.

What the heck?

Dane is coming through the front door so I run into the backyard like a burglar caught in the act.

"Sarah, I see you."

Okay, this is not fair. Shouldn't the alarm have gone off when I entered the house? I crouch down next to a bougainvillea (far too thin to hide me) and wonder if my cousin saw me. Maybe he'll rescue me.

The alarm ceases and my cousin sticks his head out the back door.

"What are you doing?" His expression shows how insane he thinks I am.

"I promised Dane I'd turn on his water heater."

"I did that last night."

"I just wanted to be certain. I didn't want him taking a cold shower. He has to be tired from all that traveling." I stand up and brush off a leaf. "Can you get me out of here?"

"I can, but does that mean you're done stalking him?"

"I'm not stalking him. I told you, I was checking the water heater."

"Even you can do better than that."

This exchange has given Dane time to join us. He looks at me and lifts his brows. Oh, those eyebrows. So much expression and gorgeousness . . .

What kind of person falls in love with eyebrows? I must be cracked.

"Sarah." He places his hand over his heart. "Sarah."

"How could you not tell me? You had every opportunity to tell me." The strength of my voice surprises even me.

"I did," he admits.

"That's what drunks do, you know. They lie about who they are. You lied to me, Dane."

He nods. "I knew you'd run, but you're right, I lied. I didn't tell you my truth."

I shake my head, but my hands are trembling. He steps closer but Scott stops him with a palm. "Leave her alone."

Once again I realize my cousin has only been trying to protect me. All along. He knew I couldn't stand to be with Dane and his daily struggle.

"Sarah, how can I prove to you—"

"You can't. You talked to me about God. You stood there as we bared our souls and didn't tell me that you struggled with drink. Even when you knew my mother was lost in LA and you knew why, you sat there and listened, and you did nothing to tell me the truth."

"I told God to give me a chance. I asked Him every time I sat there to just let me prove it to you so that you'd never have to know."

"But that's not love, Dane, if I don't know you. That's just you pretending some more."

He nods. "You're right. I know you're right."

Scott stands inside the door. "Let's go home, Sarah Claire."

My eyes start to water, but I hold steadfast. "I'm coming."

"Can I talk to you for a minute before we go? In the kitchen," Scott directs.

"I'll just get myself unpacked," Dane says before marching off to his bedroom.

"This house is incredible," I whisper to Scott.

"He's worth a fortune. His parents had all this artwork, and they died when he was sixteen in a plane crash."

"Again with the surprises!" I exclaim.

"If it means anything to you, Sarah Claire, I think he's figured it out. I can't promise you, of course, but I've known him for years. Even when he was a drinker." He shakes his head. "He loves you, and forgive me for this—"

He looks up the ceiling. "I don't think he's going back. He's worked through his grief. I'll meet you back home."

I spin around. "You're not taking me home."

He shakes his head. "Hear him out. You owe him that much."

"What made you change your mind, Scott."

He smiles and walks out the door. At the slam, Dane fills the bedroom doorway.

"You're still here!"

"You sound surprised."

"I am surprised. Naturally."

"Is it true?"

"It is, but Sarah, I've changed my entire life. I don't go into bars. I've even taken to drinking Pellingrino in France. Do you know how weird that makes me?"

I look into his eyes and I think about Mrs. Gentry's words. Dane is the only one I want to travel the road of marriage with. What is wrong with me? Do I have no common sense whatsoever?

"I believe in you, Dane."

"I never want to ruin that trust." He grins at me in that way that makes his eyebrows rise. "Do you have the book for me?"

"It's my book."

"I told you I wanted it back. It was like a library loan. I lent it to you until you were done with it. Are you done with it?"

"Meaning?"

"Are you willing to trade in the poor man's version of love for the real thing? The kind that promises to love, honor, and cherish you as long as we both shall live?"

"I have terrible luck, Dane. What if I promise that and you get run over by a garbage truck tomorrow. That's how my life works, you know. You pledge to be sober and I promise my heart and there's a garbage truck calling your name."

"Then you'll have your unrequited love, and you'll be no worse for the wear. 'Here's looking at you.'"

"I beg to differ." I walk toward him and we dance back and forth, unsure of what's appropriate. Eventually, I melt into his embrace. His arms surround me and I have never felt safer. For once in my life, there is someone here on earth to protect me.

I'm not throwing His blessings back at Him. I'm grateful for Mrs. Gentry, for Scott, and for Kate, but it's not the same. Dane is just for me. I'm his priority, the one he'll seek to protect above all else. He won't protect a cheating husband's promise first like Mrs. Gentry did. He won't protect his business first like Scott did. And he won't be threatened by who I am, like Kate and Ryan were.

He won't be perfect, but if there's anyone I want to ride the storms of life with, it's him.

He slips down on one knee. "I'll ask one more time. Did you bring the book?"

"I did." I go to the counter and get my beautiful antique version of *Camille*. "I don't want to give it up, though. It was a gift."

"If you don't give it up, I can't give you what's in box number one." He pulls a velvet box out of his suit pocket. I grab for the box and he pulls it away. "If you want box number one, the unrequited-love fascination is over."

I nod.

"And the only time traveling we'll be doing is where we fast-forward through *Somewhere in Time*?"

"You're killing me! What's in the box? I agree, I agree. You can have my firstborn; just give me the box!"

He holds my hand. "Do you know why Scott told us both we were off-limits?"

"I understand now."

"He told me on the way here we were both so stubborn, but for once he hoped we'd listen to reason. As if he'd know reason."

"Open that box," I say through clenched teeth.

He lifts the lid to reveal a dazzling diamond stick pin in an art deco-style setting I've never seen before.

"It's a cushion cut. Would you like some historical perspective on the cushion-cut diamond, also known as the miner's cut?"

"That depends. Would you like—never mind. I'm going to be demure. You can tell me all about it, its history, who's worn it, why it was made, every inch of detail about it. After—"

"Good. I like my women—ahem, woman—demure. You have to let me get through this; my knee is killing me. Sarah Claire Winowski, you have made me a *have*. I loved you the moment you walked into my life. When I stepped off that elevator, it was like traveling into my future. I won't rush you; I need to prove to you that I'm a man of my word. But you name the day, and this stick pin becomes an engagement ring."

I can only nod, and dang it if I'm not going to ugly-cry. Dane slides the pin into the lapel of my Chanel blouse. "I am a *have*."

"See that. I told the jeweler in Paris it had to be perfect. What do you say to a walk on the beach with your fiancé? Well, eventual fiancé, once you're quite certain of my stability. And I am stable, Sarah. I'm the rock of Gibraltar because I know how quickly I fell."

"I've been waiting for the beach." *With you,* I add silently.

He laughs. "Not the fiancé?"

"Well, maybe once in a while I thought of it in passing. Getting married."

He kisses me with a passion I didn't know could exist outside of a Cary Grant movie. Dane is truly notorious. Then he grabs his fedora, which I brought for him from Scott's house, places it on his head, and opens the door to the sunlit path. I can hear the ocean's waves crashing along the shore. The spray of salty sea air hits us as we walk down the path toward the Pacific.

My entire life's work is strewn on the pages of *InStyle* for all to see. I'm proud of what I have to show for my life, and my ending will be whatever I want it to be. God might send a few road bumps and a few forks, but I'm going to be better for it.

"Kiss me, Sarah. From here to eternity." Dane wraps me in his arms.

Sometimes apparently, men do marry Winowski women.

A single girl's search
for being content with
who she is . . . with or
without a man.

kristin billerbeck

what a
girl wants

All she want is a cute Christian guy who doesn't live with his mother
and maybe a Prada handbag.

kristin billerbeck

she's out
of control

kristin billerbeck

with this ring,
i'm confused

THOMAS NELSON, INC.
Since 1798

also available from Kristin Billerbeck

what a girl wants
an Ashley Stockingdale novel

"*This is Rick Ramirez, reporting for* Entertainment This Evening." *The announcer rolls his "R's" to emphasize his Latin heritage; he's a cross between Ricardo Montalban and the used car salesman up the street.*

"*We're live in Silicon Valley at the celebrated wedding of Ashley Wilkes Stockingdale to the world's most eligible bachelor, John Folger, heir to the coffee fortune. Not since JFK, Jr. have the world's single women mourned a wedding as today, but Ashley is the woman who stole his heart—the woman who left the sworn bachelor no other option but marriage. And we hear the ladies cry, Who is this woman? For more on Ashley, we go to Jen Jenkins in 'copter 7.*"

"*Rick, we're live over the Stanford University chapel, awaiting the much-anticipated arrival of the enigmatic Ashley Stockingdale: A woman who brought Manolo Blahnik, shoemaker to the stars, all the way to California to design her diamond-encrusted bridal slippers. Who is this Ashley?*" *Jen leans into the camera's lens, "I'm glad you asked.*

"*Ashley Wilkes Stockingdale came from humble beginnings, and grew up in a quaint California bungalow. The child of a homemaker and a carpenter, Ashley always knew she was destined for something great. Although there was time for frivolity, like high school cheerleading, Ashley was a serious student, passing the California bar her very first time out. And she hasn't forgotten her roots; when asked if Franklin Graham might perform the ceremony, Ashley declined, choosing her beloved pastor instead. Rumor has it she'll arrive in a cream-*

colored, body hugging Vera Wang gown. The world waits . . .
back to you, Rick."

～

Yes, the world waits. And so do I. There's single for a
season, and single for a reason. My singles' pastor used to
say that and laugh like staccato Spongebob. I remember
thinking it was hilarious until the day I turned thirty.
Then my thoughts turned much darker, like hey, maybe
I am single for a reason. That's a depressing day, when
you realize Prince Charming isn't riding in on a white
horse, and J. Vernon McGee is starting to sound awfully
handsome on the radio.

I gaze around the singles group and it's rife with its
reasons. Tim Hanson has those hair plugs that look like
he's sprouting rows of corn on his head. Jake Henley has
been pining over an ex-girlfriend that no one's ever seen,
for going on three years now. He still talks to her on the
phone, and I just want to say, "Wake up, dimwit! She's
moved on!" To waste your life on an emotional relationship
that is going nowhere is such an easy out, don't you think?
It makes him unavailable, and avoiding commitment is
now that much simpler.

There's Kay Harding, resident organizer and anal-
retentive of the group. She can run everyone's life perfectly
and is content to do so. The sad thing is we all go along,
without enough will of our own to plan our social lives.
Kay does a fine job, and we always have something to do
on Saturday night, so who's complaining? Kay's home looks
like Martha Stewart lives with her, but she's alone. Just like
me. So here I'm left to wonder, if all their reasons are so
blatantly obvious, what's mine? And why can't I see it when
I see everyone else's so clearly?

When I graduated from law school from Santa Clara University and became a patent attorney, I thought the world was my oyster. My head had a hard time fitting through the doorway, it was so grossly oversized. It's been shriveling ever since with the daily rejection that is my reality.

My mother told me that no man wanted to marry a lawyer. "You're too educated," she'd say. Like I was supposed to dumb myself down for Mr. Right. I laughed at such a ridiculous concept. After all, I'd dated plenty in college, but I waited on real romance because I knew there was someone out there who would make my feet tingle and my brain fog. Alas, I'd settle for a phone call at this point. My mom's intellectual theory is starting to gel like her aspic. But I live in Silicon Valley—it's not like intellect is a bad thing here—so where's my knight in shining silicone?

Family support is everywhere. Besides my mother, there's my brother who calls me "bus bait"—as in, I have more chance of getting hit by a bus than married after thirty. They've proven that study is totally bogus, but does that mean anything to my brother? Absolutely not. I just pity the poor woman who eventually gets stuck with him. He's a bus driver, by the way. And probably the one to run me down just to prove his point.

Don't get me wrong. I live a full life as a Christian single, and I'm not waiting for life to start when I get married. I just can't stop wondering, what is my reason? Do I have some glaring flaw that I cannot be witness to? This kind of thing just drives me crazy, like when men my age marry twelve-year-olds fresh from college. Okay, so they are in their early twenties. But I remember rooting for *The Bachelor* when he chose a woman twenty-seven. Finally, a man who saw a little age like a fine wine, rather than vinegar past its prime.

Yet here I sit, with all the same single people I've been sitting near for years. Once in a while, we'll get some cute young thing in her twenties and some single guy swoops out of nowhere and whisks her away. Leaving us "reason" people wondering what strange scent we give off. Maybe it's desperation.

I don't feel desperate. I sing in the worship band, I work at the homeless shelter, and I'm busy nearly every night of the week. Granted, my busyness translates into which reality television show is on that night, but I still have my routine.

Kay Harding has taken the podium and her familiar voice breaks into my thoughts. "Saturday night we're going to the local Starbucks for a talent night. If anyone wants to sign up, please see me after Sunday school." Kay takes the pen from behind her ear and attaches it to the clipboard. "I'll send the sign-up sheet around, but see me if you're performing."

The thought of invading a local coffee house and humiliating myself sends my stomach surging. At the same time, I know I'll be there. What else do I have to do? I'm in such a rut. It's like when an engineer tries to explain a new segment of technology to me. I know I'll eventually get it, but the early frustration leaves me wondering why I do what I do.

Jim Henderson is clapping. I call Jim "Wild at Heart Man" because he can't seem to say a thing without quoting John Eldredge. Trouble is, I think Jim missed the message of that book because he's not more masculine, just more annoying. Of course, I'm not one to judge because I've been sitting here, same as him, waiting for someone to bear witness to my feminine wiles.

Seth Greenwood stands up. Seth is the one anomaly

in the group. He's handsome, albeit bald, but that doesn't bother me. He has crystal blue eyes and a heart as big as the San Francisco Bay. He's a programmer—read: Geek. But who isn't in the Silicon Valley? He's thirty-four—granted his baldness makes him look a little older—but he's always there for anyone who needs him. Including me. Right now, he's got an out-of-work salesman friend living with him. And that guy brought two cats along. Seth's "reason" is probably just fear of commitment, the universal fear of single men everywhere, but something tells me he won't stay in that trench forever. So I guess maybe he's a "season" man. Time will tell.

Seth takes center stage over the rickety music stand. "On Wednesday night, after Bible Study, we're watching *Notorious*. It's an old movie with Cary Grant," (the women coo here) "and Ingrid Bergman," (now a few guys whistle). "Anyone interested"— Seth looks over at Kay and her organized clipboard and winces just a bit. "Well, anyone interested can just show up on Wednesday night. We'll know why you're there. Bring a snack, or be at the mercy of my fridge." Seth sits back down, and I feel my smile break loose. Seth encapsulates an invisible charm, like Fred Astaire. You can't really see his attractiveness in a Hugh Jackman way, but there's something about him that throws you off, in a good sort of way.

☙

Seth is back to discussing video games with Sam in the front seat of the Saab. They're talking about some secret key in some corner chamber, and I smile dumbly, like I have any notion as to what they're talking about. Or any care.

When I was in eighth grade and boys discussed video games, I understood. Now that I'm thirty-one I think to myself, If you boys would grow up, you might be having sex by now instead of playing Super Mario XXXIV. But as an aging virgin, who am I to judge?

"You want me to drop you off at church or home?" Sam looks at me in the rearview mirror. His Asian eyes are pleading with me silently to save him the extra jaunt to church.

"I kinda need my car," I say, trying to keep the "You're an Imbecile" out of my voice. Although it should be obvious that I'd like to be taken to where I left my vehicle, I've learned that engineers do not understand simple math: A+B = C. After all, B is an unknown, right? And if B takes an engineer out of his desired path, then the equation just doesn't add up.

I rail on engineers, but if you lived here in Silicon Valley where the men are engineers, and the women are hopelessly single, you'd understand my point. When a new science-fiction movie opens here, it's an event worthy of a costume. A nice dinner out is considered Dave & Buster's, the local grown-up arcade. Just once I want to meet up with a man who knows it's good manners to open a lady's door and let her enter first. Not a race.

Seth turns around, his blue eyes shining with laughter. He instinctively knows where Sam should be driving, but he keeps it all inside. As though he enjoys the private joke of how clueless his friends are. "We're watching *The Matrix* tonight, Ash. You want to come over?"

"No thanks. I'm doing dinner at my mom's house tonight." My birthday dinner. I don't add that I'll be home in time for Masterpiece Theatre, or that I think *The Matrix* is stupid. That's blasphemy around here. "Don't you guys ever get tired of our lives in Silicon Valley?"

We're at a traffic signal, and they both turn around and stare at me as if I have whipped cream on my nose.

"What do you mean?" Sam asks.

"I mean, we always do the same things. We hang out at the coffee shop, we see the same movies, we—you know, I can't even think of what else we do. We should plan a trip to the beach and have a wild volleyball game or something."

The light has changed, but they're both still staring. "*The Matrix* is an allegory, a worldview, if you will."

"We've still seen it a few times," I try half-heartedly. I've started it. Now we'll get into the deeper discussions—like why Spock, without feeling, would sacrifice himself for mankind in *Star Trek Genesis*.

"Do you want to watch *Lord of the Rings*?" Seth asks.

I can't help my audible sigh. "No. I'm going to my mom's. Never mind. I was just thinking out loud." That must be the burning smell in the car.

Seth's face screws up into a tight knot. He cannot understand my problem today, and I can't fathom my own lack of interest in the life around me. Engineers have their own language, their own culture. My fear is that I speak it fluently, and if I ever leave, will I still be able to speak English? Or will I revert to discussions about the battle for Middle-earth? These are my people.